S IS FOR SPANKING

Lucy Salisbury

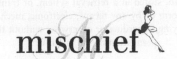

mischief

This novel is entirely a work of fiction.
The names, characters and incidents portrayed in it are
the work of the author's imagination. Any resemblance to
actual persons, living or dead, events or localities is
entirely coincidental.

Mischief
An imprint of HarperCollins*Publishers*
77–85 Fulham Palace Road,
Hammersmith, London W6 8JB

www.mischiefbooks.com

A Paperback Original 2013

First published in Great Britain in ebook format by
HarperCollins*Publishers* 2012

Copyright © Lucy Salisbury 2013

Lucy Salisbury asserts the moral right to
be identified as the author of this work

A catalogue record for this book is
available from the British Library

ISBN-13: 978 0 00 753334 3

Automatically produced by Atomik ePublisher from Easypress

Prologue

Lucy, Juliette and the Cane

I could remember every detail of the day Juliette Fisher first gave me the cane. It was an experience so full of shame and yet so exciting that I had never been able to come to terms with it, any more than I'd been able to get over the feelings of subservience she'd generated within me. Obedience to a strong, cruel will had become the key to my sexuality, along with the pain and shame of physical punishment, just as that first caning became the key to her relationship with me.

The chill of the air on my bare legs as I ran, the faint tang of burning leaves, the autumn colours on the trees along the river, every detail has remained clear in my mind ever since. Juliette was leaning on the rail of the bridge, tall and poised in black jeans and a sweater, Sunday clothes, her long dark hair caught up in a ponytail, a faint but wicked smile on her lips. I already knew I was in trouble, and just as surely I knew that I'd fight, and lose.

'Hello, Lucy.'

She sounded cheerful. My own voice was a sigh.

'Hello, Juliette.'

1

'Why didn't you report to my study this morning?'

'Because ... because I didn't want to be spanked!'

'You didn't want to be spanked? And what did we say about your spankings?'

'But somebody might have heard, and then they'd know, and ...'

'What did we say about your spankings, Lucy? Answer me!'

I was looking at my feet as I answered, barely able to mumble the words.

'We said they had to be real, so you could do it whenever you felt I needed it, or ... or if I'd been naughty.'

Just to say the word made me choke with shame, but there was no denying the sudden heat between my thighs. It was ridiculous that I went to her for spankings, impossibly inappropriate, let alone as punishment for my supposed naughtiness. Yet it happened and it was going to happen again, because however small and stupid and weak it made me feel, I needed it and I needed it from her. She knew, and she was enjoying herself, drawing out my humiliation as she went on.

'Yes, Lucy, if you'd been naughty, and you had been naughty, hadn't you?'

'Not really, no.'

'No? Going about with no knickers on under your skirt?'

'You made me take them off!'

'That's irrelevant. It's disgraceful, going about with no knickers, but it's not as bad as failing to report for your spanking. You're in big trouble, Lucy, but I'm not going to spank you.'

'No?'

My disappointment showed in my voice even as relief

washed over me. I'd been imagining how I'd look, laid across Juliette's knee with my knickers pulled well down and my bare bottom stuck up in the air, my cheeks bouncing to the slaps as she spanked me, a vision at once horrible and deeply compelling. Now it looked as if it wasn't going to happen, or so I thought for a moment.

'No, Lucy, I'm not going to spank you. I'm going to cane you.'

'Cane me? What do you mean, cane me?'

'I mean, Lucy, exactly what I say. I'm going to cane you. I'm going to make you touch your toes, I'm going to turn up your skirt and pull down your knickers, supposing you have any on, and I'm going to give you six of the best on your bare bottom.'

I tried to answer her, but all that came out was a squeak as she took me by the ear. There was every chance that somebody would see, and I was struggling immediately, but she didn't seem to care. I was led up the bank towards the main buildings, where altogether too many people were milling about and she was forced to let go. Not that it made any difference. She had me, and I followed like a puppy at heel, across the quad and indoors, where she took hold of me again, this time by my arm, to march me up to the first floor and along the corridor to the study she shared with two other girls.

Nobody seemed to be about, to my immense relief, but that came to an abrupt end when I was pushed in through the door to find both Emily and Claire seated at their desks. Both knew there was something between me and Juliette, while Juliette had already told me that it would turn her on to punish me in front of somebody else, so my fear and chagrin turned to something close to panic as I realised I was about to have an audience. It never even occurred to me that I could have walked away, or told Juliette she'd have to wait. Instead I began to babble, and so robbed myself of my last chance of escape.

'No, Juliette, please! Not in front of them, that's not fair! It's just not fair!'

She might have done it anyway, more likely not, but she couldn't possibly back down in front of her friends. Claire looked up.

'What are you going to do to her?'

Juliette didn't even hesitate, replying as if what she was about to do was perfectly acceptable, even normal.

'I'm going to cane her. Touch your toes, Lucy.'

I might have hoped they'd come to my rescue, or at least had the decency to leave the room, but they weren't Juliette's friends for nothing. Claire laughed for the thought of what was to be done to me, but Emily was worse.

'Go on then, do her hard!'

Juliette pushed me into the centre of the room and closed the door behind her, not even bothering to put the latch on.

'I said, touch your toes, Lucy. Come on, feet apart and over you go.'

I hesitated, full of misery for my own weakness but badly in need of the beating Juliette was about to give me. The window was right in front of me and I could see out across the quad, where two of my friends were talking together while the warden stalked across the grass, his black gown flapping around his ankles. The scene was so calm, so normal that it seemed insane that I was about to bend over to have my knickers pulled down and a cane used on my naked bottom. Still I went over, burning with shame as I put my fingertips to the toes of my trainers, but quite unable to stop myself.

My hair had fallen down around my head, so I could hardly see at all, save for my socks and shoes where I was stood on a patch of dark-red carpet. Juliette spoke from somewhere above and behind me.

'You see, I told you I'd find a use for this.'

She laughed, so cruel, and I found myself twisting my head around to look out from under the curtain of blonde strands that obscured my face, to find her holding a long, crook-handled school cane. I'd never seen anything so terrifying in my life, and it looked old too, making me wonder how many other unfortunate girls had been forced to adopt the same humiliating position while it was used across their bottoms. Whatever the answer, I was next, terrified of the thing but unable to move, even with the two girls watching, delighted by my fate and not even bothering to hide their reaction. When Emily spoke her voice was rich with excitement.

'Strip her, Juliette. Make her go bare.'

Juliette was as cool as ever as she answered.

'Naturally I'm going to make her go bare. You don't think I'd leave her any modesty, do you? Her skirt's coming up and her knickers are coming down, aren't they, Lucy? If you have any on today, that is. Now open wide.'

I shook my head in a denial as pathetic as it was point-less, and I'd barely taken in her final instruction, only to have the long, hard bar of the cane pressed to my lips as she spoke again.

'Hold it in your mouth, stupid.'

I obeyed, taking the cane between my teeth. She stood up once more, to take hold of the hem of my skirt, her voice now full of laughter as she lifted it to show off the seat of my panties.

'Here we go, up comes the skirt. Oh, she has got knickers

5

on, that makes a change, rather pretty ones too, don't you think, girls? Oh, but look at this, she's all wet! What a disgrace you are, Lucinda Salisbury!'

Claire and Emily were giggling as they moved to inspect the gusset of my knickers, which I'd known was embarrassingly moist, and why, but I couldn't help but try and defend myself, pulling the cane from my mouth to speak.

'I was running!'

Juliette laughed.

'A likely story! You're wet, aren't you, you slut, not sweaty, wet, *wet*, wet with juice? You're wet because you get off on having your bottom smacked, don't you?'

I shook my head, and with that I'd begun to cry, overcome with emotion for what was being done to me and for my helpless reaction. Juliette gave a short, curt laugh, pure contempt.

'What a big baby, and her knickers aren't even down yet! Come on then, let's have you bare … and down come the knickers!'

She'd done it as she spoke, taking hold of my knickers and peeling them down off my bottom, not just around my thighs to leave me bare for the cane, but all the way to my knees so that they remained stretched taut between my open legs. I knew my sex was visible from behind, just as the gusset of my knickers had been and, worse still, I could feel the cool air between my cheeks where the sweaty little dimple of my anus showed. Claire gave an excited giggle, Emily a low purr.

'Go on, Juliette, beat her.'

Juliette didn't answer, but she'd begun to touch, her hands pressing to the flesh of my bottom, then exploring my cheeks and between as the others watched. There was no restraint, her fingers digging deep to spread me open and loitering on the mouth of my anus before moving lower, to penetrate me. She'd already had my virginity and her fingers went in easily, adding to my choking shame as my secret was revealed to the two watching girls, with my soaking hole held open for their inspection. By then the tears were streaming down my face, but Juliette knew me too well to stop, continuing her exploration of my bottom and sex, then finishing by hauling my top up over my breasts to strip me of every last vestige of dignity. Only then did she bend down to take the cane from between my teeth.

I braced myself, expecting the agony of the first stroke at any instant. Just to take a spanking from her was all I could bear, and I was sure the cane would hurt a thousand times more. As she laid the awful thing across the flesh of my bottom I began to tread up and down on my feet in an agony of apprehension, and to babble.

'Not too hard, please, Juliette. I'll be good, I promise. I'll do anything ... anything you like, but not too hard, just not too hard!'

She lifted the cane and I screamed as I heard it swish down, only for Claire and Emily to dissolve in laughter as Juliette deliberately missed her target. I tried to say something but couldn't, my breath now ragged and my body shaking and wet with sweat as she brought the cane up a second time. Down it came with that awful swishing sound, only to miss once again and leave me stamping my feet and bawling my eyes out in fear and consternation. Again she lifted the horrible thing, and this time when it came down it hit the target, a hard stroke delivered full across the crest of my bottom to make me scream once more, then leap to my feet, clutching at my cheeks and jumping up and down like some mad

7

kangaroo to the tune of all three girls laughing.

Finally I managed to present myself once again, my head hung low, my breath coming in gasps, my knickers now around one ankle, but my bottom pushed out for the second stroke of Juliette's cane. I didn't know if I could take all six, but I was going to try, and when she was done with me I was going to get down on my knees, with my bare red bottom showing behind, and lick her to ecstasy in front of both her friends. Again the cane settled across my bottom as Juliette spoke.

'That's one, Lucy, and now ... no, on second thoughts get up and go and stand in the corner with your bum on show. I'll give you the remaining five next week.'

Chapter One

Five years had passed since my relationship with Juliette Fisher, but what we'd done together had left an indelible mark. For all my success at university and in the jobs market I'd never been able to get over my love for shameful erotic situations, and the slightest mention of spanking still made my tummy flutter, while the thought of the cane terrified me. As PA to the boss of an old, established and traditional company I'd had to keep my feelings to myself, aside from a few glorious moments of self-indulgence with boyfriends and with my colleague, Stacey Atkinson.

Stacey was a carefully guarded secret because for all that the company paid lip service to tolerance and equality we both knew full well that a lesbian affair would hurt our careers, while even a hint of anything kinky was likely to bring them to an abrupt halt. We both knew the risks, but I needed my fix of punishment and humiliation just as she needed hers for sex with another woman, which made us an ideal match. Otherwise I'd kept a strict rule of never accepting a proposition from anybody within the company or associated with the company. It was a shame, because I'd had several tempting offers, but I knew what would happen if I accepted. If the night was a success I'd let myself go, demanding the satisfaction of my deeper needs, including having my bottom smacked. Boys will be boys, and they do like to boast, so it was sure to be all over the office within a few days, with disastrous consequences.

When I was put up for a management training course in the West Country I was delighted to find that Stacey would be there too, but I was less happy to discover that three of our male colleagues were also going. There was Alastair Renton, a busy young man who looked as if he ought to have been a Spitfire pilot and was plainly fast-tracked for the top; Daniel Chambers, pushier still and even better looking, with a bad reputation to match, but just not as good, and Paul Yates, a great bear of a man said to be brilliant on computers but with a reputation as the office clown. The course was all about leadership and involved a lot of running around in the countryside, while every second word in the brochure we'd been given seemed to be 'team', but I still hoped to find the occasional private moment with Stacey during what looked like being a highly physical and challenging couple of weeks.

The great thing about having a clandestine relationship with another woman is that you can get away with far more than an ordinary couple could, or even two men. When Stacey and I said we'd forego our places in the minibus and take the train down the day before my boss made a comment about sticking with the team, but that was all. Nor did the staff at The Plough, a remote country pub where we'd chosen to stay the night, show any surprise when we booked a double room. We were in a tiny village more than five miles from Camp Aspiration, where the course was happening, and as we unloaded our bags I was looking forward to a delight-fully naughty afternoon.

Our room was tucked in under the eaves at the top of the building, with a single, small window looking out over the beer garden and across the woods and fields of the Exe Valley, with the loom of Dartmoor beyond. Just to breathe the air was a pleasure, after being stuck in London all winter, while I couldn't help but feel carefree, even irresponsible. We hadn't quite had the nerve to ask for a double bed, but both the ones we'd been given were big enough for two, at least while we were up to no good. I bounced down on the one nearest the window and lay back, my arms and legs spread out in a star.

'This should be a lot of fun, being with you anyway. I expect the course will be pretty silly.'

Stacey turned from where she'd been investigating the bathroom.

'Why silly?'

'Oh, you know, all this team business and outdoor stuff, when management's really all about who you know and how you look and that sort of thing. Do you think Mr Scott would have chosen me as his PA if I'd been short and dumpy with a thick Birmingham accent?'

'No, probably not, but going on the course will look good on our CVs.'

'Oh, I know that, but I don't expect it to be of any real practical value. It's just boys' games, really, you know, an excuse to show off a bit of machismo.'

'You are going to try, aren't you?'

'Yes, of course, if only to show Daniel and Alastair up, but don't expect me to volunteer for anything that involves getting unnecessarily wet or muddy. The boys can do it while we look on in admiration, staying nice and clean and dry.'

She laughed.

'You know your trouble, Lucy. You've had it too easy. I bet you were daddy's little princess, weren't you?'

'I was at public school, most of the time, and it wasn't easy at all.'

'Oh, you poor baby! Weren't the servants sufficiently respectful? Was the caviar not of the best quality?'

It was my turn to laugh, remembering what it had really been like, but her mocking tone had got to me and I couldn't resist answering her back.

'We didn't get caviar, but the servants were mostly girls like you, only they knew their place.'

I knew what was going to happen and was already snatching for a pillow as she scrambled across the other bed to get at me. My blow caught her full across the side of her face and from that moment I was in serious trouble. She called me a bitch as she pulled back to grab one of the pillows from the other bed, which left her in a crawling position for one perfect moment, with the seat of her tight blue jeans a perfect target. I brought my pillow home with every ounce of my strength, full across her bottom, a small victory but a very satisfying one. It was also my last.

She was on me in an instant, twisting around to bring her pillow down on my head, and once again before she stood up, towering above me as she rained down blows. I tried to defend myself, smacking my pillow at her legs and hips, but she was bigger and stronger. She also wanted to win, while my will to resist was fading with every smack of her pillow on my body. I soon rolled back, my efforts to hit her ever more pathetic as she laid in, hard and accurate, until I lost my pillow and curled up, my hands covering my face, my bottom on offer as a target. She took full advantage of my surrender, pummelling me with the pillow as I begged for mercy, although that was the last thing I wanted. I didn't get it either, smack after smack applied to my back and legs and arms, but with ever more attention to my bottom, until at last she threw her pillow aside, twisted one of my arms into the small of my back and began to use her hand instead, talking to me as she gave hard, purposeful slaps to the seat of my jeans.

'Girls like me, were they, Lucy? Girls who knew their place? I bet they did, and I bet they knew yours too, miss high-and-mighty, hoity-toity public school girl, swanning around like the stuck-up little bitch you are. Giving out orders and having them run around after you all day, was it? Yeah, sure, that's really you. More like over their knees with your panties pulled down and your bottom bare for a good spanking, which is exactly what you're about to get!'

'No! Please, Stacey, not that. Don't spank me, please!'

She just laughed at me, enjoying my discomfort as I began to squirm in her grip but knowing full well that the only way to really punish me would be to stop. That wasn't going to happen, because whatever my reaction, she was going to thoroughly enjoy taking her feelings out on my bottom. Her sense of social inferiority was very real, which meant it was going to hurt, and that she'd do her best to humiliate me as well. Sure enough, the spanking stopped and her hand burrowed in to tug at the button of my jeans as she spoke once more.

'Right, you little snob, let's have these trousers down and see how superior you look with your knickers on show. Get your legs down, now!'

A hard slap to my thighs and I'd done as I was told, uncurling to let her get at my jeans, which had quickly been pulled down around my thighs to leave the pretty pink silk panties I'd chosen that morning on display. She gave a tut of mock disapproval and treated herself to a quick feel of my bottom before she went on.

'Oh very fancy! Quite the little princess, aren't you? I bet you even wear a matching bra, don't you?'

'So do you!'

She ignored my comment as she pulled up my blouse to inspect my bra, gave another scornful little tut when she discovered it was in the same style as my panties, then abruptly tugged it up to spill out my breasts. I couldn't help but protest.

'Not my tits, Stacey! Why do I need my tits bare to be spanked?'

'Maybe I want to spank your tits?'

My response was a squeal as she suited action to word, slapping her open palm across the side of one bare breast and then the other. It stung far worse than across my bottom and I couldn't help but defend myself, only to have my wrists caught and my arms pinned under her legs as she climbed up onto the bed. With me squirming helpless in her grip she began to slap my breasts again, her face full of excitement and cruelty as she watched my flesh jiggle to the smacks.

'Ow! Stacey, that hurts!'

'It's supposed to hurt, you silly bitch, and it's much more satisfying than smacking your fat little arse. You enjoy that too much.'

'Don't be a bitch, please, Stacey? Ow! Ow!'

She just laughed and gave another hard slap across both my boobs, which had now begun to pink up, while my nipples looked as if they were about to pop. I closed my eyes, trying to resign myself to my punishment but unable to hold back my cries or stop myself from wriggling about as she continued work on my chest, slapping my boobs up to a rosy pink colour before she finally decided to turn her attention to my bottom.

'Right then, enough of that. Roll over.'

I obeyed, snivelling slightly and feeling very sorry for myself indeed as I turned face down on the bed. She straddled my back, seating herself so that she could keep me in place and get at my bottom. I could feel the heat of her sex through her jeans, bringing to mind what was sure to be done to me once I'd been punished, but I had to get through my spanking first. Stacey knew she had me helpless, both physically and mentally, and her voice was calm and amused as she spoke again.

'Right then, let's see shall we, what's to be done with you? First, as you have such pretty panties on, I think they'd better come down, don't you? It would be a shame to ruin them, after all. There we are, bare bottom, and don't you look pretty?'

She'd pulled my knickers down as she spoke, inverting them around my thighs to join the tangled cloth of my jeans and leaving me bare and ready, my smarting breasts already naked and now my bottom too. My spanking began, Stacey laughing as she started to slap my cheeks, one hand on each to make my flesh bounce and my slit open to show off my anus. I buried my face in the coverlet, letting the awful shame of my position sink slowly in, a smart, professional woman stripped and spanked by her friend. It was hard to imagine a more undignified position, for all I knew that there were plenty of ways she could have made it worse for me, like stripping me nude, making me kneel so that my wet, open cunt showed to the room, or sticking something up me while I was beaten. None of it would have been any more than window dressing, just as having my jeans and knickers pulled down was, and even the pain of Stacey's increasingly hard slaps. What really mattered was that I was taking a spanking, willingly, and the way I reacted to it, so turned on that in no time at all I'd begun to stick my bottom up for more. Stacey laughed to see the state I was in.

'Oh dear, what a little slut you are! You really like it, don't you?'

She never had fully understood, but that made it all the more exciting when she did it, along with the faint contempt she could never quite conceal. This time she didn't even bother to try, her voice openly mocking as she continued to spank me.

'How can you get off on this, Lucy? I mean, seriously, to let somebody spank you, as if you've been a naughty little girl, and to get off on it! And all the business about having your panties pulled down and being made to go bare afterwards, with your little red bum on parade around your own fucking flat! You are such a dirty little slut, but I do love you for it, and I've got to say, I love doing it to you.'

I'd given in completely, my bottom stuck high to the smacks, every word she'd said burning in my mind. She was beating on my cheeks as if she was playing the bongos, another way she liked to play with my bottom, but I wanted it harder, and I wanted to come.

'Use something on me, Stacey. Make me come.'

She gave a curt little tut, but leant across to where I'd put my hairbrush down on my bedside table, half hoping it might end up being used on my bottom. I knew I could make it, if she got the smacks just right, across the tuck of my cheeks so that every impact sent a jolt to my cunt. The very first made me cry out in mingled ecstasy and pain, because it hurt a lot more than her hand, and as she set up a firm, even rhythm across my cheeks she'd begun to talk to me once more.

'Just look at you, Lucy. You really should be ashamed of yourself, shouldn't you? I know you are, deep down, and that's what really gets you off, isn't it? But just think how much worse it could be. If only the boys in the office could know. Imagine it, Miss Lucinda Salisbury, the ice princess, the one woman who never, ever lets her guard down, and she likes her bare bottom spanked! Imagine if Daniel and Alastair and fat boy Paul were here to see you now, with your panties down and your red bum cheeks spread open to show off your little pink arsehole and your lovely wet cunt.'

I'd begun to moan, unable to hold back my excitement even as my body jerked to the hard smacks now being delivered full across the fleshy turn of my bum cheeks. My thoughts followed the scene she was painting, with the three young men watching me being punished just to add to my awful humiliation, enjoying the view of my bare, smacked tits and my wriggling bottom, my twitching bumhole and open cunt, as well as my helpless arousal and the thought of how they might take advantage.

'They'd fuck me, Stacey. They'd push you off and fuck me.'

'Oh no they wouldn't, darling. They wouldn't need to. I'd sit on your back while they did you, taking turns to make you suck their cocks hard while I spanked you, then spit roasting you, with Daniel and Alastair in your mouth and up your cunt, from behind, Lucy, with your sweet little bottom spread to show you off while he fucks you. That's right, darling, one in each hole, and Paul would take photographs to put on the net, photographs of you getting your smacked bottom fucked while you suck cock, you filthy, darling little bitch! That's right, Lucy, come, come while I spank you!'

As she spoke she'd been spanking all the time, harder and harder, until I finally hit my peak, screaming out in ecstasy as my body locked in orgasm. She let me finish, just, before tossing the hairbrush aside and lifting her bottom to let me twist around beneath her. I knew what was coming, still in breathless ecstasy as she pushed down her jeans and straddled me once more, squatting over my face with her cunt against my mouth as she spoke again.

'You're right, Lucy, I do know my place, sat on top of you with my pussy in your face. Now get licking!'

* * *

Once she was done, Stacey and I got into bed, meaning to cuddle for a little before going out to explore the area. Drowsy with sex and the warm, spring air, we were soon asleep and didn't wake up until nearly six. We showered together, slipped on light dresses we'd both brought in the hope of relatively civilised evenings and went downstairs to eat. The Plough was a typical old-fashioned country pub, with a large public bar and a saloon that doubled up as the restaurant. We chose an alcove where a window opened out through one of the immensely thick walls, allowing us to sit in comfort and privacy while watching what was going on around us. Part of the public bar was visible through an open door, and as we sat sipping wine and waiting for our food we'd both begun to study the locals. Stacey knew my tastes and couldn't resist teasing.

'Which one for you then? How about the one who looks like a lumberjack boss?'

'Stacey! If you mean the man in the red shirt, he has to be sixty, at least.'

'So what? He's big, he's rough, and just look at his hands.'

I couldn't help but do it, my eyes going straight to where Stacey had indicated. He'd just lifted his pint of beer, and I had to admit that she had a point. His hands were huge, his skin rough and dark from the sun and the wind, his fingers at least twice as thick as my own. If he'd been holding me, each hand could have cupped most of my bottom, and I immediately found myself imagining how it would feel to be across his knee, which sent the blood rushing to my face. Stacey laughed for how easily she'd got to me and tried again.

'Or how about Redbeard the Pirate over there, at the table next to the bar? He must be six foot six, and he looks just the sort to carry you off over his shoulder and do unspeakable things to you in the bushes.'

She knew full well it was one of my favourite fantasies, while the man also looked quite like my boyfriend, Magnus, back in London, so I stuck my tongue out at her and tried to get her back.

'How about you then? Maybe the old boy drinking red wine, the military type. He'd soon have you doing drill, and when you messed up ...'

She knew what I was implying, as she was from an army family, and her mouth came open in shock as the blood went to her face in turn.

'Lucy, you are the limit! Anyway, I don't go for older men, unlike you. There's only one man I'd even consider, Mr Blue at the far end of the bar.'

It was obvious who she meant. He was a little over six foot tall, with a pale-blue top that showed every detail of a superbly muscled torso, baggy white tracksuit bottoms that nevertheless hinted at an intriguingly large bulge in his crotch, and obviously expensive trainers. I couldn't really deny that he was attractive, but while he undoubtedly radiated confidence, even arrogance, he seemed to me to lack the charm a man like that needs in order to appeal to me. There was something else too, perhaps in the way he held himself, maybe simply the way he was dressed, or something less easily defined.

'He's gay.'

'What, because he's showing off his muscles? He's probably been running.'

'Why isn't he sweating then?'

'OK, so he's about to go for a run.'

At that moment the man turned in our direction too suddenly to allow us to hide our rather obvious attention. I found myself blushing again, but Stacey merely smiled, far better able to handle the situation than I was. Fortunately we were saved by the landlord, who'd just asked Mr Blue a question, and the arrival of our food. Nevertheless, I was feeling a little uneasy as we settled down to eat, and all the more so when I was obliged to make a trip to the loo and found his eyes following me all the way and all the way back. Stacey was merely amused, and a little excited.

'He's not gay then, is he? His eyes were glued to your arse, not that I blame him, if you must wiggle like that, you little show off.'

'I wasn't wiggling! What if he makes a pass at me?'

'Turn him down. Maybe he'll try me instead.'

'Stacey, you wouldn't! You're supposed to be with me, at least while we're away together.'

'That's OK, you can watch. Or maybe I'll spank you in front of him to get things going. I bet he'd love that, right after you'd turned him down.'

'Stacey!'

'I'm only joking, silly. He is nice, but like you say, we're together. Besides, if he approached you first I'd hardly take him up on an offer later, would I? I do have some pride. Shall I get another bottle?'

'Yes, why not?'

The man continued to watch us as we drank our wine, sometimes from the corner of his eyes, sometimes openly. Stacey had grown bored with the game and ignored him, but it was harder for me because of where I was sitting; I found it impossible not to glance in his direction from time to time. He noticed and his interest increased, making me ever more flustered and less able to look away. I was sure he was going to come over to us at any moment, and wasn't at all looking forward to the embarrassment of having to turn him down. Finally Stacey got fed up with my behaviour.

'Look, Lucy, if you want to go three in a bed that's fine, but either go and invite him over or stop flirting with him.'

'I'm not flirting with him!'

'Yes you are, and you know it. OK, I'll go and talk to him then.'

She'd already half risen and I quickly reached out to put my hand over hers and stop her, although I was no longer sure what I wanted. The wine we'd drunk had started to get to me, and he did have a very fine body, while Stacey's threat to spank me in front of him had triggered one of my favourite fantasies, punishment in front of a man who then got to do as he pleased with my body, which would be more humiliating by far if I'd turned him down earlier. He'd seen it too, and now he knew that something was up, bringing my feelings of shame and uncertainty up further still. Stacey spoke as she sat down again.

'You go then. Look, he's looking right at you.'

21

He was, leaning against the bar with his drink in one hand, watching us with open admiration. I imagined his amusement as I was turned over Stacey's knee in front of him, and how he'd be thinking what a little pervert I was to get off on being spanked by my friend even as his cock started to grow to the sight of my rear view being exposed. Or maybe he'd want to do me too, and once I'd been reduced to a red-bottomed, tear-stained mess he'd certainly want me to take his cock in my mouth and complete my humiliation by sucking him off. I could do it too, if I just had a few minutes of easy, friendly conversation to let me know that whatever his reaction to my sexuality he genuinely thought of me as more than just a sexy body with a set of conveniently wet holes to stick his erection into.

'OK, I'll do it.'

I got up, less than perfectly steady on my feet and feeling very insecure indeed. He saw and gave me a grin that was pure, arrogant self-assurance, to which I returned a nervous smile. I reached the bar and he said something I didn't catch as the landlady spoke to me, asking if Stacey and I would like any dessert. The moment was broken, and once I'd politely refused and she'd moved away I found myself standing next to him at the bar, completely lost. He wasn't, moving close and putting one strong hand on the small of my back as he spoke.

'Hey, Blondie, how about I slip eight inches of rock-hard dick up your sweet little cunt?'

As he spoke his hand had strayed down to the turn of my bottom. It was far too much, far too soon. Before I really knew what I was doing I'd swung around, to plant a slap full across his face, hard enough to knock him back and leave a livid handprint on his flesh. For one awful moment

I thought he was going to hit me back, but he got himself under control just as the landlord returned to the bar, while three men at the nearest table had half risen from their seats. There was a brief, aggressive exchange of words, which I barely took in save that the other four males all seemed keen to take my side. Then Mr Blue had swallowed his drink at a gulp and walked out even as the landlord told him he was barred, which left me trying to assure four men and Stacey that everything was alright.

It wasn't. I felt guilty, both for the way I'd reacted, which wasn't really fair, and for the way everybody else had turned on Mr Blue. Stacey and I had been flirting, and even if he'd overstepped the mark he hadn't deserved his face slapped and the very public humiliation of being thrown out of the pub. I wanted to apologise, and I felt drunk and off balance too, so pretended I was in need of a trip to the Ladies and then slipped outside. It was dark, with a single yellow light illuminating a double line of cars and trees showing black against a starry sky beyond. There was no sign of Mr Blue, save possibly a pair of red tail lights moving away down the lane, but the fresh air was very welcome indeed.

I walked to the end of the car park, where an ancient and wheel-less Volkswagen camper van had been left to rust beside the hedge. It gave me the shelter I felt I needed and I propped myself against it, drinking in the cool, clean air in an effort to clear my head, only to jump at the sound of approaching footsteps.

'You OK, love?'

'Yes, really …'

It was Redbeard the Pirate, who'd been among the men keen to take my side. We spoke for a moment, and there was no mistaking his desire for me. I half wanted to give in, but couldn't overcome my own ill feelings for what had just happened until he put an arm around my shoulder, an arm like a tree trunk. I stiffened automatically, but only for an instant before I'd allowed myself to be gathered in against his chest. He began to talk, in a rumbling bass, attempting to comfort me with clumsy words that I barely heard. Yet I couldn't help but react to his touch, my body trembling badly, and it was just too easy to accept the comfort of his arms.

I could feel a hard bulge swelling against my belly even as he assured me there was nothing to worry about. Had he simply taken me then and there I wouldn't have resisted. My defences were down and I was drunk and horny, as well as feeling guilty for being a tease, and he was so very obviously turned on. Yet I knew that it would have to be me who made the first open move. I didn't say a word as I slid his zip open, nor as I went down on my knees to pull out his cock, straight into my mouth. He reacted with a low moan, but accepted his tribute, letting me suck as he leant back against the side of the camper van. The feel of his cock in my mouth was more comforting than anything, at first, but as he began to stiffen up I was getting increasingly eager. My hand went up my dress and down the front of my panties as I began to masturbate him into my mouth.

His hand settled on the back of my head, to take me gently but firmly by the hair, holding me in place. I had no intention of stopping, but it felt nice, a big, strong male hand to make sure I gave my blow job properly. He'd already begun to groan, and I began to rub harder, my fingers bumping over my clitoris as I sucked and licked and kissed at his straining erection, trying to be a good girl for him but determined to keep him back from the edge until I too was ready to come. Only when I felt my cunt begin to tighten did I take him deep in once more, as far as I could, deliberately squashing his helmet into my throat to make myself gag, a gloriously dirty thing to do and one with inevitable consequences. I felt his grip tighten in my hair and he gave an urgent grunt, jamming his cock yet deeper into my throat as he came. Spunk erupted into my gullet and I was struggling to swallow and delighting in my own filthy behaviour as I brought myself to a long, hard orgasm with my mouth still full of come and thick, hard cock.

Chapter Two

I was glad to leave The Plough the following morning, as the entire incident was acutely embarrassing and not in a good way, although I did have Redbeard's number tucked into my back pocket. Stacey agreed, and we settled up as soon as we'd finished our breakfast and called a cab. The driver had never heard of Camp Aspiration, but we finally managed to work out that it was what he called the old airfield, which didn't sound particularly promising. It didn't look it either, to judge by the high chain-link fence running through dense pine woods, or the ancient gate, complete with rusting red- and white-striped barrier and sentry box, outside which our own company minibus was just pulling up. They stopped and Daniel climbed down from the rear doors as Stacey and I got out of the cab. Beyond the gate a stretch of eroded tarmac ran between a pair of massive concrete blocks. A group of shabby wooden huts was visible in the distance and I found myself grimacing in distaste as I turned to the others.

'Are you sure this is the right place? It looks pretty primitive.'

Daniel pointed to a new and brightly painted sign which

had been hidden by the minibus, stating that we'd reached 'Camp Aspiration, Management Training Centre'.

'It's supposed to be primitive. They're big on self-reliance.'

He flexed his muscles and drew in a deep breath of air, then strode to the barrier and pushed down on the counterweight. Nothing happened, but he pushed harder and it finally rose with a rusty groan. I shared a despairing look with Stacey before we threw our bags into the back of the minibus and climbed in behind. Alastair was driving, with Paul slumped across a triple seat, fast asleep with his hands closed over his ample stomach.

We drove in, with Daniel jogging alongside us, between the double line of huts to a crossroads with larger buildings to either side. Some were obviously disused, others freshly painted in a dull, dark green with white numbers or lettering that appeared to have been applied with a stencil, and suggested exactly the sort of pseudo-military attitude I'd been dreading. There was even an assault course, visible among the trees to one side, which looked as if it included water, mud and hair-raising apparatus. I hid a sigh as I climbed down to the ground, but the others seemed full of enthusiasm, except for Paul, who was still asleep. Alastair gave him a shove.

'Wake up, Porkchop, you're showing us up.'

Another group had emerged from one of the buildings, grinning as they approached us. We exchanged greetings, all doing our best to show how energetic and confident we were. Paul hauled himself upright and tumbled out of the minibus to look around with an expression of open horror.

'What the fuck is this?'

One of the other group answered him, a tall, slim man with square shoulders, a crew cut and sunglasses.

'Camp Aspiration. Hi, I'm Chad.'

His accent was pure Midwest American and he'd extended a hand as he spoke. Paul ignored the offer, blinking in the bright sunlight.

'I'm in fucking Alabama.'

I'd shaken Chad's hand myself so as not to give offence, but I could see he was less than impressed by Paul's attitude. He carried on anyway.

'Good to see you guys. We were the first here and there are two more groups to come, fifteen people in all, according to the roster. We're going to be in four competitive groups, eleven guys and four gals. That's Mess, the big hangar's Assembly and the gym, we bunk as teams in the huts.'

He'd been pointing to various buildings as he spoke, each of which was clearly labelled, as was a shower block and a general office, while another bore a large and rather worrying red cross. Paul spoke up.

'Where's the bar?'

Chad answered him with open disapproval.

'No bar. No alcohol.'

Paul sat back heavily on the floor of the minibus, looking more horrified than ever. I found myself sympathising with him, and very glad indeed that I had Stacey's company. Not that the others were entirely unappealing, at least to look at, but all the men seemed to have the same air of forced confidence I'd disliked in Mr Blue. Another minibus was approaching down the entrance road and I turned to greet the newcomers, three men and a woman with striking red hair. Chad seemed to have appointed himself group spokesman and did most of the introductions, which gave me a chance to wander off and look at the assault course.

It was every bit as unappetising as I'd expected, with

massive walls and complicated obstacles built of old railway sleepers, wires stretched between trees at dizzying heights, great nets made of rope and several deep pits filled with water and glutinous reddish-brown mud. Just to look at it made me feel cold, and scared, for all that I knew I could do it easily enough and possibly even without getting completely filthy. That at least I had school to thank for, while I'd also have Stacey with me, who'd been brought up on far worse.

Nobody was paying any attention to me, so I moved deeper into the woods and around to the rear of the buildings. Those furthest from the centre of the camp were clearly abandoned, including concrete pillboxes long overgrown and surrounded by trees, shelters half hidden beneath the ground and the huts themselves. I decided to investigate the one nearest the gate, numbered as twenty-six, but in faded yellow paint rather than a smart new stencil. After pushing the door open with some difficulty I found myself in a long, arched room with a row of double bunks to either side. The windows were green with algae and had several broken panes, which had allowed a scattered drift of pine needles to build up on the bare, concrete floor, but it was still easy to imagine it in use. With six of the double bunks to either side there would have been twenty-four men, young, fit men.

I let my mind wander, imagining myself as a local girl brought back to camp, drunk and happy and excited by so much male company. They'd have been nice boys, presumably, but maybe not too nice. Before long I'd have been teased out of my clothes, or perhaps found myself obliged to go nude as the loser in a game of strip poker. With that it wouldn't have been long before their arousal got the better of their manners and inhibitions. I'd have found myself promising kisses, at which the bolder spirits would have taken the opportunity to stroke my bottom or touch my breasts.

One of them would have got out his cock, demanding a toss, and I'd have given in, slightly frightened, not at all sure of myself, but very, very aroused. I'd do it on my knees, pulling him over my breasts, but before long I'd have been eased down to take him in my mouth. When they saw what a slut I was the last of their reserve would vanish. I'd be made to service them all, sucking cock after cock as I knelt on the hard, bare floor, or perhaps they'd spread me out on the bunk in the corner as they took turns with me, mounting me one after another until I was dizzy with sex and slippery with their spunk.

It was a nice fantasy, and I moved to the window, wondering if I dared slip down my jeans and knickers to enjoy a hurried climax. Nobody was about, but then again there was no shelter at all. Anybody who walked in would be sure to catch me, which was going to make for a highly uncomfortable fortnight with a reputation as the girl who couldn't resist frigging herself off ten minutes after turning up. It was better to wait, but the abandoned huts certainly offered some hope of private moments with Stacey, especially if we could find any deep in among the trees.

I turned back towards the centre of the camp, but came to a stop as I saw the group. Another man had joined them, a man in loose-fitting white tracksuit bottoms and a pale-blue top that showed off his muscles. He also had a tracksuit top and a bright-red peaked cap, but there was no mistaking him. It was Mr Blue, and if that wasn't bad enough he was carrying a clipboard and had a whistle around his neck, which seemed to suggest that he was an instructor. The blood had rushed straight to my face, but there was nothing I could do except continue walking as he led the others towards the Assembly building. I was the last there, and crowded in behind the others, to a big, square room with a wooden floor.

There were no chairs, and Chad and his friends had formed a line, so the others fell in behind, myself included. Two men stood against the end wall, both in the blue tops that seemed to denote staff, both solid and well muscled, one short and white, one tall and black. Mr Blue was busy with his clipboard and didn't notice me as I took my place in the back row, but I knew it was only a matter of time, and not long at that, as he'd begun to call out our names.

'Ackland, Wendy?'

The red-haired girl raised her hand and Mr Blue made a mark on his clipboard.

'Atkinson, Stacey?'

'Sir ... I mean, yes, I'm here.'

'Sir will do nicely, or Mr Parker. That goes for the rest of you too. Respect is a vital part of leadership, and you will show me respect. Maybe you'll earn mine, maybe not. OK, Graham Boothe?'

He carried on through the alphabet while I did my best to hide behind Paul, who was considerably wider than me and taller too. I knew it was hopeless, but that didn't stop me wanting to postpone my fate. Then he reached the Fs.

'Fisher, Juliette?'

I let out a gasp, completely unintentional and the tiniest fraction of a second before I realised that there was no reason at all to think it would be my Juliette Fisher, but it was already too late. Mr Blue, or rather Mr Parker, had moved a step aside to see who he thought had answered.

'Fisher, Juliette?'

He was looking right at me and could hardly fail to realise

who I was. I managed a sheepish smile in response to his brief glare of annoyance, but he quickly mastered himself.

'Are you Juliette Fisher?'

'No. Sorry.'

He shook his head.

'There's always one. Haynes, Sam?'

I was blushing hot as he moved on. Evidently Juliette Fisher wasn't there, and nor were two others. Parker had obviously introduced everybody to the camp while outside, as he launched straight into a sort of pep talk.

'Three missing. They go down as late. That's how we do things here. You're late, you lose. We take no prisoners and we make no exceptions. Everybody is equal, and that means equal. If you girls can't keep up, tough. If you're too weak, or too fat, or too useless to make the grade, tough. We want winners, not whingers. What do we want?'

Nearly everybody echoed his remark, even Stacey, but not me, while Paul seemed to have found something more interesting outside the window, possibly a cloud. Beforehand he'd never been more than a vague shape around the building, but I couldn't help feeling sympathy, as of the people I knew there he alone seemed to resent the place. Some were even standing with legs braced apart and their hands clasped behind their back, as if they really were on parade, including Chad, Daniel, and Stacey, although she at least had the decency to look embarrassed and relax a little when I caught her eye. Parker turned to a new page on his clipboard and carried on.

'Okey dokey, let's get things together. First off, I want all mobile phones, laptops and any other gadgetry you have with you handed in, and that means now. I know you're busy people, but I want you focused and I want you relying on yourselves, not on technology. My colleagues here are Mr

Straw and Sergeant Reynolds, who will collect everything in, and I do mean everything.'

The two assistants moved forward as he carried on.

'Second, this is a team exercise, so we form teams. Teams, not individuals, that's what matters, and that's why each of you is going to be given a letter. That's your letter and your name for the duration. It's what I'll call you by and it's how you'll appear on the rosters and on the results boards, so learn it. Use your ordinary name and you get marked down. Team leaders will be A, B, C and D, each one leading a team of the same name. We put the girls together, but otherwise we go in reverse order of salary. That's reverse order, which ought to put the bigheads in their place. I have your CVs and I have your individual company reports, so let's see then ...'

There was a stir in the ranks, some looking unhappy, others pleased, a few of the real army types holding their position without showing emotion. I for one was grateful, sure that my good position would save me from the job of team leader for the girls. Parker seemed to be having a little difficulty working things out, but finally began once more.

'OK then, tail end Charlie, bottom of the heap is ... O, Lucy Salisbury.'

Every single person in the room turned to look at me. I found myself responding with an embarrassed smile, and wondering if I really did receive the highest salary of all, or if Parker knew the implications of calling a girl O and had picked me out on purpose. It seemed likely, especially as several of the men were considerably older than me, and I found my sense of resentment flaring up, as well as fear. I told myself not to be silly, and that even if he had deliberately named me after a heroine notorious for accepting

34

sexual indignities it didn't mean he could treat me that way, but that didn't stop me feeling on edge.

Stacey was G and Wendy Ackland was E, which left the absent Juliette Fisher as A and the women's team leader. I'd already known we'd be in the same hut, and once Parker had finished his talk we gathered outside, talking formally until safely out of hearing, when Stacey spoke out.

'I'm from an army family, but I'm not putting up with this pseudo-military bullshit. I'm Stacey, and as far as I'm concerned you're Lucy and Wendy, at least when nobody else is listening.'

Wendy and I were quick to agree, although I was more concerned with our team leader, and hoping she'd turn out to be small and meek. Even having to take orders from somebody called Juliette Fisher was going to be difficult for me, at least at first, because just to hear the name had brought back all my old feelings with a vengeance. If it really was her, I was in trouble, no matter how much she'd changed or how she felt, because deep down I was still in love with her.

We were in Hut Eight, the furthest from Assembly and quite a way from the three male huts. It was much like the abandoned one I'd investigated, but carpeted, with four beds to either side, each with its own chair, along with two huge chests of drawers and a single, ancient convection heater. That was it, and Wendy immediately voiced my own misgivings.

'Where's the bathroom? Don't tell me we have to go outside to use the loo?'

She'd already thrown her things down on the nearest bed and I chose the one opposite as Stacey answered her.

'There's a ladies' shower block. The huts don't have any plumbing.'

'Oh God. Why did I let myself get talked into this?'

I was asking myself the same thing, and quietly cursing Mr Scott as I unpacked and made my area as homely as I could. Stacey had taken the bed next to mine, while Wendy seemed very easy going, making me wonder if it would be possible to get away with at least playful intimacy. There was a vulnerability to Wendy, with her fragile build and pale, freckled skin, which I was sure would appeal to Stacey, while with the door locked and the curtains across the windows we'd be in a little world of our own, opening up all sorts of intriguing possibilities. Stacey had other concerns.

'I don't know about you two, but I am not spending two weeks without a drink, especially cooped up here. They want it military, so they can have it military. Who's for Operation Merlot?'

As she spoke she'd spread out a map on the floor. I crowded close, as did Wendy, tummy down with her shoes off and her legs kicked up. We'd soon located our own position, and the three nearest pubs, which included The Plough. Stacey began to explain her strategy, first telling Wendy about the incident with Parker the night before, then putting her finger on the map where it showed a village in a valley beyond the camp.

'It's no good just telling him to get stuffed and walking out, as it will go on our reports, so we have to be sneaky. We know Mr Parker likes a drink too, so the safest thing to do is for two of us to go and fetch what we need while the third stays here to make excuses for the others. This is Venncott, which is about six miles by road but less than two as the crow flies, so we're not likely to be recognised. As long as we stick to the woods there's no reason anybody should see us at all. Hiding contraband isn't going to be a problem, even if there are hut searches. We just use the woods. Lunch is in an hour and a half, so I suggest we go.'

Wendy looked doubtful.

'What, now? We're supposed to be mingling and getting to know each other.'

I shook my head.

'We're supposed to be a team. Let's act like one. We'll go running together, around the fence, find a place to nip through and one of us can keep an eye out while the others go down to the pub.'

Stacey knew exactly what I was thinking and Wendy could see the plan made sense. We all had running kit and were soon changed and ready to go, looking keen as we jogged down the track and into the woods. Several people saw us go, but none followed and we'd soon skirted the open area of the airfield to where the ground fell away in a steep-sided valley. I'd hoped the fence wouldn't be strong any more, and sure enough, we found a way underneath. Wendy stayed put and Stacey and I began to make our way down towards the river. I waited until we were deep in among the trees before stopping where a small beech had come down to make a convenient seat. Stacey didn't need any further encouragement and was in my arms immediately, first kissing me and then allowing her hands to stray to my breasts. I hadn't bothered with a bra and my top was soon up and her mouth fastened to one nipple as I hugged her to me. As usual I'd given in to her desire and she seemed to want me nude, so I stood up, allowing her to peel my top off over my head and pull down my shorts and panties. As I stepped free I was left in nothing but trainers and socks, which felt deliciously naughty and free in the warm sun, and even nicer because she was still dressed. She gave my bottom a few gentle swats, just to keep me on my toes, before sitting down on the tree trunk to push her own shorts and knickers to her ankles. I got down on my knees in the leaf mould, to bury my face between her thighs and lick her to ecstasy while I played with myself, a brief but delicious moment made all the better for the feeling of doing something illicit.

Our bad behaviour had left Stacey in a mischievous mood and she made me climb down the next hundred yards of the slope in the nude, leaving me flustered and aroused once more. I was only allowed to dress when we were dangerously close to the edge of the trees and in sight of the pub, a pretty, old-fashioned building set beside the tiny river. The sign was just legible, showing that it was called the Venncott Arms.

The sun was now high and hot, so as soon as we arrived we ordered a glass of lager each and took them out to the beer garden. A girl was sitting at one of the tables, alone, her back to us, her dark hair cut short, a girl much like Stacey in build, while her look and something in the way she held herself were disturbingly familiar. I felt my heart jump, told myself not to be ridiculous and then found my suspicions confirmed as she turned. It was Juliette Fisher, my Juliette Fisher.

'Lucy? Lucy Salisbury?'

I tried to speak, but could only manage a gulping noise. Her eyes flicked to Stacey, then back to me as she went on.

'It's me, Lucy, Juliette. What are you doing here? Was that you coming down the slope just now? Who's your friend? Hi.'

She was smiling at Stacey, her eyes full of mischief, and I wondered if we'd been more exposed than I realised as we came through the trees. I was blushing hot on the instant, and hotter still as Stacey tried to come to my rescue.

'You're Juliette Fisher, aren't you? Lucy's told me all about you. I'm Stacey. We're on the same course, up at the old airfield on the hill, Camp Aspiration.'

'You are? That is the best news I've had in weeks, years even! What's it like? I've been dreading it, but my boss insisted I go, the common little toad.'

'It's not that bad, a bit military for some, perhaps, but we're planning to get around that. You're our team leader, by the way, so I hope you don't mind us smuggling in some drink? There's no alcohol allowed.'

'No alcohol allowed? No, I don't mind. I insist. But never mind that. You two have to be together? Trust you, Lucy! You should have known her, Stacey, back when ...'

They carried on, chatting as if they'd known each other for years as I struggled with my feelings. Just to be in Juliette's presence was making me weak, stripping away all the confidence I'd built up over the years. I could barely suppress the sense of adoration building inside me and found myself desperately eager to please, while the easy way she got on with Stacey only made things worse. They'd had me blushing from the start, and we'd barely sat down with our drinks before Juliette asked a question that turned my mild pink flush to blazing scarlet.

'Am I going nuts, or when you two came down through the woods, was Lucy in the nude?'

Stacey just laughed.

'Yes, she was. I thought it would be fun to make her go bare for a bit, but we didn't know people would be able to see!'

Juliette laughed in turn, cold and clear and cruel, just the way I remembered.

'I don't suppose anybody else did, and I wasn't even sure what I'd seen, until you came out at the bottom of the woods. I might have known it would be you, Lucy!'

39

I was smiling, pathetically grateful for her attention, exactly as I'd always been, but both she and Stacey were oblivious, Juliette carrying on blithely.

'Yup, starkers in the woods, that's Lucy's style. She's never been able to keep her clothes on for five minutes. So is this camp up on the hill?'

'Yes. This is the nearest pub. In fact, we ought to get a move on. Our friend Wendy's waiting for us and we need to be back for lunch.'

'Why don't I give you a lift? I passed a Co-Op on the main road. You can call your friend.'

'No we can't. We had to hand in our phones.'

'What? How am I going to survive with no phone? Why doesn't Lucy come with me then, and we'll get the drink?'

I made to speak, knowing exactly what she was after, but Stacey didn't hesitate.

'Sure, why not? I imagine you two have a lot of catching up to do.'

She swallowed what remained of her drink, kissed me and made for the little bridge that crossed the river, breaking into a jog on the far side. I watched as she started up the hill, already full of guilt and arousal, chagrin and excitement, all muddled together for the thought of what Juliette undoubtedly wanted. She was as cool as ever.

'She's nice. How long have you been together?'

'We're not together … not really. We just … I have a boyfriend, back in London.'

'A boyfriend, you, Lessie Lucy!?'

'Why shouldn't I have a boyfriend?'

'Well you never showed the slightest interest before.'

'No, I always liked boys. And anyway, things have changed.'

Even to myself I sounded sulky, and she just grinned.

'Not that much. You're still stripping off in the woods. Do you remember where we used to swim at Marnhoe? You'd always be the first to go naked, and the last to get dressed.'

'You used to strip me! And … and make me do rude things to get my clothes back.'

She just laughed, making my blushes hotter than ever, but I couldn't help turning my mind back to the little quarry where we used to swim together. I remembered trying not to giggle as she and her friends held me down while I was divested of my skirt and blouse, my knickers and bra, then thrown in, stark naked. And afterwards, begging to be allowed my clothes back and being made to kiss Juliette's bottom, only to be refused my knickers and to end up walking back bare under my skirt, terrified that a puff of wind would expose my shame to the world. Juliette drew a long sigh.

'Those were the days. I thought it would always be like that, and look at me now, one more rat on the treadmill. Oh well, at least I've got you, for a while. Let's go.'

Her glass was empty, but mine was nearly full and I swallowed what I could before following her to a red BMW. She didn't bother to put her seatbelt on, as heedless of both safety and authority as ever, and as I strapped up she gave me one of her brief, contemptuous glances. I could remember her driving, and was feeling nervous before we'd even got through the village, but she put her foot down hard the moment we were on the open road, only to slow down a little.

'Let's take it easy. It's not the end of the world if we don't get there for lunch.'

'The instructions said to arrive before ten o'clock. You've already been penalised for being late.'

'What are they going to do, give me a spanking?'

41

Her voice was full of derision, but just the mention of that awful word had my heart hammering in my chest and the blood rushing back to my face. She didn't see, her eyes fixed to the road as we took a long corner.

'No, they're not, are they? They're going to put a black mark against my name or make some comment about a negative attitude on my report. I don't care. Do you?'

'Not all that much, no, but I'd rather not cause any unnecessary fuss.'

'That's my Lucy, always the careful one, but always the naughty one too. Did you ever get caught for anything? No, I don't think you did, but you got punished, didn't you? Do you remember how I used to spank you?'

I nodded, unable to deny the truth but not wanting to admit just how important those memories had been to me or how much influence she'd had.

'Does Stacey do it? I bet she does, over her knee with your panties pulled down, just the way you like it, or is she really stern with you?'

This time I couldn't hold back.

'She spanks me. She ... she doesn't really understand, but she enjoys doing it, now.'

'You trained her to spank you? Wonderful! Only you, Lucy, only you. How about the cane? I used to love to cane you. Do you remember that time I did it in front of Emily and Claire? How you squealed, and then I made you wait a week before giving you the last five! Does Stacey cane you?'

'She has once, but she's not normally that harsh with me. She's sweet.'

'It doesn't sound as if she knows how to handle you at all. What does she like then?'

There was no mistaking the arousal in her voice, and she

had me in a state of toe-curling embarrassment, but I couldn't stop myself as I went on.

'She's very physical. She likes to play fight and hold me down. She's strong too, stronger than you.'

I hadn't been able to resist the dig, but Juliette merely gave a doubtful snort and I found myself backing down immediately.

'Or maybe not, and she's not really very experienced. It was her first time, with me.'

Juliette gave a low purr, another reaction I was all too familiar with. I didn't respond, wondering what would happen if she made a move on Stacey. Experience told me that poor Stacey was likely to end up on her knees, or over Juliette's, but there was also a possibility that I'd be the one on the receiving end, from both of them, a thought that made me shiver. I couldn't imagine Juliette taking anything other than an aggressive, dominant role, although the thought of her wriggling and kicking over Stacey's lap as she was spanked gave me a sudden stab of vindictive pleasure.

We'd been following the river, with dense woods on the opposite side of the road. A Forestry Commission sign came into view and Juliette immediately slammed the brakes on, slowing the car just enough to let her take the corner safely. The trees closed in above us over a gravel track, forming a gloomy tunnel into the wood. I knew full well what was going on, and that I wouldn't be able to resist her for a moment, but that didn't stop me asking, or keep the note of panic out of my voice.

'Where are we going, Juliette?'

'Somewhere I can give you what you need, for old times' sake.'

'But I don't want to be punished! Besides, you can't mark

me. What if Stacey saw? And Wendy, the other girl. We're sure to have to shower together, and they'll see!'

I was whining, and it sounded pathetic even in my own ears, but I'd sealed my fate, effectively admitting that she could do as she pleased with me as long as she didn't mark my skin. Not that she cared anyway, as she'd never had any time for the little mind games I played with myself in order to justify my surrender, except that she sometimes found them amusing.

The track was long and straight, ending in a circle of gravel wide enough to turn a lorry and completely hedged in by tall pines. Juliette swung the car around, parking so that we could look back the way we'd come. A single tug on the lever that controlled my chair and I was suddenly on my back. Now there was no mistaking her intentions at all, her eyes glittering with cruelty and mischief as she looked down at me.

'I have missed you so badly, Lucy. Roll over then, onto your front, and stick that sweet little bottom up in the air.'

I obeyed, for all that I was pouting as I did it, turning onto my belly before lifting my hips, my head burning with chagrin and resentment even as I made my bottom available to her. She either didn't realise or didn't care, reaching out to stroke the taut blue material of the seat of my shorts and shaking her head as if in wonder at the shape and texture of my bottom.

'You are lovely, so neat, so firm, but you always were so, so spankable.'

She began to smack, just hard enough to make my cheeks shiver, all the while with her gaze feasting on my bottom as if she was going to eat me. I pushed my hips up a little higher, unable to stop myself enjoying her attention, at which her fingers slipped between my legs, to stroke the bulge where my shorts were pulled tight over my cunt. What with running, and playing with Stacey in the woods, and what Juliette had been saying to me, I knew I was already wet, and exactly how I'd look from behind, with my sex lips making a horseshoe-shaped damp patch in the crotch of my shorts. Juliette could hardly fail to notice, or to comment.

'Soaking, as usual. You make me laugh, Lucy, always pretending you don't want to play and all the while you're dripping wet.'

I didn't even try to explain, because she'd never really understood my feelings and probably never would, unless she got it herself. That was never going to happen, not between me and her, because just to be with her made me want to grovel at her feet, never mind when she started to get dirty with me. Now that I had my bottom lifted and my cunt had been touched I was hers, and there was no resistance in me at all as she took hold of the waistband of my shorts.

'Let's pop these down then, shall we? I know you like me to have you bare.'

She began to pull, slowly easing my shorts down over my bottom to expose me to her gaze: the swell of my cheeks and the split between, the flesh of my bottom and the tight pink dimple of my anus, the soft crease where my buttocks met my thighs and the pouted lips of my cunt. I had no knickers on, and I knew she'd comment, but that did nothing to dilute my embarrassment as she saw.

'Still running around with no panties on, I see, Lucy. No bra either by the look of it. Don't you ever wear any underwear?'

As she spoke she pushed up my top, adding the exposure of my breasts to my woes. I was bare in front of Juliette Fisher, again, and I was no more capable of fighting the feelings she provoked in me than I had been all those years ago, perhaps weaker still, as when she began to stroke the skin of my back and bottom with her nails I couldn't hold back a sigh. She continued to explore, and when she spoke again her voice was soft.

'That's better, isn't it? I've missed you so much, Lucy, you darling little slut, but I see you've been getting your share. You're bruised.'

'Stacey spanked me with a hairbrush last night.'

'What for?'

'For being stuck up.'

'I can understand that. You always were a bit of a madam, weren't you? I bet she's rough, a big, strong girl like that. Did it hurt?'

'Yes, a lot, but not as much as the cane, not as much as you used to hurt me. She's nice, she spanks me off.'

'You have got her well trained, haven't you? You're a dirty slut, Lucy, and you need to be punished.'

There was no use denying it, with my bare bottom pushed up to the touch of her nails. As she began to spank again I was moaning in pleasure, but that wasn't her intention.

'This is no use. What you need is a good thrashing.'

'No, Juliette, please. Stacey will see.'

'What, and find out that you're an unfaithful little tart? Oh, very well, just for the sake of peace. I'll get you rosy and warm, then it's my turn.'

I knew full well she didn't mean she wanted a spanking. For her that was unthinkable, an impossible contradiction, and as she continued to smack at my bottom I was wondering what she would do to me. Whatever it was, I was in no state to resist, and she knew it, and I couldn't help but think back to some of the things she'd threatened me with but never done, leaving me as scared as I was aroused when she finally tired of amusing herself with my bottom. She jerked a thumb at me as she gave me my orders.

'On your back, Lucy, legs up and open. I'm going to sit on your face.'

It was the least of what I'd expected, and I couldn't help but feel a touch of disappointment as I rolled over to allow her to straddle my upper body. Her knees were cocked wide, her bottom a full bulge in the seat of her tight blue skirt, which she was forced to pull up before she could get comfortable. Even then it was an awkward position, but I was going to get it in the face, and that was what mattered. My own legs came up, as ordered, and she quickly pulled my shorts down properly, then right off, leaving me bare and more vulnerable than ever, with my cunt spread to the windscreen.

'Make sure to keep a lookout, Juliette.'

'I can see right down the track, and anyway, do you think I care if anyone sees your cunt? Do you think it matters? Don't be so fucking precious, Lucy.'

I knew she was only tormenting me, but it worked, leaving me imagining myself spread out in front of an audience, just as she'd had me in front of Emily and Claire, everything on show while nobody else had so much as a stitch out of place. Not that Juliette was planning to stay covered, her hands working her skirt up over her hips to expose the tops of her hold-ups and a pair of white satin panties that clung to her bottom as if they'd been painted on. With her skirt rucked up around her waist she pushed her thumbs into her panties, speaking as she began to push them slowly down.

'Take a good look, Lucy, because my bum is going right in your pretty face.'

She'd exposed herself as she spoke, baring the full globe

of her bottom and the slit between, her anus a dark wrinkle between her cheeks, her pussy lips pouted and puffy with excitement. I was going to get her bare bottom in my face, a thought that filled me with panic, almost horror, but even as she sat down my tongue had poked out, to lick between the softness of her cheeks and at the velvet-smooth dimple of her anus. She sat down, wriggling herself into my face as I began to lick harder, her voice a sigh.

'That's my Lucy, that's right, lick my bottom hole, darling. Put your tongue in ... that's right, that's my Lucy ...'

I'd pushed my tongue as deep in up her bottom as it would go, lost to all sense of decency and restraint. She gave another wriggle, delighting in my surrender. My hands had gone between my legs and I was masturbating as I licked her anus. I rolled up my legs, deliberately showing off the red flesh where I'd had the tuck of my cheeks smacked as well as my own bottom hole and my cunt, eager to show Juliette how completely she'd made me hers. She took hold of my thighs, spreading me wider still, until it hurt, with her bottom squirming in my face to a slow, lewd rhythm and my tongue as far up her hole as I could get it. That was enough, my humiliation complete, and Juliette was laughing as I started to come.

Chapter Three

Juliette and I made it back with the drink, and the excitement of sneaking it in even went some way towards keeping down my embarrassment and guilt for the way I'd let myself go in the car. I couldn't bring myself to look Stacey in the eyes over lunch, for all that I was promising myself I'd tell her the truth and hope that she'd give me some humiliating punishment but wouldn't really be cross. Our relationship was completely open, in theory, but I couldn't help feeling I'd betrayed her, not for what I'd done so much as for whom I'd done it with, and because after five years of separation I'd allowed myself to be turned back into Juliette's obedient little slut within a matter of minutes.

There was no opportunity to confess for the rest of the day, or that night. Parker and his minions kept us busy, first with arranging the camp, then an inspection and a lecture on teamwork and what was expected of us. I'd guessed he would be picking on me from the moment I saw him, and not just because of what had happened the night before. For all his talk of teamwork he was very much the type to play favourites and victims, while I always seem to be the girl who gets picked on, whether it's for good or for bad. Sure enough, he mentioned 'Girl O' almost twice as much as any other person, while his favourites seemed to be Daniel and the brash American, Chad.

After the inspirational lecture came what I'd been dreading all day, a run on the assault course, and not only because of the cold and the mud, but because completing it meant getting into all sorts of undignified positions that risked showing off the tuck of my bottom cheeks and revealing to all the world that I'd been spanked. It seemed inevitable that somebody would notice, especially with the team going one by one, which meant having fourteen no doubt highly sexed young men watch as Stacey, Juliette, Wendy and myself went over the course. I could think of only one way out, and pretended to slip at the start so that I could deliberately sit my bottom down in the first mud puddle, which drew a sarcastic remark from Parker, left the rest of the men laughing and set me blushing hot, but if I was going to be showing off a pair of red cheeks I much preferred them to be the upper ones.

With the assault course complete we were obliged to form a dishevelled, muddy line while we listened to another of Parker's talks and were given an initial assessment of our ability. Girl O got another roasting, both for being timid and not supporting my teammates, both completely unfair charges. I said nothing, standing meekly to attention as I was given what I was sure would be the first dressing down of many, then making straight for the showers. Unfortunately the arrangement of the camp created an embarrassing situation, quite possibly intentional, but made worse by the brevity of my robe. The laundry was separate from the shower block. My clothes were filthy with mud and so was my skin. If I went back to our hut to fetch my robe, stripped off and carried my dirty clothes to the laundry I'd have to squat to avoid showing my bare bottom as I put my things into the machine. On the other hand, if I stripped off in the showers I'd end up naked and wet, with only the hopelessly inadequate camp towels to cover my modesty as I visited the laundry before retreating to the hut. I didn't want to get my robe wet either, which would be inevitable if I took it into the baking, steamy shower block. The only conceivable alternative to my robe would have been my mac, except that it was a retro seventies-style one in transparent plastic.

The only chance of preserving any dignity at all was to get into the shower fully dressed, wash myself down, then strip and rinse my clothes as best I could before putting them back on, allowing me to make a dash for the hut in wet running kit. That way I managed to dry off and freshen up in peace, leaving me feeling at least vaguely human. Dinner followed, a brief social hour and then bed, with lights out at nine o'clock prompt. I'd been hoping, but also dreading, that the evening might allow what were obviously interesting possibilities between the four of us to develop, but we were all too tired to think of anything but sleep.

I was woken by the clamour of a bell, mistook it for the office fire alarm, fell out of bed, realised that there wasn't a fire but that it was six o'clock, and once more found myself cursing Mr Scott, along with Parker and everybody else who'd been involved in landing me in the situation. My entire body ached from the exertions of the day before, while if my two spankings had left me bruised it was no longer possible to distinguish the marks from the ones I'd picked up on the assault course. That only went so far to reduce the embarrassing ritual of visiting the showers, made worse because I'd expected a private bathroom and decided to sleep in panties and a top rather than a proper nightie or PJs.

51

Breakfast was served in Mess, with the sun still only just up, and followed by a parade, with the four teams now stood separately, each with the leader to the right and a little in front. We were team A, just as Juliette was Girl A, with three all-male teams stood beside us. It was obvious at a glance how Parker had divided us, and who he expected to win, and to lose. Team B included Alastair Renton and three other competent young men, but it was clear that Team C were intended to be the cream, with just three members, including Chad as team leader, Daniel Chambers and Roy Karsen, who looked like Captain America but didn't seem to speak much. If Team C were the cream, then Team D were the dregs. The leader was Graham Boothe, a big, awkward man who seemed to be all legs and arms, another man who was not only the shortest but the oldest among us all, a boy who looked like Billy Bunter and, inevitably, Paul Yates.

The temptation to step out of line and ask Parker whether he felt that classic bullying tactics were appropriate for a management course was considerable, but I knew he wouldn't understand, for all that the answer was undoubtedly yes. I didn't have the guts anyway, but stood as before, as smart and as compliant as could be, answering to 'Girl O' despite the sense that I was being somehow molested every time he said it, then bracing my feet apart and holding my hands behind my back just like the others as he began to tell us what the day had in store.

'It's a simple test, of fitness, stamina and, of course, team-work. Each team will be issued a map and a compass. You will then be driven to a base camp and given a set of field co-ordinates, which I will tell you – in case Team D decides they mark the local pub – is a tor near the third highest peak on Dartmoor. You need to get there as fast as you can. Hidden among the rocks is a jar. In the jar are twelve numbered balls. The number on the ball you take is your score for the exercise and Sergeant Reynolds will be up there to make sure there's no monkey business. The team with the highest aggregate score gets a bonus of twelve points, equally divided between them. The team with the lowest aggregate score gets a penalty of twelve points, just the same. Got that?'

As Chad and others barked out their answers I was suffering from a sinking feeling. The exercise meant a long, hard day, aching muscles, mud and scratches, not at all my idea of entertainment. Not only that, but the outcome was more or less foreordained. Team C would not only win but with just three members they would gain an unfair benefit from the scoring system. Team B would come in behind them, then us, and last of all Team D, which made the whole thing futile. Stacey was keen though, and determined that we should do our best, so I kept my thoughts to myself as we got ready and drove out to a car park beside a reservoir in the middle of a vast forestry plantation. One glance at the map showed that the situation was worse than I'd thought, with miles of rough, boggy ground to cross, most of it steep. The others obviously had no such qualms, even Juliette and Wendy caught up in the moment, so I swallowed my feelings and joined them as they clustered around our map and Stacey worked out the co-ordinates.

'We're here, in Fernworthy Forest and our objective is here, Fur Tor. That's about seven K, as the crow flies. So let's go.'

She set off at a jog and the rest of us followed, quickly overtaking Team D, who knew where they were going but didn't look too happy about it, and leaving the others still studying their maps. I couldn't help but smile as I saw that Juliette was doing her best to outrun Stacey, who responded in turn. Wendy and I were soon well behind and I kept pace with her just to be friendly, running between ranks of tall pines and clearings of freshly cut stumps and broken wood. The sun was well above the trees in a clear blue sky, while the air was gloriously fresh and carried a faint tang of pine resin, all very lovely.

Left to my own devices I'd have spent the morning walking and enjoying my thoughts, perhaps even found a quiet place to strip off for the sheer joy of being in the nude, or to bathe in one of the little streams that ran down to the reservoir, a prospect that made me all the more resentful of Parker and his pointless exercise. I was getting hot too, my thighs already aching as I pushed myself up one slope after another, and by the time I reached the stone wall that marked the edge of the forest I was forced to stop to catch my breath, while my hair was wet with sweat and my top plastered to my breasts.

Wendy was no better and we shared a rueful grin as we sat down together at the top of a big wooden stile. Beyond was bare moor, stretching up to a line of big open hills, with Stacey and Juliette visible a good half-mile ahead, like two little dolls with their black ponytails bobbing behind them. Some of the men were also visible, but they'd taken a different route through the forest and were some way to the north, too far to be sure who was who, although I could recognise Chad's cries of encouragement to his teammates. To the south the ground sloped down to a broad valley speckled with sheep and cattle, some of which were being herded by a man on a quad bike, presumably a farmer.

'That's the way to travel.'

Wendy's thoughts echoed my own, and I immediately found myself wondering if the scheme was practical. Parker hadn't said anything about how we got to our objective, and it struck me that borrowing a quad bike would be showing initiative rather than cheating. Getting the farmer to lend it to me was another matter, but that sparked another thought, a very naughty one. One of my favourite fantasies had always been to find myself in a situation in which I had no choice but to hitch a lift and was made to pay by sucking the driver's cock. Usually I imagined myself ending up penniless in somewhere like Italy or Turkey, and having to pay my way across the width of Europe with some bastard who liked to come three or four times a day and insisted on making me swallow. The situation with the farmer and the quad bike wasn't as good as that, but it had the great advantage of being real, and attainable. It had the disadvantage that sucking a farmer's cock in return for a lift wasn't going to do much good for my precious reputation, but that was only a problem if I got caught, which begged the question: could I trust Wendy? I decided to test her.

'Yes, but I can guess what he'd expect in return for a lift, let alone borrowing the thing.'

She giggled, which meant she knew what I meant and wasn't as sweet and innocent as she looked.

'Pussy as currency.'

Her voice was soft, wistful even, and I found myself slightly shocked, for all that I'd been thinking almost exactly the same thing.

'You bad girl!'

She'd gone pink, but she'd caught the tone of my voice just as I'd caught hers, and went on.

'We haven't any money, so what else are we supposed to pay with?'

I nodded, then swallowed the sudden lump in my throat. Maybe it comes of living a secure life, maybe it's the way I can't help but link sex and shame, but I've always found the idea of having to prostitute myself appealing. Wendy seemed to be the same, but I wasn't sure how far she'd go.

'You wouldn't dare.'

'Would you?'

I made a face at her. She'd put the ball straight back in my court, neither of us wanting to be the first to admit to being capable of actually doing anything so inappropriate.

'We could always ask. Maybe he'd be nice about it, or maybe …'

She smiled as I trailed off, perhaps thinking the same as I was, that maybe he was the sort of dirty bastard who'd put us on our knees together, side by side as we worked on his cock and balls with our mouths and lips and tongues. Without speaking again we climbed down the stile and ran on, angling down towards the valley. I wasn't sure what I was doing, let alone if I would dare to actually proposition the farmer, with or without Wendy there, but even to be heading towards him felt brave and naughty, a pleasant combination after my earlier feelings.

We soon lost sight of the men, then of Stacey and Juliette, with the flank of the hill sheltering us from the high ground. I was half hoping the farmer would drive away in a different direction, allowing me to escape my decision without losing face in front of Wendy, but he'd stopped beside the little stream at the bottom of the valley and was pouring what was presumably tea into the lid of a thermos. As we drew closer I saw that he was quite young, maybe younger than me, but well built, with a mop of untidy black hair and several days' worth of stubble, giving him just the sort of rough edge I've never been able to resist. Even then I'd have run past with just a nod, only he was far less shy.

'Morning, girls, out for a run? Time to stop for a dish of tea?'

I came to a halt, leaning my hands on my knees for a moment to get my breath back and let Wendy catch up before I spoke.

'Thank you, that would be lovely. It's hot.'

He nodded, his eyes flicking from my face to my chest, where my nipples showed stiff through my top, then to Wendy, who was in a similar condition although she at least had a bra on. I accepted the thermos lid and took a swallow before passing it to Wendy as he went on.

'I don't get it myself, all this running about. I get enough of that working.'

It was just the feed I needed, and I couldn't resist.

'We're on a sort of exercise, but I'd much rather hitch a ride on your quad bike.'

He seemed to think about it.

'Where to?'

'Fur Tor, it's ...'

'Oh I know Fur Tor, right up on the tops, that is. I can take one of you, two if the other doesn't mind clinging on the back.'

I gave the quad bike a dubious look. It was a big square thing, obviously designed for agriculture rather than sport, with plenty of room for a pillion passenger and even a low rail to cling on to, but anybody standing on the ledge at the back while it went over rough ground was almost certainly going to end up getting thrown off.

'Perhaps one of us could sit on your lap?'

Wendy shot me a meaningful glance, which he didn't see. I hadn't expected him to proposition us on the spot, as few men are that rude, but there was no mistaking his tone as he answered.

'I can't say I mind a pretty girl on my knee, if it's alright with you? I'm John, John Runyon.'

'Lucy, how d'you do? This is my friend Wendy.'

I was far from sure of myself, but excited, and fairly certain that if I showed the slightest interest I was going to end up riding more than just the quad bike. He was keen to go too, and no surprise, with Wendy's thighs spread across his backside and my bottom perched on his leg, so close in that I could feel the bugle of his cock and balls beneath his trousers. I couldn't even move, or he'd have been unable to drive properly, and from the moment we set off the vibration of the engine and the motion of the bike on the rough ground had my bottom bouncing on his leg and his cock rubbing against my crotch.

He didn't say anything, at first, beyond laughing or cursing as he negotiated obstacles, but I could feel him getting hard against my thigh. Obviously he knew, and he must have guessed that I knew, because as we reached a narrow part of the valley he came to a halt, his voice full of embarrassment as he spoke.

'I suppose you'll be wanting to get off? I'm sorry, only some things a man can't help.'

In my fantasies the men were always assertive, even downright rude, ordering me to get down on their cocks or down from the cab, but it was far easier to respond to his shy, almost apologetic manner.

'I don't mind at all, really. In fact, it only seems fair, as you're taking us all the way to Fur Tor, that we ought to, er … pay …'

My face was hot with blushes and I couldn't bring myself to finish, but Wendy was no better. I was hoping he'd realise and take control of the situation, but unfortunately he wasn't very quick on the uptake.

'Oh no, I couldn't take any money.'

I had to do it, and I was red-faced and babbling as I replied.

'I mean pay by ... by being nice to you, and anyway, if you're getting ... getting a bit of a problem, it only seems sensible for us to help you with it, and fair.'

His eyes had gone round.

'You're offering me a hand job?'

I nodded, reaching out to squeeze him through his trousers, only for Wendy to interrupt.

'Er ... shouldn't we get up to Fur Tor first, Lucy? Otherwise the others will beat us.'

'Are you in a race?' John asked as his hand closed on top of mine. 'I'll get you there, but you don't do this to me and leave me. I've got to come.'

He was certainly hard enough, and I glanced at my watch, then at Wendy.

'I'll get him off. You pose for him or something.'

'No! I'll get him off. You can pose!'

'OK, but ...'

I'd been massaging John's cock through his trousers as we spoke and his voice was little more than a moan as he cut in.

'Just pull your tops up, that'll be fine, and you can both do it, but let's get out of sight first.'

We stopped just a few feet away from a stand of rocks and quickly moved in among them, not completely sheltered but probably safe for a few minutes. I could see Wendy's point about hurrying and didn't waste any time, quickly tugging my top up to bare my breasts as John pulled his cock and balls free of his fly. Wendy hesitated only a moment before she too pulled her upper clothes high, exposing two rounded, pale boobs, both splashed with freckles. I already had John

59

in hand, tugging on his stiff shaft, and she took hold of his balls. His hand went around our waists, then lower, pushing into the back of my shorts, and Wendy's, to squeeze and stroke our bottoms as we masturbated him.

I wanted my shorts down, and I wanted to suck, so I quickly got to my knees, stripping myself behind as Wendy took hold of his erection and opening my mouth to let her guide it in. John gave a deep moan for the feel of his cock in my mouth and Wendy giggled to see me so urgent and so dirty, her eyes full of laughter and mischief as she masturbated him in time to the motions of my sucking. I was wishing we had more time, so that I could suck him properly, and perhaps more, maybe even find an excuse to play with Wendy, but I knew we had to hurry. My hand went to his balls, I slid one finger between his muscular bum cheeks and I found his anus, teasing the tiny hole even as I wondered at my own filthy behaviour.

Wendy gave a little gasp of shock as she saw what I was doing, but began to tug faster on his shaft as he reacted with a groan of ecstasy. I pushed my finger in up his bottom, he grunted and suddenly my mouth was full of salty, slimy spunk, more than I could possibly swallow. Most of it came out from around my lips and over Wendy's hand and his balls, the rest exploding from my nose as I began to gag, losing my balance at the same instant, to sprawl, thighs spread, on the turf. Wendy reacted first.

'You dirty bitch, Lucy! It's all over my hand.'

'Sorry, I couldn't help it. Wash it off in the water.'

She made a dash for the stream, bare boobs jiggling as she ran, while John relaxed back against the rock with a long sigh. I had to join Wendy, who still hadn't covered herself up, and as I knelt down beside her I saw that she was shaking, for all her disgust when I'd spat spunk over her hand. I needed more and I was sure she did too.

'Later? Perhaps in the woods?'

She responded with an urgent nod and we hurried back to the quad bike. We'd taken just a few minutes to get John off, but it had left me badly in need and Wendy the same. As we rode on I was wondering how long he'd take before he'd want us again, and whether he'd be able to cope with us both. I also wondered if he'd like to watch us together, because there's no better excuse for lesbian sex than pretending you're only doing it to please a man. What little I'd seen of Wendy's pale, delicate body appealed, but I could only hope that she returned my feelings. If she did, then a whole world of possibilities would be opened up, involving Stacey and Juliette too.

Now that we'd got him despunked, John gave his full attention to driving the quad bike, and he'd obviously had plenty of experience and knew every inch of the moor. He was able to find tracks where I hadn't been able to see anything but tufts of coarse grass, and take advantage of areas of short, hard turf that I'd have ignored because they didn't run in quite the right direction. When we came out onto the shoulder of the biggest of the hills we'd been able to see from the forest I found myself looking down over a huge area of open ground, with the competition visible as tiny pale dots against the vastness, too small for me to see who was who.

At the top of the hill a new vista opened out, to the west, with a great irregular pan of land surrounded by big hills, and right in front of us an impressive pile of granite that could only be Fur Tor. I could see Sergeant Reynolds too, his blue Camp Aspiration top quite distinct, and I told John to stop and wait for us out of sight, not wanting to have to defend my choice of transport unless I had to. Wendy and I ran on, quickly reaching the tor and digging out the jar of balls from among the rocks. Sergeant Reynolds looked on, impassive, as we chose numbers twelve and eleven, although he was looking at his watch with a somewhat puzzled expression.

I was keen to get away before the others came up with us and ran back as fast as I could, leaving Wendy well behind as I rejoined John where he was sat astride the quad bike in a shallow gully between banks of peat. He was clearly enjoying the game, and no surprise when Wendy and I were more or less obliged to do anything he wanted once he got us into the shelter of the forest. I kissed him as I reached the bike and was rewarded with a squeeze of my bottom as I climbed onto his lap. We started immediately, swinging around to collect Wendy, and for one brief moment I could see some of the men across the rough turf of the hilltop: Alastair, Chad and a couple more I couldn't be sure of. They were plainly exhausted, and I couldn't help but laugh as we started back, bouncing over the turf at a speed I'd have found frightening if it wasn't for the exhilaration of what we'd done. Wendy was laughing too, and I saw that where she'd put her arms around John's waist to hold on she'd also pushed her hands down the front of his trousers. I could feel her massaging his cock as we rode, and for all the concentration he was putting into his driving he was soon getting hard.

As we reached the little valley where we'd first met she unzipped him, to pull his erection free in full view of anybody who happened to be passing. I thought he'd stop, but there was nobody in sight and he was obviously enjoying the attention, and maybe showing off. She'd got his balls out too, and I risked letting go with one hand so that I could squeeze and stroke them, only for the bike to hit a bump and knock me backward, completely off balance, to land spread-eagled on the turf, still laughing.

John pulled the bike to a stop, his face full of concern as he dismounted, until he saw that I wasn't hurt. His cock was still out and still hard, a sight that filled me with a sudden impulse to be fucked where I lay, for all that I'd gone down in something soft and squashy and knew I'd be filthy with mud. We were in a steep part of the valley too, not exactly hidden, but safe enough, while our companions were all a mile or more to the side. As he approached I pushed down my shorts, all the way to my ankles, and spread my thighs, offering myself to him. He'd been apologising, but immediately went quiet. Wendy giggled and called me a slut, then told John to fuck me.

He didn't need instructions. I was bare and wet, his cock was hard, and that was enough. I opened my arms to him as he got down between my legs, his cock pressed to my cunt as we came together, and he was in me, pushing deep up without any trouble. My arms closed around his back, our mouths met in an open kiss and I surrendered myself completely, my thighs spread as he pumped himself into me. Wendy came close, her eyes wide with arousal and excitement but not sure what to do. I wanted her to play too and reached up to grab her shorts, which came down as I pulled, panties and all, to bare the furry ginger triangle between her thighs.

She squeaked in surprise but went to her knees, unresisting as I pulled her in, to kiss first John and then me as my hand went to her bottom. I could tell she was unsure of herself, reluctant even, but with John's cock thrusting in and out of my open pussy I simply didn't have the patience to take it slowly. Her panties were still up at the back, but I quickly got them down. She gasped as my fingers burrowed between her bottom cheeks, to brush her anus before finding the wet slit of her cunt, but when I touched her clit her resistance vanished. Her mouth opened against mine and we were kissing, with John staring in amazement and delight even as he continued with my fucking.

He also saw the position Wendy was in, kneeling with her pale little bottom stuck up in the air and her shorts and panties pulled down to leave her vulnerable from behind as we kissed. I pointed at her, trying to signal that I didn't mind if he took turns with us, but he misunderstood, still pumping into me as he put a hand to her bottom and slid one large finger in up her cunt. Her body shivered and her kisses grew more passionate as she was filled, but I wanted her as badly as I wanted him, and wasn't content with just a kiss.

John's cock slipped from my cunt as I wriggled in underneath Wendy's body, my arms encircling her waist to lock her into a sixty-nine. Again she seemed hesitant for a moment, until my mouth found her pussy, and after a single gasp of what might have been simple passion, or more likely dismay for her inability to hold herself back, she returned the favour. John swore as he saw what we were doing, and called us dirty bitches as he pushed his cock in up Wendy's cunt. I saw it go in, and the way her hole spread to take him, before his balls pressed to my face.

With that I was truly in heaven, at the bottom of the heap where I've always felt I belonged, licking my new friend's cunt with a man's balls squashing in my face as he fucked her. Even if she hadn't been licking me I'd have had to masturbate, but with her tongue flicking at my clitoris and her hands holding my bottom cheeks apart the consequences were inevitable. My thighs went tight around Wendy's head as the muscles of my belly and legs went into contraction and I was coming, with my cunt open to her face, utterly shameless and still licking for all I was worth as I gasped out my ecstasy.

I heard John grunt and I knew he was going to come too, but I was taken completely by surprise as he jerked his cock free of Wendy's hole. He was already coming, and the first spurt went in my face and the second in my mouth as he jammed himself deep, making me gag and retch with my orgasm still singing in my head. I could taste his spunk, and Wendy's juice, and the thought of sucking a cock freshly drawn from her body pushed me up to another peak before I collapsed back on the turf, soiled but happy.

* * *

Parker was frowning as he looked down at his clipboard, clearly less than happy with the data in front of him. I waited, with my feet braced apart and my hands behind my back, the at-ease position he favoured and which everybody else seemed happy with, although it made me feel as if I was being forced to make myself vulnerable. After a long while he looked up, right at me.

'Girl O, twelve points. Girl E, eleven points. Now how did you manage that, O? Did you outrun all these fine young men?'

I wasn't sure how much he knew, and I wasn't about to enlighten him, for all the sinking feeling in my stomach for his openly sarcastic tone. Nevertheless, it was obviously pointless to pretend I'd done it under my own steam. Alastair, Chad and perhaps others had seen me and Wendy on the quad bike, while even after our urgent little sex session in the gully we'd got back to the vehicles long before anybody else.

'I used my initiative.'

'You used your initiative? Are you sure you didn't cheat?'

I didn't answer, because I knew it was pointless. Parker was a bully and he was sure to behave like a bully, imposing his will simply because he knew he could and relishing his victim's attempts to escape. I had no intention of giving him the satisfaction of seeing me squirm, for all that I knew full well that if it had been his precious Chad who'd hitched a lift on the quad bike it would have been a different story. The thought provoked an image of Chad on his knees as he sucked on John's erection, which brought an involuntary smile to the corners of my mouth. Parker had been waiting for me to say something but carried on.

'What Girl O and Girl E did, boys and girls, was to hitch a lift with a local farmer. Fortunately Chad saw them and reported the matter to Sergeant Reynolds. Team A is disqualified, which means …'

It was exactly as I'd expected, but Juliette wasn't having it, speaking out without bothering to raise her hand.

'What do you mean we're disqualified? You didn't say anything about not using vehicles, and anyway, Stacey and I got the six and five balls.'

Parker didn't even bother to acknowledge her, but began again.

'Team A is disqualified.'

'That's completely unreasonable.'

'Team A is disqualified.'

Juliette would have carried on, but I reached out to touch her arm, hoping to stop her before she lost her temper, which would only make matters worse. She understood and went quiet, allowing Parker to read out the results, with Team

C firmly in the lead with twenty-six points and the bonus of twelve, making thirty-eight in all, and Chad on top with fourteen. We were last and collected the penalty, leaving us with a team score of minus twelve, only for him to suddenly change his mind.

'On second thoughts, I'm going to allow Girls A and G their individual scores, which leaves them on two and three points respectively, which is fair, but that also means Girls O and E have to take full penalties, which leaves them with minus fifteen and minus fourteen.'

The decision was arbitrary, and clearly intended to humiliate me and Wendy, but again I held my peace, determined not to give him the pleasure of having me react. With the scores read out he went on to discuss the exercise, but I wasn't listening. He had got to me, and there was a big lump in my throat, but I was determined not to cry and turned my thoughts to the fun I'd had with John and Wendy. It had been a wonderful experience, dirty and spontaneous, risky too, which always added to the thrill, while the discovery that Wendy was willing to play opened up all sorts of possibilities for the future. We also had John's number.

We hadn't been given a chance to tidy ourselves up before being put on parade and my first thought on being dismissed was to head for the showers, quickly, so as to minimise the embarrassment of trying not to show myself off too much. The others weren't in such a hurry, staying back to talk to the men, so I was on my own in the hut as I peeled off my wet things to wrap one towel around my body and use a second to make a turban for my hair. Wendy was the first to join me, having made the dash from the shower block in nothing but a towel and complaining immediately.

'I'm sure that man Parker's done it on purpose. I virtually

had to streak, and with most of the men looking on.'

'You're probably right. He's a dirty so-and-so, I know that for sure, and not in a nice way. The first thing he said to me was that he wanted to fuck me. He was really crude about it too.'

'What a pig! John was nicer. I don't think he'd have pushed it at all if we hadn't given him the green light.'

'He was good. Polite when it mattered, forceful when it mattered.'

Her response was a low purr, then a mischievous smile, only for her expression to turn to a frown as she began to dry her legs.

'How are we supposed to manage with one towel each? I mean, this one's already soaking, and how are we supposed to do our hair?'

'One towel each? Aren't there more?'

'No. I asked Mr Straw and he was really sarcastic about it. He asked if I thought I was at a hotel. Apparently it's all to do with learning self-reliance.'

'More like keeping the costs down.'

I'd pulled one leg up onto the bed to dry between my toes, and was just reaching for the powder when the door opened again, to admit Juliette. Like Wendy, she was wrapped in a single towel, but being taller she'd only just been able to cover her nipples and the tuck of her bottom at the same time. She did not sound happy.

'OK, which of you jokers took all the towels? Oh, I see, I might have known it would be you, Lucy.'

'But I need one for my hair.'

'Fine, but try telling that to Stacey. She's just got into the shower and there are no towels.'

'I'll take her one. I'm nearly dry.'

I made for the chest of drawers where I'd put my clothes, only for Stacey to come in, still in her dirty running kit, and also wet. She took in the scene, Juliette and Wendy wrapped in their towels, me with one around my body and one around my head, then spoke.

'Oh, thank you very much, Lucy. It's supposed to be one towel each.'

'I'm sorry, Stacey. I didn't realise. These are a bit wet, I'm afraid, but …'

Juliette laughed, cutting me off, then addressed Stacey.

'I know what I'd do. I'd spank the little brat.'

I found myself colouring up immediately, just at the mention of the word, with my stomach tight and a lump in my throat. Wendy gave a short, nervous giggle, and I hastened to reassure her.

'She's only joking, Wendy. Sorry, Stacey, I didn't realise there was only one each. Here, have this one.'

Stacey took the towel I'd had around my hair, but Juliette wasn't done.

'And she got us disqualified. Go on, Stacey, spank her. I'm not bothered.'

Wendy obviously was, pink-faced and looking nervously between us as Stacey examined the towel.

'This is soaking, Lucy. You might have some consideration!'

I shrugged, genuinely contrite but painfully embarrassed and not at all sure what to say. Juliette had an evil little smirk painted on her face and was plainly taking a lot of pleasure in my discomfort, but to my relief Stacey seemed more worried about getting her shower as she went on.

'Maybe I'll be OK with two. Give me your other one.'

I did as I was told, for all that it left me stark naked. She turned for the door, only for Juliette to speak up again.

'By the way, Stacey, how do you suppose these two little tarts paid for their quad-bike ride? She's got to be spanked.'

Stacey turned on her.

'I'll decide when a spanking is necessary, thank you very much.'

I'd been blushing hot already, but I must have been the colour of a beetroot as I saw Wendy's mouth come open in horror at the realisation that Stacey really did spank me. She looked as embarrassed as I felt, while she'd let her towel slip slightly to expose one little pink nipple, which looked painfully stiff. I had to say something.

'It's … it's just something we do, to … to balance our relationship, you know, if we have a row or something.'

Juliette's smirk would have done credit to a witch, but she knew when not to say anything. Stacey hesitated, genuinely cross, obviously wanting to do it, though not at all sure about Wendy's reaction, but the truth was out and we were going to have to deal with it sooner or later. Stacey had to ask.

'Do you mind?'

Wendy shook her head.

'I … I suppose not, not if it's something between you, as girlfriends.'

I realised I'd put my foot in it and was wishing I'd used a different excuse, something Wendy would have objected to, but it was too late. Stacey tossed the two towels on the nearest bed, which happened to be mine, and sat down.

'Come on, Lucy, you deserve this. Over my knee.'

Juliette's smile had grown more wicked than ever, but I didn't mind her seeing, not when she'd done it to me so often and knew how it all worked. Wendy was another matter entirely, and the fact that we'd played together with John only made it worse. She still looked horrified, but also fascinated, and she clearly had no intention of missing the show. I found myself begging.

'Please, Stacey, no, not like this, not in front of Wendy!'

Stacey cocked one eyebrow at me, but spoke to Wendy.

'Would you like to watch me spank her?'

Wendy nodded, shook her head, nodded again, then started to speak.

'I ... I don't know. I've never seen a girl spanked before, not like this. Are you going to hurt her?'

'Oh, it's going to sting, but it's more to do with her embarrassment, really. That's why I'd prefer to do it in front of you, if you don't mind? Besides, if we're going to be living together for two weeks life's going to be a lot easier if I can give Lucy her discipline in front of you two, and I know Juliette doesn't mind.'

Wendy nodded again, now tight-lipped with excitement. I threw my hands up in despair.

'Oh, all right, if you have to, and they both obviously want to watch. And yes, Wendy and I did do the guy on the quad bike a little favour for our ride, and it was just as much her idea as mine, so really she ought to get it too!'

Stacey shook her head.

'Wendy is not my girlfriend, and anyway, who said anything about you being punished for getting us disqualified, or for your dirty behaviour? This is for pinching my towel, you selfish little brat, now get over my knee!'

I knew from the tone of her voice that I'd be going over anyway, whether I liked it or not, so that trying to fight would only mean making an even more undignified display of myself. Besides, there was no denying my arousal, for all that I was feeling bitterly sorry for myself as I got into position, draped nude across Stacey's knees with my bottom lifted as one more name was added to the list of people who knew I got my bottom smacked.

Stacey took a grip around my waist, settled her hand across my cheeks, and it had begun. I'd already been close to crying, just for the shame of my predicament, but from the first firm smack of Stacey's hand across my bottom the tears began to come, rolling heavily down my cheeks. It just wasn't fair, when I'd made her my playmate, at least with John as well, and just a few short hours later she was watching as I got spanked across my girlfriend's knee, not just bare bottom, but stark naked, with my cunt and bumhole on show to her, all my mystery and all my dignity stripped away. She was enjoying it too, smiling as my punishment continued, until she realised I was crying.

'Is she alright?'

It was Stacey who answered first, directly followed by Juliette.

'Don't worry about it, she likes to let her emotions out, don't you, darling?'

'More like she's a big baby! Oh dear, poor little Lucy, getting her botty smacked, again, are we? The thing is, she'd like to be little miss perfect, who everybody looks up to and everybody admires, but the truth is she's a bratty little princess type who needs regular spanking, and she knows she does. Don't you, Lucy?'

I shook my head, unable to speak for my choking tears but desperate to deny what she was saying, for all that it was true, or mostly true. Juliette carried on.

'She does, but that doesn't make it hurt any less, and believe me, she is thoroughly ashamed of her own reactions, which makes it all the more fun to spank her.'

'So, she sort of loves it and hates it at the same time?'

'You could put it that way, I suppose. Better to say she hates it but she knows she has to have it anyway.'

Stacey took over.

'The way I see it, is that she's a bit of a princess, as Juliette says, so she needs a good spanking occasionally to put her back in her place, and she knows it so she accepts that it needs to be done. It makes me feel better too, and she's always at her nicest after she's had her bottom smacked, and her naughtiest.'

A fresh stab of humiliation hit me at her words. My bottom was warm and I knew I was starting to get wet and excited, and that Wendy could see. I tried to tell myself that we'd already been together, that she'd even seen me suck her juice from John's cock, but it didn't do any good. Dirty, indulgent sex is one thing, being spanked across my girlfriend's knee quite another, especially when it was a punishment for being a selfish little brat. Now Wendy knew I got it, and to her I'd always be the girl who got spanked, keeping me constantly aroused and constantly ashamed of myself. She giggled.

'I must say, you do look funny, Lucy.'

Stacey laughed.

'She does, doesn't she? I love the way her bum wobbles, but if you spank her really hard, and in just the right place ...'

'No, Stacey, please, not that!'

She ignored me, tightening her grip around my waist and applying her hand to the tuck of my cheeks. I knew exactly what she was up to, bringing the great bubble of shame in my throat up to bursting point, so that I was blubbering pathetically and begging her to stop even as the urge to stick my bottom up to the smacks grew stronger. Still Stacey paid no attention to my pleas, spanking me harder and harder still, full across the softest, most sensitive part of my bottom, every single smack sending a sharp jolt to my cunt.

Juliette was laughing in open enjoyment for my plight and knowing exactly what was going to happen, while Wendy was watching in ever-growing fascination, giggling for my helpless antics and utter inability to control myself, then gasping in shock and delight as I started to come, spanked to orgasm in front of her. I cried out in raw, agonising shame as I felt my cunt and anus tighten, calling Stacey a bitch before I finally broke and began to beg her to spank me harder, with both girls laughing in delight as they watched me go through my helpless, shame-filled orgasm.

Chapter Four

I woke to a sharp pang of elation instantly followed by deep shame. Both emotions came from allowing myself to be spanked in front of Wendy and Juliette, and to a lesser extent from what we'd done with John. I'd behaved like a vulgar little slut, to borrow one of my mother's pet phrases, then given in to what has to be the most inappropriate, undignified punishment a woman can possibly receive, bare-bottom, over-the-knee spanking.

It was hardly the first time I'd suffered from the same ambivalent blend of feelings, and matched such memorable incidents as the first time I'd woken up in bed with Juliette, the aftermath of pretending to be bullied into sex by the huge black teddy bear I had at home, and of course being spanked for masturbating. I was fairly sure it wouldn't be the last, either, and lay still in bed for a while, staring up into the darkness in rueful contemplation of my sexuality. Only slowly did a much more immediate worry penetrate my consciousness with the patter of raindrops on the windows, while the light which had begun to filter in around the curtains was the colour of dull pearl. It was going to be a wet day.

The warmth and comfort of my bed suddenly increased

its appeal and I snuggled deeper in, still half asleep, only to be jerked into full wakefulness by the din of the bell, immediately followed by a loud rapping at our hut door and the sound of Parker's voice telling us to get up. He even tried the handle, but we'd bolted the door the previous evening to guard against male intrusion while we sat up and talked in our night things. Juliette pulled herself up in her bed.

'Go away, you pervert!'

There was no response, and with the bell going it was unlikely he'd even heard, but I found myself smiling at her. Stacey was awake too, rubbing the sleep from her eyes, but Wendy showed only as an irregular lump beneath her covers. Juliette reached out to snatch the blankets back, exposing a little round bottom as white as cream and barely covered by bright-green knickers. Wendy squeaked in surprise as she was stripped, then turned an accusing glare on her persecutor.

'OK, OK, I'm getting up. What are we doing today anyway?'

Stacey was already out of bed, and looking offensively fit as she did her morning exercises.

'Negotiation bridge building. We're in four teams, as usual, and we have to build a bridge across a ditch. They'll supply us with poles, planks, rope and tools, but each team will only have one thing, so that we have to bargain to get what we need to complete the bridge. I'm not sure how they do the scoring.'

I knelt up in bed to get at the window and pulled the curtains a little to one side. Directly outside was a large puddle, stained by the red Devon soil, with tufts of grass sticking up through water spotted with rain. Not far beyond was the wet brown flank of the next hut along, while the concrete paths were the same damp grey as the sky. A faint marbling in the western sky suggested that the weather might eventually improve, but there was no sign of the sun whatsoever. For a long moment I considered getting back into bed and telling Parker exactly what he could do with his team-building exercise, but Stacey was now doing press-ups on the floor, while Juliette and Wendy were discussing the exercise.

'... the knack has to be to get what we need without giving too much away, and in the right order, but it has to depend on what material we get.'

'I bet Team C gets whatever's most useful.'

'Everything ought to be essential, especially if we have to build a particular sort of bridge, but whoever gets the poles is going to have a head start, especially if they trade with whoever's got the rope.'

'Surely it's best to have the tools?'

'If you've got the poles you can get the framework ready in advance. You're right though, I bet it's C and B ...'

She continued to explain her strategy, but I was more concerned with getting to the shower block and back, which looked like being a constant source of embarrassment throughout our time at the camp. My robe was not only too short but would also get soaked in the rain, but it struck me that I could manage with a pair of panties under my robe and my transparent mac on top of it, which meant I'd stay dry and reasonably decent. That way I'd also have a warm, dry towel ready when I came back to the hut.

Just to think about the towel brought back memories of my ignominious spanking and I was blushing as I got ready. The others didn't seem to care, mainly discussing the exercise, but then they hadn't had their bare red bottoms on show. I had, and it was impossible to shrug off the feeling that I'd become very much the junior member of the team, deferring not only to Stacey and Juliette, but to Wendy too, so that I even found myself asking if it was alright to go over to the showers.

The feeling stayed with me as we washed, dressed and breakfasted together in the mess before going over to the big Assembly hangar. By then it had stopped raining and the cloud had begun to break up, to my immense relief, although the ground was still wet and the water had come through the roof in one place, to leave a large puddle in the corner. Parker was already there, with his clipboard as usual, and to judge by the mud on his legs and his wet clothes he'd been running before the rest of us got up. So had Team C, and Chad gave us a look of pure contempt as we took our place in the line, before coming smartly to attention as Parker stepped forward to address us.

'Good morning, teams! As the triers among you will know, today's exercise is Negotiation Bridge Building, which means ...'

He began to explain, much as Stacey had done, only in far greater detail, including that half the points would go according to the order in which we finished, by making a bridge we were confident to walk across, and half according to his judgement on our performance. That seemed rather arbitrary to me and I was sure he'd do his best to help his favourites, Team C, who were also in the lead. I leant over to whisper to Juliette.

'We need to make sure Team C don't finish, or make a mess of it.'

Parker turned towards me.

'Yes, Girl O? Did you having something to say? Are you worried about breaking a nail, or getting your pretty pink trainers muddy?'

'I was discussing tactics.'

'Tactics? I wouldn't worry too much about that, O, as your team is in last place and likely to stay there, even with the mighty Team D in contention. You won't be able to wiggle your little bottom at any farmers today either, as the exercise is in the camp. It's at the north end of the old airstrip, to be precise, where you'll find a long ditch and the four piles of equipment. You run there, and you stake your claim to whichever sort of equipment you prefer, first come, first served, so let's go, go, go!'

His remark about wiggling my bottom at farmers had come much too close to the truth, so I was blushing and got caught off guard as people started for the door, most of them running. I'd decided what we needed and was determined to get my choice, telling Juliette and then breaking into a sprint the moment I was through the door. More than half of the others were ahead of me, making directly across the grass, but I turned to one side, staying on the concrete of the old runway. One or two others had made the same decision, including Daniel, who was soon ahead of me. I had no chance of catching him, but as we came to the shallow slope at the end he angled off to where the tools had been stacked into a neat pyramid. The rope was right in front of me, a big pile of hanks and coils of different thicknesses, and I flopped down on top of it just as Alastair arrived to claim the planks for Team B.

Chad was close behind him, and others, all spattered with mud up to their knees, while I was still clean and fairly fresh, a minor triumph in its own right. Not that it looked likely I'd be staying that way, as the ditch was half full of soupy red water, while the sides were raw, slippery mud. The miniature digger they'd used still stood nearby, with Mr Straw seated in the cab, while Sergeant Reynolds had run up to the top of the bank to watch the stragglers come in. Team D were last, and hadn't even bothered to run, chatting nonchalantly as they strolled down to the pile of poles that remained as the final choice. Juliette gave them a doubtful glance.

'I still think we should have gone for the poles.'

I shook my head.

'We need poles, but it doesn't matter about Team D. The important thing is not to let Team C complete their bridge.'

'But they've got all the tools. We'll have to trade.'

'No we won't, and we don't really need to trade with Team B either. We're going to build a suspension bridge, using rope with two tripods made of poles at either end.'

Stacey had been looking around as we spoke, and now joined in.

'That ought to work, but there's another problem. There isn't nearly enough stuff to go around, not for four bridges.'

She was right. The ditch was a good eight feet across and maybe as much as six feet deep, while neither the poles nor the planks were long enough to cover the gap. I couldn't help but grin, as with my solution it didn't matter, as long as we got our twelve poles from Team D. Juliette was thinking the same thing.

'We'd better go and talk to the nerds then. You come with me, Lucy, and you two can start on the rope work.'

Paul and his teammates were at the end of the ditch, next to us, but he and the one I thought of as Billy Bunter had climbed up the bank, taking several poles with them. Both were grinning as we approached, and Paul spoke up.

'This is the pole bank. How may I help you, girls? We have eight-foot poles and we have eight-inch poles, both of the highest quality.'

The Billy Bunter lookalike sniggered and I found myself blushing pink, then red for the embarrassment of being seen blushing at such a puerile joke. Juliette simply ignored them.

'We need twelve poles, for which we're prepared to trade you all our leftover rope.'

'Twelve? That's a lot of poles. We're only reckoning on using eight.'

'Good for you. We need twelve.'

'There are only twenty-four of the things, and we need to trade for planks and tools.'

'Hang on.'

She drew me back and the boys began to whisper together even as we did.

'Could we do it with just one tripod at each end?'

'No … yes, maybe, but it wouldn't be nearly as stable. We have to try and get twelve, or at least as many as we possibly can, to make sure B and C fail.'

She shrugged and turned back to the boys, who were still whispering together, with the occasional glance towards us, their faces working with a sort of idiotic, lecherous mirth I didn't like the look of at all. Finally they broke apart and came towards us, Billy Bunter looking embarrassed and shifty, Paul grinning.

'We want to see your tits.'

I'd guessed something of the sort was coming, but that didn't keep the shock from my voice as I answered him.

'What!? Don't be such a pervert!'

'There's nothing perverted about wanting to see a girl's tits. Perverted is like when you're into shoes, or splosh, or sheep. Come on, tits out and you get two poles.'

I drew my breath in, about to deliver a stinging lecture about inappropriate behaviour and learning to show respect for women, only to be interrupted by Juliette.

'Don't be so fucking precious, Lucy.'

Even as she spoke she'd pulled up her top, taking her bra with it, to show off her firm, heavy breasts. I saw Paul swallow, and Billy Bunter couldn't resist a comment.

'Whoa, nice!'

'Thank you. That will be twelve poles, please.'

Paul wagged a finger.

'Uh, uh, one pole at best. Now you, Lucy, and don't worry, what goes on in camp stays in camp.'

Juliette wasn't satisfied.

'You said you'd give us two poles if we showed you our tits.'

'Yeah, two poles for two sets of tits, yours and Lucy's.'

'How about a pole a tit?'

I'd been listening in horrified silence, but finally found my voice.

'No! Juliette, I can't ...'

'Don't be silly, Lucy, of course you can. What's the problem? I know they've probably never seen a girl's breasts before, except on a computer screen, but ...'

'Paul's in my company, and ... and ...'

Paul licked his lips.

'What goes on in camp stays in camp.'

'Jedi's honour,' Billy added.

'What!? Oh God!'

'Come on, love, just a little peek? I can see you've got nice ones.'

'You dirty little ...'

'OK, four tits, four poles, but we've got to see Lucy's.'

It was Paul who'd spoken, his voice firm and really quite commanding, in sharp contrast to Billy Bunter's wheedling drawl. I still wasn't going to do it, but Juliette drew a deep, patient sigh and pointed towards the far end of the ditch.

'Come on, Lucy, don't be such a princess! Chad's coming, so get on with it.'

'But Juliette ...'

'Just do as you're fucking told!'

I nearly did it, just for the tone of command in her voice, which I'd always struggled to resist, but instead I glanced around to where Chad was approaching, still some way away. Paul spoke again, his voice now urgent.

'Tits out, both of you, and it's six poles.'

Juliette's top was up in an instant, her back turned so Chad wouldn't see, then so was mine, jerked up more by instinct than design, my breasts bare in the cool morning sun, my heart hammering and my face and chest burning with blushes. Paul gave a long, low sigh and Billy Bunter a startled squeak, then a grunt so heartfelt I couldn't help but wonder if he'd come in his pants, a thought which filled me with disgust and left my blushes hotter than ever as I quickly covered myself up. Juliette spoke up again as she too lowered her top.

'Satisfied, you dirty little boys? So that's six poles, and another six for our rope.'

'Take these, then come back when we've spoken to Chad.'

I'd grabbed two of the poles they'd brought as I answered him.

'Don't give any to Chad. That's important.'

'We need tools, Lucy.'

'Yes, but ... look, put him off, at least until we come back.'

He laughed.

'That's going to be worth more than a flash of your tits, Miss Salisbury.'

83

Chad had broken into a jog as he drew near and I didn't say anything else for fear of provoking some embarrassing response in his hearing. Juliette was already halfway down the slope with the four poles she'd picked up, and spoke as I caught up with her.

'What a fuss! No wonder Stacey has to spank you.'

'Sorry. I ... I just get a bit embarrassed, and Paul's from our company, and I'm sure some of the others noticed.'

'It's only a pair of tits, Lucy. We all have them, including Paul and William.'

'But we're girls. So, he's called William?'

'Yes, why?'

'It suits him. He looks like Billy Bunter.'

'That's for sure, now stop being so fucking precious and let's get on with this. I want to win.'

I did too, both because I wanted to wipe the smug grin off Parker's face and because if I'd had to bare my breasts in public I didn't want it to be for nothing. It was all very well for Juliette to call me precious and a princess, and I do like going bare, but to have to do it for Paul and William was bitterly humiliating. Unfortunately that's just the sort of thing that gets to me, and I was having trouble keeping my mind on my work as we lashed the poles into two tall tripods and set them up on either side of the ditch.

Stacey had been hard at work on the rope bridge, with the main lines laid out on the ground as she knotted connecting lines into place with skilled fingers, while Wendy was talking to representatives from the other two teams and standing firm in the face of increasing irritation. Chad didn't seem to be doing too well up on the slope either, his voice loud and aggressive as he tried to dominate Paul and William. Juliette laughed.

'Fat chance he's got. There's nothing quite so proud as a nerd who's just seen a girl's tits, except maybe one who's had even more. If you want to win, just go and offer them blow jobs. They'll do anything you say.'

I shook my head, not wanting to speak and let my voice betray my agitation for what I'd already been made to do. Unfortunately Juliette knew me far too well.

'What if I made you do it, you know, held you by the hair to force you down on their cocks? Think how weak you'd feel, think how ashamed of yourself you'd be as their cocks began to grow and you started to get horny and willing.'

'Juliette! Not them, please.'

It was the wrong thing to say, and I knew it. Juliette merely laughed and carried on, her voice like honey.

'Come on, Lucy, you loved it that time when I made you lick Emily and Claire. Don't you remember, on your knees in my study with your panties rolled down and your smacked bottom sticking out under your skirt? Don't you remember the feel of your hair twisted into my fist, and the way the harder I twisted the harder you licked? You really loved that, didn't you, you bad, bad girl.'

'No I ... OK, I did, but that's hardly the same thing, is it?'

'Why not? You like cock, don't you? You said you had a boyfriend.'

'He's six foot six and looks like a Viking warrior, and he's my boyfriend, not some pasty-faced fat boy I've only just met. And there are four of them!'

'OK, so you don't want to suck nerd cock, I get that, but it will be me who's in charge. I don't suppose you'll have to suck all four, anyway, just Paul and William. Anyway, think how ashamed of yourself you'd feel with some fat nerd's cock in your mouth. Think, Lucy, the sort of man who'd barely dare to dream of getting with you and you're on your knees to him, sucking his big fat penis while his friend watches you, sucking and licking and ...'

'Juliette, stop it! Stacey, help!'

Stacey got up and quickly walked across to us. Juliette stepped back, looking a little cross and a little uncertain. I wanted Stacey to put her in her place, allowing me to salvage at least some pride, although she'd already got me in such a state I'd have happily gone down for both of them, and fantasised about what she'd said as I licked.

'What's the matter?'

'Juliette's trying to make me offer to suck Paul off, and the little fat one who looks like Billy Bunter, so that they'll refuse to sell Chad any poles.'

Stacey hesitated in surprise, allowing Juliette to speak first.

'I was only teasing her, and I don't mean to intrude on your relationship, but if we want to win ...'

She trailed off, leaving the sentence unfinished, and in doing so pushing Stacey's buttons almost as skilfully as she'd pushed mine. Stacey glanced up to where Chad was now waving his arms in furious expostulation at Paul and William.

'You flashed your boobs, didn't you, to get the poles?'

'Yes, but ...'

'At least go and talk to them. Make an offer. After all, they can't very well take you up on it here and now, so you don't even have to go through with it, and it doesn't have to be that heavy either. I bet they'd kill to see you do a striptease.'

'What, Stacey?! I can't do that. Paul works with us, and anyway, if you're so keen, why don't you do it?'

She made an offhand gesture.

'You're the one they'd want, the boss's PA, the office ice

maiden. But I tell you what, if they ask me, I'll do it. You too, Juliette.'

Juliette hesitated before answering, and even then she sounded far from certain.

'OK, if I'm the one they want, it's a deal.'

'You wouldn't!?'

'Why not? You must have stripped for men before, Lucy.'

'She let her boyfriend, Magnus, cane her in front of me, and another girl.'

'You did? She's such a slut. I used to make her lick my friends out. Come on, Lucy, stop trying to pretend you're something you're not.'

'You don't understand! This is Paul we're talking about, from our own office.'

'So what? Just remind him that if he says anything you can deny it and accuse him of harassment. He's not stupid.'

Juliette nodded thoughtfully.

'That makes sense. Who's going to believe little miss goodie-two-shoes sucks cock for favours? Oh, and I've promised I'll hold her head, if that's OK with you, Stacey?'

'To make her suck? I suppose that's OK, but I ought to do it, really. I mean, we're not an exclusive couple or anything, but still ... hush, here they come.'

Paul was approaching, his face split into a smug grin, with William and Chad behind, still arguing. The three of us turned to face them and I folded my arms across my chest in an effort to look calm and determined, which was the exact opposite to the way I felt. Paul cocked a thumb over his shoulder.

'Chad says we can use all the tools we need in return for six of the remaining poles, which leaves us four to trade for our planks. That makes sense, unless you want to top his bid?'

Chad broke in before we could reply.

'What the heck is this? We're supposed to negotiate, girls. That's the whole point of the exercise, to negotiate and see who does it best.'

Juliette answered him.

'Absolutely, and we aim to win. Come and talk to me, Paul.'

She put her arm around his shoulder, talking in a low, soft voice as she steered him away. I knew perfectly well what she was saying, which put an agonising knot in my stomach and brought me to the edge of tears. She'd taken the decision out of my hands, and I knew that once it was made there would be no backing out. I desperately wanted to go and speak to them, to tell Paul I wouldn't suck his horrible little cock for every last penny on Earth, but Chad was still talking to me and Stacey, while the memory of being held by my hair as my face was pushed between Emily's thighs was burning in my head. Chad quickly realised he didn't have my full attention.

'At least try and take this seriously!'

Stacey answered him.

'We are, and we intend to win.'

'Oh yeah? Let me tell you this, I saw what you two dirty bitches did over there, and I tell you right now, two can play at that game, so put that in your pipe and smoke it!'

He'd turned on his heel as he finished and strode away, picking up Roy Karsen as he passed Wendy. Stacey blew out her breath.

'Well, I don't think much of his negotiation skills.'

'No, but what do you think he meant by two can play at that game? I don't see Paul and Billy wanting him to pull his top up.'

Stacey just laughed, leaving me to ponder but only for a moment. Juliette had finished talking to Paul and was coming back, while he was actually running for his team's section of the ditch. Juliette's grin was pure evil.

'It's all arranged, after lights out tonight, in one of the abandoned huts, number twenty-six at the end. You're going to suck his cock, Lucy.'

She said it slowly, relishing every word and leaving me feeling so weak I had to go and sit down on the rapidly diminishing pile of rope. Stacey went back to work and was quickly joined by Juliette and then Wendy, leaving me to think on how I was going to feel with Paul's cock in my mouth. He was the company joker, a bit of a clown, and very definitely not one of the men the girls were keen to be with, and yet for all his weight he was big and solid, the sort of man who'd easily be able to dominate me physically. Billy was worse, a real butterball, with a dirty, wheedling manner that made me think of dirty magazines and spunk stains on clothing, which sent a powerful shiver the full length of my spine and put a sick feeling in the back of my throat.

I grabbed up a hank of rope and joined the others, desperate for anything that might help me keep my mind off my fate. It was easy-enough work, looping the strands back and forth and tying them off to the main ropes. By the time Paul came over with the other six poles Juliette had negotiated we were half done and he gave an approving nod as he came close.

'It's a rope bridge, isn't it, like the one in *Indiana Jones and the Temple of Doom*?'

He was quite close to me, and as I was kneeling to work my head was level with his crotch, making me think of blow jobs once more. I quickly got up, blushing, and he gave me a lewd wink as he went on.

'You need some planks, really. Can I have some rope then?' Stacey answered him.

'Go ahead, we've got plenty. We can't do the planks though, because we'd need a saw to cut them and we're not trading with Team C.'

'I don't blame you. They're arseholes, especially Chad. See you later.'

He'd been gathering up rope as he spoke and gave me another slow wink before lumbering back towards the rest of his team. The lump in my throat was bigger than ever as I got back to work, but I tried to console myself that we were going to win. Team D obviously had a plan, but they all seemed to want to give instructions rather than do any real work, while both the other teams were foundering in the ditch, every single one of them filthy with mud and soaking wet, while their haphazard constructions built of planks fixed together with nails looked positively dangerous.

They hadn't got much further an hour later, both having had to restart several times when their half-built bridges collapsed, although they were muddier than ever. Paul and Graham had finally decided to get into the ditch and Team D's bridge was nearly complete, but ours was finished, with four tall tripods supporting a span that crossed the water with no more than a foot of sag. We stood back, thoroughly pleased with ourselves, and I was about to point out that Wendy was probably the lightest when she spoke up.

'Go on, Lucy, you designed the thing.'

I hesitated only a moment, then stepped out onto the bridge, thankful for the ballet lessons I'd taken as a little girl as it began to sway, but I'd always had a good sense of balance and was soon across. Wendy followed, clutching the sides and placing every foot as if the drop below her was a thousand feet onto jagged rocks instead of a short fall into muddy water. She made it, and gave us a little bow, just as Parker appeared at the top of the bank. He was in his tracksuit bottoms and the blue camp top, fresh and clean, also rather smug until he'd taken in the scene along the ditch. Chad had seen him and immediately ran over, talking excitedly and pointing towards us. Juliette sighed.

'Oh dear, it looks like we've just been sneaked on again.'

Chad returned to his team while Parker jogged down the slope towards us, addressing Juliette as she stood up.

'What's this, Girl A? I'm told you're refusing to negotiate?'

I stood up, determined to defend what was really my decision, and my design.

'We did negotiate, with Team D. We don't need any tools, or any planks.'

'Yes you do. This exercise has been designed by people a great deal cleverer than you, designed to test your negotiation skills in such a way that only the best succeed, because, Girl O, there are only enough materials to build two effective bridges. The idea is to negotiate, Girl O, to negotiate, not to refuse to co-operate at all.'

'I thought the idea was to win? Anyway, we've built a bridge, and crossed it.'

I stepped out onto the bridge a second time, deliberately showing off as I skipped across the plaited ropes that stood in for planks. At the far side I turned and curtsied, enjoying his discomfort. He gave the bridge a doubtful look, obviously trying to think of a way he could disqualify us. Juliette followed me, rather more cautiously, then turned back to him.

'Have a go.'

He stepped carefully forward, allowing his weight to settle on the ropes, took another step, and a third, now more confident as he reached the centre of the bridge, which twisted, turning completely upside down and depositing him into the mixture of water and mud in the ditch below.

* * *

I lay over Stacey's lap, my skirt turned up and my panties well down, even my top pulled high so that my boobs were on show as well as my bare, hot bottom. We'd shared a bottle of wine from our stash before I'd been put over the knee, and the drink didn't seem to have affected me at all, but had left the others merry and full of mischief, especially Wendy. She'd been giggling openly as she watched my spanking, while Juliette had helped by holding my legs to stop me kicking, and to give herself a prime view of my squirming cheeks and the rear of my pussy. It had been hard too, much harder than the day before, to leave me tear-stained and shaking, but still not penitent.

'It's just not fair! Why is it my fault that Parker's a complete bastard?'

Stacey began to spank again, a dozen firm, even swats that set me gasping and wriggling again before she stopped once more and spoke up.

'I don't care. You got us disqualified again, so you're getting spanked, and I'm not going to stop until you say you're sorry.'

'But it wasn't my fault! Only a complete idiot would have fallen off like that!'

'Maybe, maybe not, but you didn't have to laugh quite so loud, did you?'

'I couldn't help it! Ow! Ow! Ow! Stacey, please! This just isn't fair!'

She began to spank once more, then paused to pull my knickers down a bit further, making sure that every single rude detail of my rear view was on full show to the others. My voice was a sob as I continued to plead.

'It isn't fair ... ow ... really it's not, ow! You know you can spank me whenever you like, but please say it's not a punishment for us getting disqualified, please Stacey? Ow! Ow! Ow! Stacey!'

'Oh alright, it's not a punishment, but that's not going to stop me, because spanking your bottom makes me feel a whole lot better. And now will somebody please shut her up?'

'My pleasure.'

It was Juliette who'd answered, and as her hands went to my panties I realised what she was going to do, gag me the same humiliating but effective way she'd once used to stop the neighbours hearing my screams as I was caned.

'No, Juliette, not in my mouth! Please?'

'Shut up and open wide, or do I have to pinch your nose?'

She did it anyway, squeezing my nose until I was forced to open my mouth and then cramming my panties in to leave me chewing on damp cotton. Wendy couldn't help but comment.

'That is such a dirty thing to do, poor Lucy!'

Her voice was full of laughter and arousal, adding to my consternation as my spanking continued. It was bad enough to be punished for nothing, but far worse to have all three of them laughing at me, especially considering what they had in store for me once I'd been spanked. It wasn't over yet though, with my cheeks bouncing to hard, accurate slaps from Stacey's open palm as I squirmed on her lap, until I was faint with reaction and from being held almost completely upside down, and all the while with her talking to me.

'How does it feel, you little brat? How does it feel with your bare bottom on show to all three of us and your fancy little panties in your mouth? Are you regretting teaching me to spank you? I bet you are!'

Juliette laughed as the spanking grew harder still, on a crescendo of furious smacks that left me thrashing in Stacey's grip before she finally stopped to allow me to slump to the floor, shaking and sweaty, too far gone even to bother to cover my bottom, although I did manage to spit out my now sodden panties. Stacey blew her breath out.

'That was fun. Right, Lucy, are you warm enough yet?'

I gave a single, weak nod, acknowledging the true reason for my spanking, or at least part of the reason. As I'd explained to Stacey, with Juliette's backing, if I was to be made to keep my promise and suck Paul and Billy off I needed to be beaten first, or I simply wouldn't be able to do it. As it was my bottom was hot, my head was burning with shame and arousal and I'd have done anything she ordered me to, however unspeakable. She nodded to Juliette.

'OK, let's go. Wendy, make sure the coast is clear and we'll follow you out.'

Wendy nodded, threw a towel over her shoulder and made for the door, opening it casually, as if she was going across to the shower block, then beckoning us forward. Stacey and Juliette took hold of my arms, hauled me to my feet and quickly hustled me across to the door. They'd left my panties behind, in the middle of the floor, and my top was still up over my boobs, but I was too far gone to care.

It was almost completely black outside, with only the dull yellow hut lights to see by, and we'd soon moved into the shadows. Only gradually did my eyes become accustomed to the gloom, as I was led behind the line of huts to the one at the very end, and inside. At first I could see nothing at all, and my heart jumped in shock as a voice spoke out of the darkness.

'Lucy?'

A light came on, a big torch placed beam down on a plastic container, so that all it gave was a dull red glow. Paul and William were both there, seated on battered old chairs and illuminated from below, which highlighted their crotches and bellies, as well as making their features more pronounced, so that it was as if I was looking at two fat, lecherous imps. Both were in tracksuits, and both had their legs braced apart, showing off the bulges of what I was expected to attend to. Stacey's grip tightened on my arm.

'We've got her. OK, boys, who's first?'

They glanced at each other, sharing dirty but embarrassed grins, just as I'd have expected of the two dirty little boys I imagined them to be at heart. It was left to Juliette to get things going.

'Let's see what you've got then. Come on, drop your trousers.'

She started to pull me forward as she spoke and I found myself stumbling close to the boys, who shared another grin before rising as one to push down their tracksuit bottoms, leaving William showing off a pair of bright orange Y-fronts and Paul quite bare. He was huge, with a fat, fleshy cock lying on a pair of balls the size of plums and encased in a heavily wrinkled sac. He was also completely hairless, making it all seem bigger still and even more grotesque. I swallowed hard, horrified by the thought of having to work on him with my mouth, and my words came out as a weak croak.

'I'll ... I'll do Billy first.'

William's grin immediately grew broader, and dirtier than ever. He made some peculiar hand signal to Paul, then pulled his Y-fronts open to flop out the most miserable penis I'd ever seen, along with a fat little scrotum. I winced in involuntary disgust, wishing I'd chosen to start on Paul's obviously virile member instead, but Juliette and Stacey were already pushing me down.

'On your knees, slut. You know what you have to do.'

'Yes, you have to suck their little cocks, Lucy, all the way ... well, not so little in your case, Paul. I might even get you ready.'

I glanced up in surprise as Stacey moved aside to sit down on Paul's knee and take his cock in her hand. His arm went around her as she began to knead his genitals, but both of them were looking at me. I'd thought she wanted to hold my hair, and felt an immediate pang of jealousy, which she must have seen in my face.

'Don't worry, darling. I'll hold you for Paul, but this is Juliette's turn.'

Even as she spoke Juliette had put a hand in my hair, twisting so hard I cried out in pain, while she now had one arm locked behind my back. I was on my knees too, directly in front of Billy, my eyes fixed in genuine horror on his ugly little cock and bloated ball sac, but my mouth already open. Now I knew why Juliette had to hold my hair, because otherwise I could never have done it, but as it was she'd begun to push, her voice rich with sadistic pleasure as she forced me down.

'Come on, Princess Lucy, in it goes, right in your pretty mouth. Oh I am going to enjoy this, Lucy. I should have made you suck cock years ago, when you'd only been with girls and would have really hated it, maybe the gardener's boy, or that dirty old bastard who used to do the odd jobs. Come on, you little bitch, get your mouth around it and suck!'

She pushed, hard, forcing my head down into Billy's crotch and suddenly my mouth was full of rubbery male flesh, turning my squeal of alarm and protest into a muffled bubbling noise. For one awful moment I simply couldn't handle the shame of what was being done to me, jerking in panic and revulsion as I struggled to pull back, but Juliette wasn't having it, twisting her fist harder still in my hair and shoving my head back down.

'I said suck it, you little bitch, now do as you're fucking told! Sorry, Billy, she's normally quite obedient. I don't know what's got into her. Ah, that's better, good girl.'

I'd given in, my will broken by the sound of Juliette's voice, mocking and authoritative at the same time. My lips and tongue worked on Billy's horrid little cock, although it wasn't him I was in thrall to, but her. As I sucked I thought of Stacey too, my girlfriend, who'd just spanked me across her knee, but she was sat on Paul's lap, stroking his cock, a naughty girl like me, while Juliette was cool and aloof, far better suited to control me. Not only that, but she wasn't really getting off on the men at all, but on my humiliation, her voice full of cruelty and delight as she went on.

'That's right, sweetheart, suck his little cock, suck it well, like the dirty little tart you are, Lucy. That's it, good girl, now peel his foreskin back with your lips and kiss his helmet. Oh you dirty, filthy little bitch! Yes, that's right, suck on it, make him stiff. Now kiss his balls. Good girl. Now in your mouth. Go on, you know you want to ...'

I was sobbing with emotion as I did it, utterly ashamed of myself as I opened my mouth to take in Billy's plump little scrotum. He gasped as I began to suck on his balls, as much in pain as pleasure, but his reaction didn't really matter to me, save that I was being forced to service him by my beautiful Juliette and I wasn't going to be allowed to stop until he'd come, probably in my mouth.

'That's my girl. You do look good with a pair of balls in your mouth and a little stiff cock pressed to your face. Go on, Billy, why don't you have a nice wank while she sucks your balls? Go on, Lucy, suck the dirty little bastard's balls while he wanks in your face.'

Billy's hand went to his cock, tugging on the weedy little shaft with his fingers rubbing on my cheeks and slapping against my nose as I continued to suck on his balls. Juliette gave a low, satisfied sigh to see how obedient I was, and how dirty, twisting her hand harder still into my hair and tightening her grip on my wrist, so that I was utterly helpless. Billy was getting urgent and had started to make a piglike grunting noise, so I shut my eyes, ready to take it in the face as Juliette continued to encourage him and to taunt me.

'Go on, Billy, do it, right in her face, right in her pretty face. Go on, do it, you little wanker, spunk in her face ... Oh yes, you filthy fucking pig, Billy! That's right, rub it in, and now in her mouth, put it in her mouth. Oh God, how does that feel, Lucy, sucking his spunky cock when he's wanked off in your face?'

It felt revolting, with his little slimy cock deep in my mouth as she held me in place, but that didn't stop me licking and sucking at the stiff little shaft, deliberately degrading myself by eating his spunk, or at least as much as I could get, because most of it was trickling slowly down my face or in my hair. Finally Juliette pulled me off.

'You dirty little bitch, Lucy! Right, number two, and he's big. Look at him, Lucy.'

Billy had spunked over my right eye and I didn't dare open it, but my left was OK and I took a cautious peek, to find Paul's cock fully erect in Stacey's hand. He'd been impressive limp, but now that he was stiff he was huge, a great, fat column of male meat straining up from his ball sac, his shaft gnarled and threaded with veins, his helmet a bloated, purple knob just made for pushing up into some hapless girl's cunt, or sucking on, which was what I had to do.

I couldn't have stopped myself, even if the girls hadn't had me under control, my need too great for all my shame. As it was I didn't have any choice, Juliette forcing me to crawl across to where Stacey could take me by the hair and drag me forward into the same kneeling position I'd been put in to suck Billy. My mouth was wide though, and I couldn't help but sigh as I was pushed down onto Paul's erection, taking it as deep as I could and immediately starting to suck. Juliette came close, to squat down behind me, her thighs spread across my back as she watched me work on Paul's cock.

'That's the way to do it, Lucy, you dirty little cocksucker. Did you know Stacey had to spank her first, Paul?'

He gave an interested grunt as I shook my head frantically, far from keen on letting him know that I got spanked. Juliette ignored me, slipping a hand under my skirt to stroke my bottom as she continued.

'Her bum's still warm. Oh you should have seen her, Paul. I bet you'd like to, wouldn't you? Imagine her, bare bottom across Stacey's lap, with her skirt turned up and her panties pulled right down so you could see everything. She wouldn't shut up either, so I took her panties right off and stuck them in her mouth. That's why she hasn't got any on, look.'

She'd pulled up the front of my skirt to show off my bare pussy as both Paul and Billy craned forward to get a look.

It was almost too much, and I threw an urgent glance at Stacey, hoping she'd come to my rescue, but she was staring in fascination at the junction between Paul's huge cock and my mouth as she pulled my head up and down to force me to suck. It was going deep too, making me gag and starting my eyes watering, although that was mixed with tears for the added shame of Juliette telling the boys my secret and showing them my cunt. She wasn't finished either, tucking my skirt up into its waistband to leave me showing back and front, then tugging up my top to bare my breasts as she went on.

'There, that's how a girl ought to suck cock, isn't it, Paul? Isn't it, Lucy? Tits out and pussy bare so you can fiddle with yourself while you do it ... umm, you're lovely and wet.'

Her finger had gone in up my cunt as she spoke, and she'd begun to move it in and out, making me wonder if she was going to let Paul fuck me, but at that Stacey finally reacted.

'Leave her for now, Juliette. I want her to concentrate on sucking cock. Are you ready to come, Paul?'

Juliette's finger slid from my hole as Paul gave a low, pleased grunt. My head was pulled back and Stacey caught me by my jaw, squeezing my cheeks to force me to hold my mouth open. I realised what was going to happen as she took hold of Paul's cock, tugging it with the fat purple knob aimed straight at my open mouth, but I stuck out my tongue of my own free will. Paul caught hold of his balls, squeezing them as Stacey tossed at his cock, faster and faster, until at last a jet of thick, white spunk erupted from the tip, missing my mouth to splash across my nose and cheek, but the second spurt went in, full on my tongue, and the rest. Juliette was giggling in demented glee as she watched Stacey milk Paul's cock onto my tongue, and both of them were talking.

100

'What a good girl! Oh you do look good, Lucy.'

'Cocksucking little bitch, more like, but that does look rude. Come on, Lucy, swallow it all down, you know you want to.'

'Yes, eat it all up, Princess. You know polite girls always swallow, so down it goes.'

Stacey had let go of my cheeks, and before I could even think to stop myself I'd closed my mouth and gulped down what Paul had done on my tongue, drawing gasps of delight and disgust from my audience, then a crow of laughter from Juliette as my face screwed up in response to the horrible taste.

'Ah, has little Lucy been made to eat the nasty boy's spunk? What a shame! Let me make you better.'

Stacey had let go, and Juliette began to stroke my hair, a caring gesture that destroyed any lingering resistance or resentment I might have had. I sank down, spunk and spittle dribbling from my lower lip to splash over my top and breasts, my thighs wide in surrender as she slipped a finger back in up my cunt. This time there was no objection, Stacey dropping down to kiss me before she spoke to the boys.

'You've had your fun, so out you go, but send Wendy in and keep a lookout.'

'Sure thing.'

I was fairly sure they'd find some way to watch us, but I didn't care, not when I'd sucked them both off and had my body put on show for their amusement. Juliette and Stacey didn't seem concerned either, cuddling up to me before helping each other strip off my clothes, so that by the time Wendy appeared I was in nothing but socks and trainers.

'Did she do it, both of them? Oh my!'

She'd seen the state I was in and her hand had gone to her open mouth in shock. I managed a smile in an effort to reassure her, only to have my head pulled around once more so that Stacey could use my discarded top to wipe my face.

'I'm first. Come on, Lucy, get busy.'

Her hand was back in my hair and she'd sat down on the chair Paul had been using, with her thighs well spread and her skirt rucked up to show off the front of her panties. I was pulled in, my face rubbed into her crotch through the damp cotton before it was pulled aside to allow me to lick her properly. She gave a pleased sigh as my tongue found her clitoris and I was in heaven, first spanked, then made to suck off two men before being put to work at making my girlfriends come, used and abused, but in just the right way.

They took turns with me, Stacey, then Juliette, and finally Wendy, each sitting with her pussy bare to my mouth as I knelt in the nude with my spunk-soiled boobs swinging under my chest and my spanked bottom stuck out behind, constantly masturbating as I brought myself to one orgasm after another over what had been done to me. Even Wendy was rude with me, holding me by the hair as the others had done, telling me how to lick her properly and calling me a slut and a bitch as I took her to orgasm.

Only when she'd come did I give in to my aching, exhausted body, slumping to the hard concrete floor with my fingers still between my thighs, and the others had to help me dress before we started back for our own hut. The cool night air and the worry of being caught perked me up a bit and I was the first through the door, to find the hut exactly as we'd left it except for one crucial detail. My panties were gone.

Chapter Five

'It couldn't have been the boys,' Stacey assured me the next morning. 'They were with us.'

'They might have nipped back.'

'What, to steal your panties instead of watching you lick us out? And they were watching, the dirty little sods.'

'I know. Who then?'

'I don't know. Not Parker, he'd have wanted to make a song and dance about us not being in our hut, and I don't think he's that much of a perve anyway.'

'Graham Boothe, or that other guy, Martin?'

'Paul swore they didn't know what was going on. Anyway, Graham's far too shy and Martin seems a bit of a dull fish. Don't let it get to you. That's exactly what gives people like that the biggest kick. Anyway, we need to concentrate on this exercise.'

I made a face, imagining one of the men we'd just had breakfast with masturbating into my stolen panties, probably while he imagined me naked, or maybe performing a sex act on him. Even after what had happened the night before it was embarrassing, and a little frightening too, when I didn't know who it was or what else they might do. Stacey was right though, our team was still in last place after two disqualifications in a row, so we badly needed to pull up. Juliette was less determined.

'What's the point? We should have won the orienteering and the bridge building, and you can bet Team C would have done if they'd used the same tactics. Parker's the worst sort of misogynist and he's not going to let us win no matter what we do.'

'I still want to try, mainly to show the bastard we can do it, but we need to think about our reports too.'

I nodded my agreement, as did Wendy, but Juliette wasn't convinced.

'We're all going to get bad reports anyway. He thinks we ought to be barefoot, pregnant and in the kitchen, and whatever fancy newspeak he uses that's what it'll boil down to. I don't want to let you down though, so OK, let's get on with it and think about today's exercise. We have to get to our objective without ...'

A new thought had occurred to me.

'Panty raiding is an American thing, isn't it? What about Chad?'

Stacey considered the idea.

'I doubt it. He's obviously gay, if nothing else, and anyway, it wasn't a panty raid or they'd have taken ours too.'

'Maybe, but still ...'

Juliette broke in.

'Will you shut up about your wretched panties, Lucy, or I'll take off the ones you've got on now and stuff them in your mouth to shut you up, like I did last night. Assuming you're wearing any, that is?'

'Of course I am. We're in our camouflage gear.'

'With you, one never knows. Now, as I was saying, we

have to get to our objective without being caught by the opposing team, the defenders, who have these puff stick things to make a mark with coloured dye.'

Stacey gave me a wink.

'A bit like paintball, eh Lucy, only for chickens.'

I winced, remembering the feel of paintballs smacking into my flesh on the occasion she and her friends had hunted me down and shot me. Juliette carried on.

'Yes, something like that, although I think if we made Lucy choose between a paintball and a puff stick she might have a hard time. They're effectively canes with some coloured cotton wool glued to the end, so watch out for your bums girls, because if I had one of those things I know what I'd do with it, and I'm sure at least some of the boys would be tempted.'

I'd started to blush at the mention of the cane and Wendy was giggling, presumably at the thought of me being forced to choose between two painful punishments. Stacey raised her hand.

'How does team play come into it?'

'I suppose we're meant to work out tactics that give us the best overall chance, like making one of us a decoy so the others can get through or something, but only those who get to the objective and take a numbered ball get any points.'

'I get it. It's all about being prepared to make sacrifices for the good of the team.'

'Something like that, and because the balls are worth twelve, nine, six and three it makes a big difference to individual scores. When we're defending it's more like playing hockey.'

I winced for a second time, remembering her tactics as a defender for the house, when I'd always been very glad indeed to be on the same side. Wendy had raised her hand, and seemed oddly nervous as she spoke.

'Um ... can I make a suggestion? Perhaps ... perhaps we ought to have our own little competition, only instead of points the loser pays a forfeit ... like a spanking, or something.'

Her face was flushed red, and she'd obviously found it difficult to say what she had, which meant she needed to do it, badly. For all my surprise I could guess what was going on in her head, because I'd been there many times before. She'd watched me being punished, and seen how I'd reacted. That had intrigued her enough to make her want to try it herself, but she wasn't sure about it and didn't want to admit to something as shameful as wanting to be spanked. By suggesting a game she could seem daring and playful rather than openly dirty and submissive, while it's always easier to take a punishment if you can find an excuse to pretend you have no choice in the matter. It was a good idea too, exciting and humiliating for the thought of losing, while there was always a chance that it would be Stacey or even Juliette who ended up in trouble, which provoked all sorts of interesting emotions and made me wonder if I was quite as deeply in thrall to Juliette as I'd imagined. Wendy carried on, stammering out her words.

'Don't you think it would be fun? Maybe if the loser gets as many smacks as she falls short of the winner's score, so if Stacey comes in first and gets the twelve, but Lucy gets caught ... or maybe I do, we get twelve spanks. That's fun, isn't it?'

She was plainly desperate for support and I was quick to help out.

'I'm up for that, but we all have to take a risk.'

Juliette answered casually.

'Sure, why not, but why be such a baby? Twelve spanks is nothing. We can use a puff stick as a cane and really have some fun. Stacey?'

'I suppose if I dish it out I'd be a coward not to be prepared to take it, and yeah, it makes the competition a lot more fun. OK?'

It was what I'd have expected of Stacey, who might not have understood punishment for pleasure but would never let herself look weak. Juliette was another matter, as she always liked to be the one to dish it out.

'You'd really take the cane, Juliette, if you lost, even from me?'

'I've been caned before, and believe me, I make a lot less fuss about it than you do. Anyway, I don't intend to lose.'

Wendy spoke up again, even more nervous than before.

'I ... I've never even been spanked, let alone caned, um ...'

She trailed off as Juliette put an arm around her shoulders.

'Don't worry, I'll be gentle, and if a big cry baby like Lucy can take it, then I'm sure you can too.'

Mr Straw was coming towards us and Juliette turned to speak to him and get our instructions. We were up against Team B, certainly the hardest to beat when Team C only had three players, which somehow didn't surprise me at all. The jar of balls would be on a rock somewhere in the woods beyond the old runway, which again gave whoever defended first an advantage, as they at least would know where they were going.

Fortunately so did I, as I'd glimpsed a big rock among the trees when Wendy and I had gone to get essential provisions and it seemed very likely to be the one we were after. My first thought was to move the jar when our turn came to defend, but Mr Straw was looking right at me as he concluded his remarks.

'… and if you don't play by the rules you'll be disqualified. That means you, Girl O. Look, seriously, I don't know why Mr Parker's got it in for you, but he has. My advice is to lose gracefully, or you'll just piss him off. Start when the bell goes.'

Both Juliette and Stacey had begun to speak, but he'd already turned away, and despite what he'd said I couldn't help but feel grateful, as he plainly thought Parker was being unfair. We also needed to get into the woods before the bell went or we'd risk getting caught in the open, which was probably exactly what Parker intended to happen.

'Come on, let's go. I think I know where the rock is.'

We ran across the airfield and into the shelter of the woods, mature pines well spaced out and providing very little cover, although I knew it got denser further in. There was no sign of the men, only a slightly eerie silence. The other two teams were playing in the woods behind the buildings, well out of our way, although I could see Paul standing by one of the disused hangars, looking lost. Juliette called us to order.

'Gather round. Right, never mind this crap about teamwork, I say it's every girl for herself, especially as we're playing the caning game. One exception – if you're being chased and you don't think you can get away, run this way, not towards the rock, which at least gives the rest of us a better chance, OK? So where's this rock, Lucy?'

'That way, if it's the right one.'

'And if it isn't?'

'I'll probably end up getting caned.'

She made to reply, just as the bell sounded from across the field. I'd guessed that Team B would have been watching the open field from the woods, hoping to catch us off guard, and so would know where we'd gone in. That meant they'd be coming for us, probably along the edge of the trees, so I made for the deep wood, intent on finding some cover and then sneaking slowly towards the rock.

The others had headed more or less directly towards the rock and I was soon alone, and thinking out the possible consequences of the game as I went. I wanted to win in order to prove myself against Parker's determination to keep me down, but that would mean caning one of my friends. I knew I could do Wendy, and enjoy it, but the idea of beating Stacey didn't feel right at all, while to think of doing Juliette seemed at once impossibly outrageous and hugely satisfying. For all my natural tendency to be sexually submissive, she was the one who'd moulded me, who'd taught me to grovel at other women's feet, to enjoy the appalling indignity of a bare-bottom spanking, to feel it natural to have my face sat on or my legs held apart for my cunt to be penetrated. The idea of giving her a dose of her own medicine terrified me and seemed completely against the natural order of things, but there was no denying that it would be justice. On the other hand she might end up caning me, which made my stomach churn with fear and desire at the same time, leaving me wanting to run as far away as I possibly could and to strip naked then and there to await my fate.

I pushed on, forcing myself not to allow my private thoughts to interfere with what I was doing. Beyond the pines I came to thicker, older woodland, with ferns pushing up among hazel trees and patches of rhododendron between huge oaks and beeches. The ground had begun to slope too, and I knew the fence couldn't be far away, but I didn't want to follow it and risk running into somebody, or cross it only to get caught and disqualified. I froze as a male voice called out, to be answered by another, then a female shriek, but they were a long way away and I soon moved on, creeping from tree to tree and bush to bush until at last I made out the grey bulk of a rock about fifty yards up the slope.

There were three problems. It wasn't the rock I'd seen before, which had been close to the fence and almost completely shrouded by trees, while this one was in a small clearing with the big pines on one side. The other one had also been smaller, while this was a great tower of weathered granite, at least twenty feet tall and not at all easy to climb, which was the second problem. Alastair Renton was the third problem, pacing back and forth across the clearing, the puff stick held in one hand as he tapped it against the palm of the other, for all the world like an old-fashioned schoolmaster preparing to give a naughty girl six-of-the-best, although the puff of bright-red cotton wool at the tip of his weapon somewhat spoilt the effect.

I stole forward, placing one foot in front of the other with agonising care until he was hidden from me by the bulk of the rock. There was a scatter of pine cones near the edge of the clearing and I paused to put a few in my pockets, intending to throw them at Alastair to buy me the time I needed to get clear if he saw me. A dash across the soft grass of the clearing and I was at the rock, scrabbling for purchase and jamming my toes into a vertical fissure that opened to a good-sized gap a few feet above my head. I climbed high, forcing myself to take it slowly, but for one awful moment I thought I was going to fall back before I steadied myself. One good pull and I was safe, a quick scramble and I was on top of the rock, triumphant.

The jar was there too, with all four balls still inside, as well as a trio of well-fixed bolts supporting a rope ladder and a safety line, which was evidently how you were supposed to get up. I couldn't help but wonder if Parker would disqualify me for not using the proper equipment, but I took the number twelve ball anyway, then lay down on my stomach to peer cautiously over the edge.

Alastair was still pacing up and down and still tapping the cane against his palm, oblivious to my success. I could see how the tactics were supposed to work, as it would be almost impossible to get onto the rope ladder, let alone get the safety line attached, without one member of the team agreeing to act as a decoy, which not only meant risking elimination but ensured a lower score. What I couldn't work out was why all four members of Team B hadn't stayed to guard the rock, making it almost impossible for their opponents to succeed.

I put it down to a general male inability to stay still for five minutes, curled myself into a comfortable lotus and relaxed, allowing my mind to wander. My victory meant I had the right to cane one of my friends, and while that came with issues it was easy to remind myself that they'd made me suck cock for a pair of fat boys, and while Paul was alright, even quite attractive in that I like men to be overwhelmingly bigger than me, Billy really was beyond the pale, appealing only to my love of erotic shame.

Stacey and Juliette had also spanked me, beaten me and humiliated me in a dozen different ways, and the fact that I looked back on every moment with relish didn't alter my delight in the possibility of revenge. It still felt wrong, and I was fairly sure that even if I found the courage to go through with it I'd soon be on my knees begging forgiveness, then bent over for a double dose of what I'd dished out. Wendy was an altogether different prospect, sweet-natured and relatively naïve if not actually innocent, and a far better candidate for having her pretty, pale bottom decorated with a dozen scarlet lines.

It was a nice thought, although it was difficult not to imagine myself lined up next to her, both touching our toes with our combat trousers and knickers pulled down at the back to get us bare as Stacey and Juliette applied the canes. I tried to compromise, imagining myself giving Wendy her forfeit and then allowing her to beat me in turn, but there was no denying that my proper place was on the receiving end, or that one or other of the girls who'd taken control of me so well ought to be wielding the cane. Wendy could be punished too, maybe even by me, but what mattered was that I was the one who ended up with a burning bottom as I took turns to lick the women who'd beaten me to ecstasy.

I soon found myself wondering if it was safe for me to slip a hand down the front of my panties and finish myself off, because whatever the others were up to they weren't nearby. Distant shouts suggested that the competition between Team C and Team D was going strong, but the woods around me were oddly silent. Alastair couldn't see me and didn't even know I was there, while his presence nearby made the thought of masturbating all the more naughty. Nobody could possibly climb the rock without me noticing either, and I'd have plenty of time to make myself decent.

With that thought I decided to do it, feeling deliciously rude as I tugged open the front of my combat trousers and pulled up my top to get myself ready. It felt lovely to have my breasts bare in the open, with the wide blue sky all around me and the air cool on my already stiff nipples, so I spent a while just holding my breasts and gently running my fingers over my skin while I got my thoughts in order.

There was no use in pretending I wanted to cane Stacey

for any reason other than revenge, much less Juliette, so I imagined how Wendy would react to the news that she'd lost. Many a time I'd been told I was to be beaten long before it happened, invariably leaving me in a scarcely bearable state of arousal and apprehension. Wendy was sure to be the same, scared and full of self-pity but also turned on, emotions that would grow worse throughout the day, until at last the time came for her punishment.

I wasn't at all sure how she'd take it, maybe doing her best to be brave as she went through the awful little ritual of baring her bottom and bending to touch her toes, perhaps asking to be held in place or even tied up so that it wouldn't be a problem if her nerve broke. It was hard to imagine her crying off, not when she'd suggested the game herself, so one way or another she'd end up bent down with her bottom on show and her neat little cunt peeping out from between her thighs just the way mine did when I got it, our dignity stripped away, our twin holes vulnerable to mocking, excited eyes and greedy fingers.

The thought was making me shake and I could hold back no more. My hand went down the front of my panties, to find my pussy wet and ready, my clitoris poking out and so sensitive I had to bite my lip to stop myself crying out as I began to stroke. I tried to think of Wendy getting ready for the cane, but it wouldn't work. Ignoring my right to dish it out, I went back to my picture of the two of us side my side, bare and ready. Knowing Juliette and Stacey they'd probably pull our tops up to add to our humiliation, or maybe even make us strip nude. What was absolutely certain was that we wouldn't be allowed to keep our panties up, and we'd be showing everything behind as the cold, hard canes were laid across our bare cheeks.

I'd be shivering even before I'd been hit, maybe even in tears. Wendy would try to be brave, but she'd start to whimper as the cane was lifted over her bottom, and she'd scream just as loudly as I did when it came down across her tender flesh. She'd have had no idea how much it hurt, and would be shaking her hair and dancing up and down on her feet for ages, much like I would, and all to the sound of cruel laughter from our persecutors. It would take all her courage to get back into position, and she'd be whimpering and choking on her tears even as she stuck her bottom out once more, but I'd be no better than her, one more snivelling little brat ready for a well-justified thrashing.

My head was thrown back, my mouth open, my fingers pinching at a nipple and rubbing hard on my clitoris. I started to come, holding the image of me and Wendy bent over together with our whipped bottoms thrust out in my head as my ecstasy rose higher and higher still, to finally burst in an orgasm that left me shaking and breathless, one of the best, and better still because there was a high chance of what I'd been imagining becoming real.

It took me a while to come down, but I soon found myself smiling for how naughty I'd been, as well as feeling embarrassed and guilty, but those were emotions I'd learnt to cope with. There was still no sign of anybody else, and I was considering calling down to Alastair when I heard voices from among the trees, men calling to each other and obviously in pursuit of one of my friends. I stood up, just in time to see Stacey burst out from among the pines with two men close behind her, both clutching their puff sticks. Alastair moved to head her off, making her position impossible, until I launched a salvo of pine cones, one of which caught him smartly on the side of the head. Stacey was past in an instant, grabbing for the ladder without bothering about the safety line and hauling herself up, just fast enough to evade the men as they came crashing up behind her. When she'd joined me and I'd helped her to her feet we came close to the edge, looking down at the men below. The two who'd chased her were still fighting for breath, but Alastair was looking up in astonishment.

'How did you get up there, Lucy?'

'I've been here ages. You should learn to look around more often! Sorry about the pine cones.'

He responded with a resigned grin and I turned to Stacey.

'What about Juliette and Wendy?'

'They got Juliette almost immediately. They'd have got Wendy too if Juliette hadn't held on to Sam Haynes.'

'Oh, dear, that's sure to get her disqualified, maybe all of us!'

'He won't tell Parker, not Sam. Hey Sam, you're not going to tell old man Parker that Juliette sat on you, are you?'

She was calling down from the rock, and one of the men who'd been chasing her looked up, shaking his head. Alastair didn't seem to mind having had pine cones thrown at him either, to my relief. I turned to Stacey again, speaking quietly so that the men couldn't hear me.

'So where's Wendy?'

'They got her too, later, when we were trying to get back here. You sent us to the wrong rock, Lucy.'

'Oops, sorry. It wasn't on purpose, but you can spank me if you feel you need to.'

'Only if you need spanking, but you have to give Juliette twelve of the cane.'

I nodded, wondering if I could actually do it, after everything that had passed between me and Juliette. Stacey seemed pleased though.

'I'm looking forward to that. In fact, I wish I was the one doing the caning. I like Juliette, but she can be a little too full of herself sometimes, and she treats you as if you're her property.'

'I was, once upon a time.'

'Don't be daft. I know you were in love with her, but she didn't own you.'

'It felt that way, and I know she can be a bitch, but ...'

I trailed off with a shrug, wanting to say more but unsure how to fully express myself. Stacey responded with a hug and we saw that Mr Straw had arrived below.

* * *

We'd come second, with twenty-one points, behind Team B, who managed to get three people past Team D, but ahead of both the others, who'd failed to get a single person through to the jar. I was well pleased with myself, for my own performance in getting twelve points, for our determined defence against Chad and his crew, but most of all because Parker was obviously furious but could find no way of adjusting the result to help his favourites. Mr Straw and Sergeant Reynolds had done the refereeing while he'd been in Exeter and both had been fair, leaving him unable to do more than accuse us of being over-cautious and unimaginative for staying close to the rock when we were defending.

Juliette had accepted my right to cane her in the same offhand manner she'd agreed to take it if she lost, but she was quieter than usual during lunch and I was sure she was suffering from the same feelings of apprehension and fear she'd inflicted on me before. It felt odd, with my emotions swinging between a vicious sense of satisfaction that quite took me by surprise and remorse and self-recrimination for exactly that. There was another problem, in that we'd had to hand the puff sticks in after the game, and by the time we'd finished dinner I was wondering if the best thing to do wasn't to let Juliette off on the grounds of not having a suitable implement to deal with her. When I suggested it to Stacey as we talked together outside our hut she was horrified.

'You can't let her off! We'll find something, even if it's only a switch from a hedge, but I've been thinking. The puff sticks are in the Stores, and I saw into the door when Sergeant Reynolds was putting them back. There are all sorts of things in there, towels for starters.'

I nodded. We'd worked out a routine to keep the amount of time we had to spend running about the camp in next to nothing to a minimum, but the shortage of towels was still a sore point. Stacey went on.

'They keep the door locked most of the time, but I'm sure you could get in.'

'Why me!?'

'Because you're the skinniest, and the best climber. There's no way I could have got up that rock the way you did. I could probably lift you up so that you can get onto the roof too, and I don't suppose the skylight's locked.'

'How would I get back out?'

'Easy. The lock's a latch. Think about it, lots of lovely towels and you get to give Juliette a proper caning.'

Again I nodded, but with far less certainty. She made it sound easy, but at the very least we were going to have to wait for lights out. Juliette was coming towards us, and there was no mistaking the tremor in her voice as she spoke.

'Come on then, let's get it over with. I'm ready, unless you'd like a glass of wine first to celebrate our win?'

She obviously wanted one, and so did I, besides having to wait before we could steal a puff stick for a cane.

'I'll get a bottle. Keep an eye out for Parker and the others.'

I made for our stash, quickly retrieving a bottle of red and making my way back to the hut without incident. Juliette was now sat on her bed with her legs pulled up, still dressed.

'I hear you're going to raid the Stores? Try and get some glasses. I hate these plastic cups, and I'm sure they make it taste funny. Give me the bottle then.'

She was trying to be brave, but her fingers were shaking as she twisted the cap loose from the bottle and she put it straight to her mouth instead of pouring out a cupful. Stacey immediately objected.

'Juliette! Leave some for us.'

Juliette took another swallow before replying.

'You're not the one who's going to get caned. I'm no cry baby, but it hurts.'

I bit back the impulse to offer to let her off, not wanting to risk Stacey's scorn. Wendy was sitting cross-legged on her own bed, and spoke up as she accepted the bottle.

'I'm sure it does, but won't you ... I mean, will it ...'

'If you mean, will it make me wet, then yes. That's just the way it is, but that doesn't mean I like it. You must remember Angela Barnes, Lucy? She was the one who did me, on my back with my legs rolled up and her hand twisted in my knickers so I was pretty well helpless. Then she gave me six with a bamboo from a plant pot. It stung like anything.'

I could imagine exactly how she'd have looked, with her knickers around her ankles and her long legs pulled high to leave her pussy showing and her bottom spread and

118

vulnerable. It wasn't something she'd admitted to before, and no surprise. She'd also dealt with me in the same humiliating position, and in front of Claire and Emily, but I couldn't help feeling sorry for her.

'Look, if you'd rather not ...'

'No. A bet's a bet, and believe me, when you lose and it's the other way around, I'm not going to let you off, not one stroke.'

I could well believe it and I responded with a nervous nod. We lapsed into silence, each thinking her own thoughts as we sipped our wine. Only Stacey seemed at all calm, but I wondered how she'd have been if and when her turn came.

An hour later we decided it was safe to reconnoitre the Stores. It was brighter outside than it had been the night before, with a crescent moon hanging low over the trees and a sky full of stars. Nobody seemed to be about, although we could hear voices coming from the hut occupied by Team D and closest to ours. Not a single window showed any light and although there were several areas we couldn't see it seemed likely that everybody else had gone to bed, exhausted after the morning's exercise and a run on the assault course in the afternoon. I still wanted to be sure, and whispered to Stacey.

'Let's go round by Parker's hut, just in case he's still up.'

She nodded and we set out, moving furtively across the path to the huts on the opposite side. It was a long time since I'd done anything of the sort, and it brought back memories of midnight scrumping expeditions and illicit visits to men's rooms while at college, always in defiance of either authority or convention. Now was no different, as the humourless Parker was sure to see it as theft, and I took extreme care, moving from shadow to shadow and repeatedly pausing to listen and look around. Every sound seemed magnified, the low mutter of voices from the huts, the occasional bird call and, as we approached Parker's hut, a sharp click.

We both froze, crouching down in the darkness cast by a squat concrete pillbox, not daring to move, scarcely daring to breathe. Somebody, presumably Parker, had opened the hut door, but it was on the far side of the hut and we had no idea if he was coming or going. A light went on, visible only as a bright slit where the curtains failed to cover one window properly, which meant he'd been prowling the camp even as we made our way towards the Stores, each unaware of the other.

My first instinct was to turn back, but Stacey hadn't moved and I didn't want to face Juliette's scorn for failing in my mission. Then I heard new voices, very low and coming from Parker's hut, which could only mean he hadn't been out at all, but had a visitor. I couldn't make out any words, but it was no open, unabashed conversation, rather a furtive exchange between two people who very definitely did not want to be heard. Stacey's hand tightened on mine and gave a gentle tug, urging me forward.

I followed her, placing one foot in front of the other with my heart hammering so fast and hard I was sure Parker and his friend would hear. We reached the hut, not daring to touch the walls for fear of giving ourselves away, and peered close to the gap between window frame and curtain. I could see part of a bed, and a vertical area of khaki and another of hairy flesh that seemed oddly out of place until it moved and I realised I was looking at somebody's back and somebody else's leg. Intrigued, I pressed close, telling myself that I might be seen but I couldn't possibly be recognised. I judged that I'd have plenty of time to escape too, as whatever was going on it was highly furtive and almost certainly sexual.

The implications sank in even as my view grew clearer.

With just four women in the camp, whoever had come to see Parker had to be another man, and he seemed to be on his knees in front of the bed. He was, and more. My mouth had come open as I took in the full scene, viewed in a long frame but still clear enough. Parker was seated on his bed, naked but for one of the blue camp tops he always wore, the material tight across the muscles of his chest and belly. Between his legs knelt another man, in khaki, his hands extended to massage a large, limp penis and a good-sized set of balls. The second man was Chad.

Stacey must have realised what was going on at exactly the same moment I did. Her hand tightened on mine and we shared a look, her face full of astonishment and delight, her free hand clamped over her mouth to stifle her laughter. I felt the same, highly amused to find that big, butch Chad liked to suck cock, which was obviously what he was planning to do, and even more so that Parker liked his sucked by other men, but if it was funny, it was also highly arousing. There was no denying that both men were physically attractive, for all my personal feelings, and the fact that I disliked them made it easier to watch, and more satisfying.

It's good to watch two men together anyway, especially when they're not openly gay, and despite not being able to see Chad clearly I could tell that he was nervous. Parker seemed more relaxed, settled back on his arms with his thighs a little apart to make his cock and balls available, and I guessed that it wasn't his first time. Not that Chad was actually reluctant, but he must have been having difficulty coming to terms with his feelings, because it wasn't until Parker actually told him to get sucking that he bent down to take the fat white cock in his mouth.

My tummy had gone tight and Stacey's grip grew harder

121

as we watched Chad start to suck. I could see his face now, with his mouth wide around Parker's shaft and his eyes closed in a mixture of bliss and shame. Both feelings were familiar to me, and I couldn't help but feel a touch of sympathy, remembering the first time I'd put my tongue to another woman's sex. Yet I'd been spanked first, bringing me up to a state of arousal so strong I barely knew what I was doing, while Chad had clearly come to visit Parker with the specific intention of sucking him off. That had to mean he'd known there was a good chance Parker was up for it, which was intriguing in itself, but for the moment I was content to watch.

Parker was getting stiff, his cock now a long, crooked pole only half in, but Chad was doing his manly best, playing with his lover's balls and tugging on the base of his shaft. It was just what I'd have done myself, when trying to suck a well-endowed man off without gagging too badly, which made me think of how Parker had promised to put his cock up me, and that I'd have undoubtedly had to suck him hard first. The thought sent a shiver through me, but more of resentment than desire, and I was very glad it was Chad who'd ended up on his knees with his mouth full of the bastard's cock and not me.

Stacey gave a gentle tug on my hand, indicating that we should move on. I hesitated, fascinated by the sight of Chad's face as he worked on Parker's erection, but we obviously needed to talk. She moved back and I followed, into the shadows of the pillbox, where I spoke to Stacey, my voice coming in a breathless whisper.

'That was rude!'

'Wasn't it just, but never mind them. Shall we go for the Stores?'

'I don't know. Chad will have to walk right past to get back to his hut. How long do you think they'll take?'

'Not long. You know what guys are like. The moment they've spunked they either want to leave or go to sleep. Chad looked embarrassed too, so I don't suppose he'll hang around for a chat.'

'Don't you think they'll take turns though, or maybe go to bed together?'

'I doubt it. I'm guessing Chad likes to suck cock but has trouble with his feelings, but you might be right. We should wait. Anyway, I'm turned on, and I want to watch.'

'Slut. Come on then.'

She took my hand once more, leading me back to the window. The scene was much as before, with Chad sucking eagerly on Parker's erect cock. He was still kneeling too, but upright, with his own cock and balls out of his combat trousers, masturbating as he sucked. I heard Stacey draw her breath in at the sight and a moment later her arm had come around me. Chad was big, and very pale, with a thick foreskin now peeled back from the glossy head. I couldn't help but imagine sucking on him, and wondered how it would feel to take a cock in my mouth for a man who was sucking his male lover's cock at the same time.

Stacey's hand moved to my bottom, stroking and patting my cheeks. I stuck it out, making myself available to her, and her hand slid between my thighs, cupping the bulge of my pussy through my combat trousers. She began to masturbate me and I cuddled close, eager to return the favour but unable to do so without breaking away from the window, and I had to watch. Chad was tugging hard on his erection, his face full of emotion as he continued to work on Parker's cock and balls, no longer simply sucking, but licking and kissing and rubbing it all against his face, as much in worship as in any attempt to give pleasure.

Parker didn't seem to mind, propped up on one elbow while he used his spare hand to stroke Chad's close-cropped hair, the same gesture many a man had used to soothe my feelings while I gave him a dirty blow job. Chad obviously needed it, because he looked close to tears, for all that he was obviously in ecstasy for what he was doing, while the motion of his hand on his erection had become frantic. He came, suddenly, a jet of thick white spunk erupting from the tip of his cock as he buried his face in Parker's lap, sobbing with emotion as he mouthed at the big prick and fat, wrinkled ball sac.

I'd never seen a man give in to that sort of need so completely, and I was squirming my bottom against Stacey's hand as I watched spurt after spurt of come erupt from Chad's cock. She caught hold of me, forcing me to keep still as her rubbing grew harder, directly on my clit, and even though it was through my trousers and my panties too I knew I was soon going to come.

The moment he was done Chad sank down, his head hung in shame, his cock still in his hand with a trickle of spunk running down over his fingers. Parker said something, then again, his tone now harsh, telling Chad he wasn't going to get away without finishing what he'd begun. Chad responded with a single, weak nod, before leaning forward again, to take Parker's erection back in his mouth, his slowly deflating cock now dribbling spunk onto the carpet as he once more began to suck. Parker called him a good boy and began to stroke his hair again, but that did nothing to reduce the look of utter disgust on Chad's face.

That was too much for me, to see a man made to suck

another's cock when he'd just come, clearly hating every moment and yet unable to stop himself. I'd been in the same situation so many times, painfully ashamed of my own behaviour even as I made an utter slut of myself or did something no self-respecting modern woman should even so much as think about. Most often it had been with Juliette, but also Stacey, the girl now rubbing my cunt through my combats and panties, to bring me up to a long, tight orgasm just as Parker grunted and came, full in Chad's mouth.

I'd thought Chad looked disgusted, but I'd seen nothing until a great mass of spunk and bubbles erupted from around his lips, all over Parker's balls and the base of his cock. Then I saw Chad's Adam's apple bob and I realised that for all his revulsion he'd deliberately swallowed, which pushed my ecstasy up to a second, higher peak, so strong I couldn't hold back a cry of pleasure.

Chapter Six

Juliette didn't get her caning. Both Chad and Parker heard my gasp when I came, and if one hadn't had the other's erection jammed down his throat they'd have probably seen me too. Stacey and I fled, with her supporting me until I'd found my feet properly, and by the time we'd reached our hut Parker's torch could already be seen flickering among the distant shadows. Wendy and Juliette had been curled together on a bed, kissing open-mouthed and already half undressed, but quickly broke apart to listen as we gasped out our story.

We were convinced there would be a hut search and all four of us had got into bed as quickly as possible, waiting for a rap on the firmly locked door. Nothing happened, and my excitement gradually faded, but we all agreed it was too dangerous to play, and to my secret relief we agreed to postpone Juliette's punishment to a more convenient time. I was exhausted anyway, but it still took me a long time to get to sleep, and when I finally managed the images of Chad down on his knees with Parker's cock in his mouth invaded my dreams.

The bell came as a sudden, harsh shock, and I hauled myself out of bed with some difficulty. It was another bright spring day, to my relief, but colder than I'd expected, which added to the trials of the morning routine. At breakfast it was hard not to be too obvious in my attention to Chad, although he was his usual, brash self, so much so that if I hadn't witnessed his emotional and dirty performance the night before I'd have had trouble believing it had happened. Parker was no different, full of energy and snide remarks as he moved among the tables, informing us we had five minutes to be on parade in Assembly when some of us were only just starting breakfast.

Chad immediately abandoned his tray, calling on his friends to do the same and jogging from the room. Others followed at a more leisurely pace, although I couldn't stop myself wanting to hurry, while Paul and his teammates took no notice whatsoever. I already knew what we were doing anyway, a tactical exercise designed to make us think about choosing the right person for the right job, but really all about strength and stamina. As Parker explained as we stood to attention, we had to nominate a runner, a climber, a swimmer and a thrower, who would then compete against members of the other teams, scoring twelve, eight, four or nothing according to how they placed. It seemed to be designed for Team C to shine, especially as they were allowed to borrow Mr Straw to make up their numbers.

Stacey was as determined as ever, speaking as soon as Juliette had led us a little way away from the buildings so that we could talk in private.

'The knack is choosing the best person for each event in such a way as to maximise our overall score. So while I'm probably the best runner, I'm not going to beat Chad or Daniel or whoever anyway, so I'd be wasted.'

Wendy spoke up.

'But we don't actually know what we're doing.'

'No, but we can make a fair guess. It's not going to be really dangerous, or anything Parker and the assistants couldn't handle, and it's going to take a while but not all day, so maybe a cross-country for the runner, or a steeplechase, but that doesn't really matter. None of us are going to beat the best from Team B or C, so I suggest Wendy as the runner and we'll go for the four points. OK?'

Juliette answered her.

'Fine, except that I'm the team leader. Let's make the most obvious choice first. Lucy's built like a spider, so she's the obvious choice for the climber, especially after yesterday. She might actually win. I reckon I can hold my own in the water and at least have a chance at second, so I'll be the swimmer. I agree that Wendy's the best choice for running, which leaves you as our thrower, Stacey, if that's OK?'

There was a touch of sarcasm in her voice, but Stacey ignored it, contenting herself with a simple nod. I wanted to ask about our punishment regime, but Wendy got in first.

'How do we rank ourselves for ... you know, for smacks, or the cane, or whatever? We might all score four points.'

Juliette considered.

'If we're equal, we're equal, but it's not that likely, so we can use the same rules ...'

Stacey interrupted.

'Let's keep it simple. Whoever does best gets to punish whoever does worst.'

'And how about draws?'

'Two with twelve are both winners, two with zero are both losers, simple.'

Juliette gave her a doubtful look, evidently trying to calculate the odds. The way Stacey had suggested we work it one or the other of them was likely to get spanked. It was also quite likely one would end up spanking the other, and I could see that the rivalry between them was building to the point at which they'd enjoy dishing out a punishment immensely, and be willing to take risks with their own bottoms to get what they wanted. It was also plain that either way Wendy was likely to end up either touching her toes for the cane or over somebody's knee, but she'd been the one who'd mentioned the punishments first and obviously wanted to find herself in a position in which she had no choice but to take what was coming to her. I was likely to win, which was a little annoying, but I was sure that whoever I ended up punishing would get me back in due course, and maybe take me further than she would otherwise have done.

'I like Stacey's suggestion. Let's go for that.'

Juliette gave me a hard stare.

'You are going to end up in serious trouble, Miss Lucy.'

'That's the whole idea, but only after you've had yours.'

'You are getting brave, aren't you? OK, let's see how things pan out, shall we?'

I managed a smile, and if she'd got to me then that was what I'd hoped for. The other teams had gathered nearby and had been doing much the same as us, while Parker was standing beside his precious Team C, taking down their choices on his clipboard. I watched, trying to see if I could detect any differences in their body language as he spoke with Chad. There was nothing obvious, but I told myself that given how Chad crawled to Parker anyway, a bit of cocksucking wasn't going to make an appreciable difference.

Parker came to us last, by which time everybody else was gathering into their new groups. I'd thought we might be climbing the same rock we'd used the day before, or perhaps just the walls on the assault course, but I was told to get into one of the minibuses, joining Sergeant Reynolds and Alastair Renton, who both represented serious competition, and William, who was the last person I could imagine climbing anything. I spoke to him as soon as we were in the minibus, trying not to sound impolite.

'I'd have thought you'd be better at … throwing perhaps, or swimming?'

'It's fixed, isn't it? We're meant to lose, so what's the point? Now make it something that needs brains and we're on it, but not this crap.'

I could see his point, and would have sympathised, but Alastair had climbed in with us, while Sergeant Reynolds was about to take the driver's seat.

'Where are we going anyway, Dartmoor?'

'Hartland Point.'

There was a nasty inflection in his voice and when we got there I found out why. Hartland Point was a massive headland of dark-red rock, near vertical in places and over 300 feet high, as he gleefully pointed out. I could only stare in horror, wishing I'd volunteered for anything else and wondering if I had either the strength or courage to make it down, never mind up, as Sergeant Reynolds seemed intent on making us do both. Alastair didn't look too happy about it either, while William took one look at the cliff, shrugged and asked if there was a decent pub nearby. I almost joined him, but there was something about Sergeant Reynolds' smug, self-satisfied manner as he rigged up a system of ropes that made me determined not to back down. When he'd finished and checked that everything was safe and secure he walked back to where Alastair and I were sitting, his face showing open contempt despite his words.

'This is an easy exercise, but it takes courage, and ... Where's the other one?'

'He's gone to look for a pub.'

'One down, two to go. Either of you two want to join him, 'cause it makes my job a whole lot easier if you do?'

'No, thank you. What are we doing anyway?'

'Abseiling, all the way down to the bottom, 309 feet, and the faster you go, the more points you get.'

'How about coming back up?'

'Use the path, smart arse. It goes round by the lighthouse. So who's first?'

I got up, trying not to show my feelings as I approached the edge and following his instructions mechanically until I was fully harnessed up and standing at the lip of the cliff with the rocks 300 feet below me. My stomach was churning, my bladder felt weak and I was shaking so badly I could hardly hold onto the rope. He was grinning at me as he took out his stopwatch, openly enjoying my discomfort, and I was about to give in and haul myself back when he shouted.

'Go!'

I went, and so did my bladder, piddle squirting into my panties as the safety line took my full weight, to leave me upside down with my legs spread wide in front of him before I'd disappeared over the edge of the cliff. For one ghastly moment I was in free fall and even the fact that I was wetting myself didn't matter, before the safety line took my weight again with a horrible jerk, to leave me dangling in mid-air with pee running down my legs. I knew what to do and I did it, working the descender in frantic haste in a vain and pointless effort to stop Sergeant Reynolds realising what had happened. His head appeared over the cliff edge and I saw that he was laughing, leaving me furious as I continued down, as fast as I possibly could, to land bottom first on a huge boulder, at which I gave in once more, letting go to release the full contents of my bladder into my panties. His voice floated down from the top.

'Are you alright?'

'Fuck off!'

He didn't bother to reply and I set about unfastening myself, which left me safe but in a very awkward situation indeed. There was no possible way anybody could see me and not realise I'd wet myself. My trousers were soaking, with the crotch pulled tight up against my pussy in a sticky V, while the pee had soaked up the back of my harness to leave both my cheeks neatly outlined in sodden cotton. Nobody was on the beach, which was entirely composed of boulders, but I'd seen the way up from the car park and knew I'd have to walk past the lighthouse, and the café beside it, and at least fifty curious tourists.

I stood up, grimacing at the squashy, sticky feel in my knickers and desperately trying to figure out how to escape my predicament with the minimum of embarrassment. There was no time to waste either, as Alastair would shortly be coming down the rope, not only a man but a man from my own company. I could only think of one way out, embarrassing enough in itself, but nothing like as embarrassing as being caught in pee-soaked trousers.

Sergeant Reynolds called down from above, warning me to get clear, but I was already on my way, jumping from boulder to boulder towards the welcome embrace of the sea. Welcome, but also cold and wet. That didn't stop me, for all that I was gasping as I waded out and when a wave caught my stomach and chest I was left cursing Sergeant Reynolds out loud, then spitting sea water as a second one caught me full in the face. I was in though, and struggling to pull down my trousers and panties to wash myself off even as Alastair appeared at the lip of the cliff.

He was cautious, to my relief, lowering himself in careful, measured jumps, under full control but far more slowly than me, so that I was able to cover myself up long before he got to the rocks. Soaking wet, but at least not in a state of disgrace, I swam out a little way, then back, by which time he was standing at the water's edge, looking puzzled. I greeted him with a grin.

'That was great, so refreshing.'

'You're nuts. You beat me down the cliff too.'

'Oh? I wasn't really trying. I just wanted to wipe the smug grin off Reynolds' face.'

'He's not that bad. You just need to win his respect.'

I didn't bother to argue, but looked up as Sergeant Reynolds himself started down the rope. He was good, and obviously experienced, coming down in a few long swoops and landing neatly on his feet, right in my wet patch. I found myself grinning despite everything, and all the more for the irritable look on his face as he approached, pulling the stopwatch from his pocket as he reached us.

'You got it, O. Never have I seen such a fuck-up, but time is time and that's what counts.'

'I won?'

'I was five seconds short on your time. Well done.'

Alastair raised his palm and I slapped it, feeling slightly embarrassed for the gesture. I was sure Sergeant Reynolds knew I'd had an accident, but he was decent enough not to say anything, despite laughing at my antics on the rope. As we began to walk he was explaining that the exercise was deliberately designed to shock people into backing out, the idea being as much to teach people to think carefully about their own aptitudes as for the team to choose the best members for the task.

'... like here. Half the people take one look at the cliff and give up. That says a lot about them. It's the same with the running. The winner is the last one to give up.'

'I see. So what now?'

'I don't know about you, but I'm going to join L in the pub for some lunch. L for loser, huh?'

I smiled, although I personally felt that whatever Billy lacked in courage he made up for in common sense. He might have scored zero, but he might have gone down the cliff and still scored zero, while he was warm and dry and had been spared a terrifying experience. I was cold, wet and shaking with reaction, as well as being badly in need of some dry clothes. Fortunately the buildings around the lighthouse included a gift shop and Sergeant Reynolds allowed me the use of his debit card. Unfortunately their selection of clothing was both limited and designed for the tourist trade, leaving me in pink flip-flops and a baggy yellow beach shirt that showed a pair of Union Jack panties from behind as we climbed back up to the car park. Both Alastair and Sergeant Reynolds were very polite, saying nothing and trying not to grin, but when we eventually found Billy he was less reticent.

'What the fuck!? Are they doing Girls Gone Wild down on the beach? Go on then, give us a flash of your tits.'

I gave him a clip around the ear, which he didn't object to, and sat down. He'd had at least two pints since he'd left us, maybe more, and his little piggy eyes looked slightly glassy as they feasted on my chest. It was very obvious that I had no bra and I found myself blushing and trying to cool my embarrassment by reminding myself that he'd seen it all anyway. That also reminded me of what I'd done, sucking his cock in front of Paul and my friends, leaving me pinker than ever.

Neither Alastair nor Sergeant Reynolds noticed, both too wrapped up in their conversation about the course, and it stayed that way as we ate lunch. I was thirsty and felt off balance, so let them buy me two pints of lager to wash down my meal, but while that quenched my thirst it only made my sense of shame worse, and gave it an increasingly erotic edge. Not only was I barely dressed in front of three men, but I'd wet myself, which had to be almost as pathetic and inappropriate a thing for a grown woman to do as letting somebody spank her. I tried to tell myself that in the circumstances it might have happened to anybody, but it hadn't. It had happened to me.

My feelings grew stronger on the long drive back to the camp, until I was promising myself I'd tell Stacey and ask her to punish me for what I'd done. It was an irresistibly arousing thought, to be put across her knee and have my silly Union Jack panties pulled down and my bottom smacked while I was told off for wetting myself, but when we arrived it was to find the place empty. Sergeant Reynolds explained that the other exercises all took longer and suggested a timed run on the assault course. Alastair accepted, Billy had made straight for his hut, saying he wanted to take a nap, and I declined, preferring to be alone.

I knew I was going to be dirty with myself even as I stepped in among the big pines behind the huts. That didn't stop me feeling ashamed, which in turn added to my excitement. Not only had I wet my panties, more or less in public, but I was going to play with myself over the memory, and outdoors, the sort of thing only a woman completely lost to any sense of decency or self-respect would do. I didn't care, and I couldn't stop myself anyway. At the time it had been a genuinely awful experience, but the memory was another matter entirely, especially the feeling of utter helplessness as the hot pee bubbled out into my panties as I swung on a rope far above the rocks.

All I needed was somewhere safe, where I could feel sufficiently secure to pull up my top, pop my panties down and bring myself to a badly needed orgasm. The pillboxes scattered among the trees seemed a good choice, but I wanted to find one deep in the woods, where there was no chance of anybody accidentally catching me while I was masturbating, although I could hear Alastair and Sergeant Reynolds on the assault course, now some way behind me, while Billy was presumably sleeping off his alcoholic lunch.

I found myself smiling a crooked grin as I thought of him and the way his eyes had feasted on my body at the pub and afterwards, walking back to the minibus. He'd stayed behind me, obviously hoping to catch a glimpse of my panties, for all that I'd been on my knees to him with his cock in my mouth just a couple of nights before. I couldn't help but react to his attention, for all that he was a dirty-minded little nerd, or really precisely because he was a dirty-minded little nerd. To think of him enjoying the sight of my body and the memory of how I'd been forced to humiliate myself to him was agonisingly shameful, and suited my mood to perfection.

Now deep in the woods, I stopped, close to where one of the pillboxes was visible among the trees. It had its own little patch of sunlight, the roof open to the sky but invisible from more than a few metres away. Even then it would normally have been much too open for the sort of dirty behaviour I was contemplating, but with the camp fenced off from the road and all of my colleagues safely accounted for I felt I could risk it. I also felt more ashamed of myself than ever as I gave my pussy a quick stroke through my Union Jack panties, now with a hard knot in my tummy for what I wanted to do and scarcely able to accept that I could be so filthy with myself.

Climbing onto the pillbox roof, I deliberately peeled my top up and off, partly for the sheer joy of going near-naked outdoors, but also for the thrill of being topless. The way Billy had looked at me had triggered a favourite fantasy, or more a reaction. I've often felt resentful for the way men can sexualise a woman, looking at her not as another person but as a pretty toy to be played with, all bum and tits and pussy, created purely for their indulgence. Billy was like that, and Paul, but while their attention would usually have been annoying, it was also embarrassing, and for me that was fatal.

I imagined them watching me, getting a kick out of the fact that I was topless, just as Billy had enjoyed seeing my panties. Now they were all I had on, and they didn't even cover very much, tight against the swell of my sex and doing more to show off the contours of my bottom than conceal anything, save for the very rudest, most private details of my pussy lips and my bumhole. I thought of how I'd have looked from behind as I knelt to suck Paul's cock, with my skirt turned up to show off my cheeks, my flesh red from spanking and the tight pink star of my anus on blatant show between.

'I'm such a slut, a dirty, cocksucking little slut.'

It was no good denying it, so I'd said it aloud, bringing home the awful, shameful truth of my behaviour. It was no surprise girls liked to spank me. I deserved it, whipped across the knee and my panties pulled down for a good smacking, by Stacey, by Juliette, by any woman who wanted to take me to task. Even if they'd made me strip in public and caned me until I screamed I'd have deserved it, for being a disgrace to womanhood, the sort of girl who gets off on showing dirty little boys her tits and likes to wet her panties.

I'd sat down, cross-legged in the sunny patch on the roof of the pillbox, and as I settled my bottom onto the warm, smooth concrete I realised that it would be very easy to make an even bigger disgrace of myself. The lager I'd drunk at lunchtime was beginning to have its effect, making my tummy swell and filling me with an urgency I'd normally have found irritating but was now gloriously sexy. All I had to do was give a little push and I'd pee in my panties, deliberately this time, to make a warm, sticky puddle under my bottom.

The thought was almost too shameful. Almost. I couldn't do it, not yet, but I knew I'd be able to once I was just a little bit more turned on. That meant playing with my cunt, deliberately being rude in order to make myself do something ruder still. I was looking down as I began to stroke the front of my panties. They were ridiculously tight, and very thin, the lips of my sex making a soft, horseshoe-shaped bulge in the cotton. I was already wet, a damp patch between my lips betraying my excitement, and I imagined Billy seeing it, perhaps if I'd bent over, or when I'd climbed into the minibus.

I closed my eyes and tilted my head back, letting the hot sun play on my face as I imagined how it might have been in a different world, a world in which men weren't polite, or shy, or reserved, but gave way to their primitive instincts without the slightest thought. They'd have had me, no question about it, then and there, bent into the door of the minibus with my silly panties pulled down, fucked from behind in front of fifty tourists and loving every second. Sergeant Reynolds was undoubtedly the dominant male and would have gone first, pushing the others aside to thrust a huge black cock right up me. He'd have fucked me hard and spunked deep inside me, to leave me with come dribbling from my open hole to act as lubricant for Alastair's cock as he took his turn.

An expression came to mind, sloppy seconds, an impossibly disrespectful description of a girl's cunt when she's been fucked by one man and is ready for another. That was how I'd be for Alastair, his cock squashing in Sergeant Reynolds' spunk as he pumped into me, both of us utterly humiliated in our own way but too turned on to do anything but fuck, until he too had come inside me. Then would come Billy, only by then I'd be so open he wouldn't be able to get enough friction to his weedy little cock, making the boys laugh at him, and at me as I begged him to fuck me properly. In response he'd slap me, tell me to shut up and pull his slippery cock free, only to immediately jam it up my bottom.

I nearly came at the thought, crying out my pleasure to the empty wood, but it wasn't the time, not yet, and I went back to my fantasy. Billy would bugger me, ignoring my urgent, disgusted protests as he fucked my bottom hole, spanking me as he did it, while the others egged him on to be as dirty with me as possible. I'd realise what was going to happen, that if I didn't stop I'd have an accident, and I'd start to beg, pleading with him to at least give me the privacy I needed to pee and promising he could take as long as he liked up my bum if I could only make a visit to the loo. He'd just laugh, and with that my will would break and I'd let go, pissing in my half-lowered panties to the sound of claps and jeers from both the boys and the tourists, all the while with Billy's cock squelching in my bumhole.

That was what I needed to get over my inhibitions in

reality and I let go, my mouth wide in shame and ecstasy as my pee came, spurting out through the gusset of my panties and all over my busy fingers. I knew I'd have to let it all go before I could come, and I allowed myself to go limp, sobbing in mingled shame and pleasure as the hot, wet piddle splashed out to soak the concrete and quickly spread into a pool around my bottom and legs. Seldom had I felt so deliciously dirty, and I'd have done more, but for a sudden, sharp noise, and as my eyes sprang open I found myself face to face with Billy himself.

I screamed, and he was babbling apologies immediately, but it only took a few seconds for my arousal to push aside the shock. He'd seen everything anyway, and I'd sucked him off, while I'd been on the edge of orgasm as I imagined him buggering me. Better still, he already had his cock out, a little stiff pink rod protruding from his trousers and exactly what I needed up my cunt. I'd turned over before I could stop myself, offering myself in the same rude position I'd been imagining, bent over with my bum stuck out, only instead of having my panties at half-mast they were plastered to my pee-soaked bottom.

They didn't stay that way for long, whipped down to bare myself for entry in maybe the dirtiest, most shameless position a woman can get in, kneeling and bare bottom, her cunt and her anus on full, open show to any man behind her. In my case it was more shameful by far, because my bottom was wet with my own piddle, with more still dripping from my sodden knickers. Billy either liked it or didn't care, muttering comments about the shape of my bottom and the length of my legs as he climbed up behind me, and worse as he put his cock to my hole.

'Oh yeah, Lucy, you are the best, such a gorgeous little

bum, and legs like a fucking giraffe, and such a sweet cunt, and your little pink arsehole ...'

He broke off with a grunt as he stuck his cock up me, but instead of starting to fuck me he did something no man had ever done to me before, and few could, something so shameful, so utterly against everything a woman is supposed to believe about sex and pleasure and what's supposed to be good that it made me gasp. Taking hold of his bulging, grotesquely obese belly, he lifted it up and settled it on my upturned bottom so that he could get right in up my cunt and fuck me properly.

I put my face in my hands, sobbing out my feelings as he began to hump me, tears of raw shame mingling with the puddle I'd made as I was fucked, doggy position in a pool of my own piss, by an overweight little nerd who got off on peeking at my panties. He was being really filthy about it too, calling me a bitch and a slut and telling me what a pretty bumhole I had, over and over as he humped me, until finally I could hold back no more.

'Go on then, you little pervert, go on ... if you like my bottom hole so much, you can put your cock up me, up my bottom, Billy.'

He didn't need telling twice, pulling his erection from my cunt and sliding it higher, into the wet, slippery crease between my cheeks. I felt his knob press to my anus and I screamed once more, in shame and despair and dirty, heartfelt bliss as I felt my hole open to his cock and knew that he was inside me. He adjusted his belly for a second time, lifting it to wedge his cock deeper into my anus and letting it settle onto my cheeks as before, his hot, soft flesh pressed to mine, wobbling as he began to push in and out of my straining ring. I felt his balls touch my sex and I snatched back, to grab them and squash them to my empty cunt hole. He gave a grunt of complaint, but that didn't stop me.

My face had gone in my puddle and I was squirming my bottom against his blubbery gut and rubbing his ball sac on my cunt, the wrinkly flesh bumping over my clitoris, to lift me up to a truly filthy orgasm so strong it left me too weak even to hold my kneeling position. I slumped down. His cock slipped from my bumhole and I was lying sprawled in the still warm puddle underneath me, only to have him jam his erection back up my bottom, give a few last, hard pumps and come in my rectum.

* * *

I could barely take in what I'd done. Billy had caught me at the worst possible moment, when I was at the edge of orgasm after working myself up over a period of hours, but that was really no excuse, certainly not for deliberately peeing in my knickers while I masturbated in the woods and really not even for letting him use me in both holes. He'd been invited to take his pleasure with me and he'd done so, exactly as I'd have expected of any red-blooded male, never mind a smutty-minded little nerd. I'd also taken his virginity, although it seemed odd to think of it that way, as I discovered later while trying every possible tactic I could think of to persuade him not to tell anybody else. He'd given me his promise, without too much difficulty, although it carried the implication that he'd expect to have a lot more fun with me before we left the camp, a prospect that brought me as much consternation as excitement.

The one good thing was that he would now do exactly as he was told, including fetching me some clean clothes so that I didn't have to suffer any further embarrassment on my return to the huts. That proved to be just as well, because while we were playing dirty in the woods all three of the remaining teams had returned and would have had a fair chance of seeing me in nothing but flip-flops, a dirty top and a pair of over-tight, pee-sodden Union Jack panties. As it was I'd put on jeans and a comfy top, in marked contrast to their mud-smeared sweat socks, sports gear and combats, and I must have looked as smug as I felt when I made my announcement.

'First place. Twelve points. How did you do?'

Wendy looked as if she'd been dragged through a hedge backward, then dipped in mud. Her legs were plastered with it, to well up her thighs, while her shorts and top were filthy and her hair was full of bits of moss and leaves. She sounded exhausted as she answered me.

'He took us running, Parker. It was somewhere on Dartmoor and we weren't allowed to stop … I tried, but I fell in a bog and got stuck and he said that was it, all over. I came last.'

Juliette blew her breath out.

'Me too. We had to play chicken fight, in a lake, taking it in turns to carry each other. Can you imagine having Paul on your shoulders? Chad's no lightweight either, or Sam. I never had a chance.'

She sat down on the ground, apparently even more exhausted than Wendy, then looked up to Stacey.

'Well?'

Stacey spread her hands. 'Sorry, girls, I came last too. We had to do basketball, and javelin, and … anyway, it might have been custom-made for men.'

Wendy shook her head.

144

'Parker is a complete bastard, and a misogynist. He's determined to make us look as bad as possible.'

Stacey gave a rueful nod and looked down to where Parker was having an animated conversation with Team C, who had presumably won out overall. I agreed with Wendy, but there didn't seem to be a great deal we could do about it, at least until the course was over. Until then the sensible thing to do seemed to be to keep trying but not to let him get to us, and to have as much fun with the situation as we could. The evening certainly looked promising, as according to the rules I was entitled to punish all three of them, although it didn't seem the right moment to point it out. That would come later.

'You three get in the showers. I'll fetch a bottle from the stash.'

'Make it two.'

I obliged and we drank the first of the bottles as they dried themselves and got dressed. The wine cheered us up, and we were soon comparing scrapes and bruises, of which we had plenty to go around, but it wasn't until we'd eaten and come back to the hut to open the second bottle that I pointed out the consequences of the day's scores.

'So, what do you think I should do with the three of you?'

They knew full well what I was talking about and Wendy had immediately begun to look nervous, fidgeting with her fingers as she sat cross-legged on her bed. Juliette simply raised one lazy finger to indicate what I could do with myself, then flopped back to lie full length with one hand over her face. Only Stacey spoke up.

'Come on, girls, fair's fair, unless you want to wait for tomorrow, Lucy?'

'No, I don't. We might well be in an even worse state.'

Juliette gave a hollow groan and stayed as she was, but Wendy uncurled herself and stood up. She was in nothing but a top and panties, her red hair still wet, which gave her a bedraggled look even I could appreciate as vulnerable. I was sat on the edge of my bed, and gave my lap a gentle pat.

'Come on, over you go then. I'll give you a spanking.'

She looked terrified, but she came forward anyway, to kneel beside me and turn her big pale eyes up in a pleading look.

'Remember, I've never had it before.'

'I'll be gentle, I promise. Now come along, over you go.'

'Don't you want me to take my knickers down first?'

'I'll attend to that. Now come on, you're stalling.'

She knew it was true, pursing her lips and nodding before draping herself clumsily across my legs in such a way that I could barely get at her.

'Not like that, Wendy. Stick your bottom up. If it's going to be spanked you ought to be showing it off properly.'

Her response was a weak sob, but she did as she was told, moving forward on my lap and lifting her bottom to make it a round, tempting ball within the taut white cotton of her panties. I took hold of her top, which had already got rucked up around her tummy, tugging it higher to leave her little round breasts dangling bare beneath her chest and provoking a response.

'Why my boobs? I don't need my boobs bare to be spanked.'

'Yes you do. Your feelings will be stronger if you've got your titties out, and besides, we like to see, don't we girls?'

It was Stacey who answered.

'You can be a right little bitch, can't you, Lucy?'

Then Juliette, who'd sat up to take notice as I got Wendy ready.

'The more they get it the worse they are when it comes to dishing it out.'

I couldn't resist a biting answer.

'It's your turn next, just remember that. In fact, I think you both ought to pop your panties down and sit on your bare bottoms while you wait.'

Stacey was going to do it, but Juliette wasn't impressed.

'Make me.'

I knew I couldn't, and that if I tried I'd be the one who ended up without any panties, and I wasn't going to give up that easily.

'Fair enough, if you won't do as you're told I'll just have to give you extra when your turn comes, with a hairbrush. Now then, speaking of panties, I think we'd better have these down, don't you, Wendy?'

Juliette ignored me, but I was pleased to see that there was a distinctly sulky look on her face as I levered down Wendy's knickers to bare her bottom to the room. She didn't say anything, but her breathing was deep and a little ragged. I knew just how emotional the experience would be for her, if my own first spanking was anything to go by, which made it all the more exciting as I adjusted her panties to make sure her pussy showed from behind and settled my hand across her pale, soft cheeks.

'Right, Miss E, spankies time.'

I began to smack, not hard, but then it doesn't have to be hard. She was over my knee, with her panties pulled down to bare her bottom while it was smacked, and that was enough. I'd only given her a dozen or so before her little squeaks and gasps had turned to moans and she'd begun to stick her bottom up to show off the tiny pink dimple of her anus as well as her now distinctly puffy cunt. Juliette laughed.

'I may be going to get it, but I hope I'll show a bit more dignity than that! You're a little slut, Wendy. What are you?'

Wendy's voice came as a muffled sob.

'I'm a slut. Spank me harder, Lucy, please.'

This time both Stacey and Juliette laughed as I did my best to oblige her, slapping upward to make Wendy's cheeks bounce and spread. She'd braced her feet apart, to stretch her lowered panties taut between her knees, showing everything as her bottom jiggled to the smacks. I'd been put in the same position many a time, and I knew how it felt, but she hadn't even had to be told, exhibiting herself in open, abandoned pleasure. My arm went around her waist and my smacks grew harder still, to make her gasp and kick in her knickers, but she didn't object.

'Juliette's right, Wendy, you are a slut. Just look at you, getting off on having your bare bottom smacked. You ought to be ashamed of yourself.'

I was spanking as hard as I could and she'd begun to wriggle in my grip and kick her feet up and down, either indifferent to the display she was making of herself or unable to stop it anyway. She was getting to me as well, making me want to be put in the same sorry condition, for all that I was enjoying punishing her and had no intention of letting the others off. Both were watching in fascination, and I could just imagine their feelings when they far preferred to dish it out but were going to have to take the same.

With that thought I decided that Wendy had had enough. I was going to do Stacey, then Juliette. The idea still seemed an outrage, but with the wine inside me and the thrill of spanking Wendy I was sure I could go through with it, while there was also the prospect of revenge, on Stacey, but far more so on Juliette. I stopped spanking and let go of Wendy's waist, to let her slide from my lap onto the floor, where she lay propped up on one arm, the other reached back to rub at her well-smacked bottom, her mouth wide and her eyes full of shock as she looked up through a ragged curtain of hair. I pointed to the corner of the hut.

'There we are, now you've been spanked, and I want you to think about what that means while I deal with the others. Go and stand in the corner, with your hands on your head and your back to the room, still with your knickers down so we can all see your red bottom, and your top up too.'

Wendy nodded, but Juliette spoke.

'That's a bit mean, isn't it, Lucy, making her do corner time after her first ever spanking? She wasn't even naughty, anyway, so what's she supposed to feel sorry about?'

'I don't want her to feel sorry. I want her to think about her spanking, and how once it's been done there's no going back. Just like you said to me after my first time, Juliette, once a spanked girl, always a spanked girl.'

Wendy had gone into the corner without protest, standing in exactly the position I'd ordered with her knickers now around her ankles. It was Stacey who reacted to what I'd said, now looking doubtful and biting her lip even as she stood up to take her turn.

'Um … oh well, a bet's a bet, I suppose, and I admit I'll feel better about doing it to you once I've had it myself.'

'That's the spirit. Come on, over you go.'

She stepped towards me, hugging her robe around her body, to get down into much the same vulnerable position I'd spanked Wendy in, with her bottom well lifted, but with her feet and hands braced on the floor. I didn't feel at all sure of myself, as if I was the one losing something, if not my dignity. That didn't stop me taking hold of the hem of her robe, or lifting it slowly to unveil her bottom, with her full cheeks straining out a tiny pair of pale-blue panties. I'd kissed her bottom so many times, and that was what I felt I should be doing, in abject apology for even daring to think about spanking her. It had to be done though, if only to wipe away the small, smug smile growing on Juliette's face, as if she was reading my thoughts. As I spoke to Stacey I was trying to sound bold and commanding, for all that my true feelings were the exact opposite.

'Let's pop you out of your panties then, darling. There we go, all bare and beautiful.'

I'd taken her knickers down, inverting them around her thighs to leave her on open show to Juliette, bare, with her full cheeks lifted and a little open to hint at the dark spot of her anus as I laid my palm across her flesh. She stayed exactly still, not even clenching her cheeks as I lifted my hand, nor when I brought it down in a firm, open slap. Juliette gave a little tut, in disapproval, or perhaps amusement, but certainly with more than a hint of contempt. I ignored her, refusing to rise to the bait as I continued to spank Stacey. She took it stoically, never moving a muscle or letting out so much as a sigh even as her cheeks began to go red, making my sense of my own inappropriate behaviour ever stronger, until finally I had to stop.

'OK, you're done. You can get up now.'

She rose, to kiss me as she pulled up her panties, then went back to her bed. I didn't have the courage to send her into the corner, and it wouldn't have felt right anyway. Nevertheless, I'd spanked her, and I was determined to spank Juliette too, especially as she was looking at me with a knowing grin.

'You don't really want to do this, do you?'

'Shut up and get over my knee, Girl A.'

I was trying hard to sound strong and authoritative, but the truth was that I couldn't even bring myself to use her real name, as if to say 'get over my knee, Juliette Fisher' was akin to blasphemy. She knew, and she laughed, even as she rose to stretch her tall, lithe body, making her breasts lift and showing off the smooth, strong muscles of her arms and torso. I could barely look her in the eyes as she started towards me, her gaze as mocking as her tone.

'Very well, Lucinda, if you insist, but wouldn't you rather be over my knee instead, with that sweet little bottom of yours pushed up high? After all, you deserve a spanking, don't you?'

'Yes, I do, but you're going to get yours first, Girl … Juliette, so come over my knee, right now! I am going to spank you, Juliette Fisher.'

It had taken all my nerve just to say it, but there was still laughter in her eyes as she reached me.

'Quite the little firebrand nowadays, aren't you, Lucy? Come on then, if you're so determined, spank me.'

She had laid herself across my lap, her bottom pushed well up, but with her body at a diagonal, so that instead of having her head dangling down by my feet she could put an elbow on the bed to support it, as if she found the whole process pleasantly amusing and nothing to be in the least bit concerned about. Like Wendy, she was in just a top and panties, and like Wendy her top had ridden up as she got into position, showing off her knickers to the room. She was looking at me as she carried on.

'Go on then, Lucy, pull down my panties and give me a good, long spanking, as hard as you can. And when you're done I'm going to take you across my knee in turn, stripped bare, and I am going to spank you until you howl, you sassy little brat!'

Stacey made to speak, but I lifted my hand to stop her. I took hold of the waistband of Juliette's panties, paused to savour the moment I bared her bottom, then peeled them down as I answered her.

'Maybe, but whatever you do to me it's not going to alter the fact that you've been spanked by me. Once a spanked girl, always a spanked girl, Juliette.'

'You bitch! Look, Lucy ...'

The tone of her voice had changed completely, but whatever she was about to say was lost as the handle to the hut door twisted. It was locked, but that didn't stop all four of us from going into an instant panic as we tried to make ourselves decent and hide the evidence of our misbehaviour at the same time. Whoever was outside tried the handle again, then rapped loudly on the door, and I'd just managed to stick the empty wine bottle down the side of my bed when Parker's voice sounded from outside.

'Open this door. Alcohol inspection!'

Chapter Seven

The four of us stood in a ragged line in front of Parker's desk, very like a gang of naughty schoolgirls brought up before the headmaster, except in one crucial respect. Parker had no real authority over any of us. Stacey at least was stood more or less to attention, although her arms were folded across her chest, while Wendy looked sulky and defiant. Juliette was looking out of the window. Our attitude clearly annoyed him, and as he told us off I'd been wondering if, given the opportunity, he'd have liked to line us up with our bottoms bare for six-of-the-best apiece. He continued the harangue he'd started as soon as we walked into his office.

'... a serious offence, in direct contradiction of the statement of conduct you signed when I agreed to accept you on this course. Despite my clear instructions to the contrary you brought alcohol into the camp ...'

Juliette interrupted.

'No. We brought a bottle of wine into the camp. Wine contains alcohol, but it is not alcohol. Please at least try and get your facts right.'

She sounded serious, but I knew she was simply annoying him on purpose. It worked too, his face turning a couple of

153

shades darker than it had already been before he went on.

'Alcohol, which is forbidden, and it is forbidden for the very good reason that it has a deleterious effect on concentration and performance ...'

I couldn't help but point something out.

'You drink. You were having a pint of beer that night at The Plough.'

It took him only a moment to rally himself.

'That is irrelevant. Besides, what is more important is that you deliberately disobeyed the camp rules, my rules. It's hardly the first time either, especially you two, Girls O and E, while you, Girl A, have a serious attitude problem.'

Juliette spoke up again.

'Blah, blah, blah. We know what you think of us, Mr Parker, and I for one couldn't give a damn. So either kick us out, and we can deal with the rest of this through our company solicitors, or let's get on with it, shall we?'

For a moment I thought he was going to explode, but he managed to get himself under control and carried on, in a particularly nasty voice.

'No, Girl A, I am not going to kick you out, but this incident is going on your report, along with every other detail of your disruptive behaviour.'

Juliette merely shrugged, but I was conscious of a sinking feeling and couldn't help imagining Mr Scott's reaction when he read what Parker had to say. I was going to have a lot of explaining to do, although I wasn't prepared to accept that we'd done anything wrong. Stacey and Wendy didn't look particularly happy either, but there was nothing to be done. Parker continued, now rather calmer.

'It would be a shame to kick you out anyway, as that would deprive me of the chance to really bring home to you how little potential you have in comparison to the serious candidates on this course. On the other hand, you can leave at any time you like, on the full and clear understanding that it will be an admission of failure. With that in mind, I've made a couple of minor changes to the usual course. Today should be an exercise in trust and confidence, but I've decided on something else, something a little more physical.'

He was now smiling, with all the friendliness and sincerity of a hungry crocodile. Not that it seemed to bother Juliette.

'What are you going to do, make us wrestle nude in a vat of custard?'

His smile grew yet more reptilian as he leant back in his chair.

'No, nothing like that, just a little racing game, and do bear in mind that you can quit whenever you like. Right, sports kit, Assembly, five minutes!'

He'd barked out the last few words, no doubt expecting, or at least hoping, that we'd run to get ready. Stacey almost did, from sheer force of habit, but stopped herself as Juliette slowly and deliberately lifted a hand to her mouth to stifle a pretend yawn. It had been the same the night before, when I'd tried to make them take their knickers down in advance of their spankings, the second time in twenty-four hours Stacey had followed Juliette's lead. I was musing on the implications as we left Parker's office, as while we were obviously supposed to consider ourselves well and truly told off, I found it impossible to take him seriously. Wendy evidently felt the same, only more so, speaking as soon as we were safely outside.

'So it's some sort of race, but how about our own game?'

I wasn't at all sure it was a good idea.

'Are we still going to play, even with Parker after us?'

Juliette answered me.

'Why not? He's not going to kick us out, he said so himself, and besides, I for one do not intend to let that oily little bastard spoil our fun.'

Stacey added her opinion.

'I agree, but I don't want to get caught, so let's make the punishment something other than spanking. It's just too noisy, and if Parker had turned up just a few seconds later last night he'd have heard the smacks when Lucy was dealing with Juliette.'

Wendy sounded disappointed as she responded.

'What then? It has to be … you know, embarrassing but nice. Spanking's perfect, and … the truth is, I want more. I don't think my boyfriend would do it.'

I couldn't help but agree.

'It is perfect, and we could always nip into the woods, or use one of the empty huts nearer the gates.'

Stacey objected.

'Parker's going to be on the lookout and might well follow us. We're better off behind closed doors, but Wendy's right, it has to be the right sort of punishment. How about being tied up?'

Wendy gave an urgent nod.

'Yes, so the others can do exactly as they please with you, and …'

She broke off, blushing for her own enthusiasm as both Stacey and Juliette turned to her in surprise. I understood exactly how she felt, having often imagined myself trussed helpless for the amusement of others, but there was an obvious problem, in that I knew exactly who was going to end up breaking into the Stores to pinch the rope we needed: me.

'I don't mind being tied up, as long as it's with bathrobe

cords and things, but I am not breaking into the Stores for rope, not with Parker prowling about.'

Juliette didn't even bother to argue.

'We'll see. Anyway, for now, I suppose we'd better get changed for Assembly.'

By the time we got into the hangar not only was everybody else there but Parker was halfway through his explanation of the day's exercise. He broke off briefly to make a remark about women always taking a long time to get ready but didn't bother to start from the beginning again, so that we only heard how the points were to be awarded.

'... thirty-six for the winners, then twenty-four and twelve, zero for the losers. Mr Straw can, at his discretion, award a bonus of twelve points if he feels you have shown proper initiative. The team leaders must then distribute the team's points among individuals as they deem appropriate, according to performance. Nominate your victims.'

I had no idea what he was talking about, and turned to Paul, who was next to me in line.

'What are we doing? What does he mean, "victims"?'

'It's some sort of rescue game, to test initiative and prior-itisation, or some bollocks like that anyway. Just pick the lightest person in your team.'

'Thanks. That's got to be Wendy then?'

I'd turned to the girls as I spoke and they were nodding agreement as Sergeant Reynolds approached. Juliette announced our choice.

'Wendy Ackland ... Girl E, but what are we doing? I thought it was a race?'

'It is a race. OK, E, come with me.'

'Where are we going?'

'North end airstrip.'

157

Parker had overheard and continued.

'Yup, the north end of the airstrip, on the far side of the ditch where you built your so-called bridge. OK, the rest of you, take two poles per team from Mr Straw and assemble at the south end of the airstrip. Go, go, go, let's see those heels twinkle!'

Most of us ran, but I'd got to the point at which every tiny defiance of Parker's orders became a little victory and hung back with the slowcoaches, including Paul and Billy, who immediately opened a conversation.

'So you girls got busted for booze? So did we.'

'I didn't know, sorry. What happened?'

'We ordered a few cases from this place in Exeter, only Chad saw the delivery van and ratted us out. What about you?'

'He did an inspection last night, but all he got was a couple of empty bottles.'

'The inspection was our fault, sorry. So you've got some more?'

'Plenty, but how do you mean you ordered it? Not by phone?'

Paul raised his eyebrows.

'You think I don't have access to the net? You think Paul Yates does not have access to the net?'

'Sorry, I wasn't thinking. So you ordered it online?'

Billy explained.

'He's got a smartphone made up like an old plastic Dalek. So what then, do you girls want to party?'

I knew exactly what sort of party he meant and gave an honest answer.

'Maybe. I'll have to talk to the others.'

He carried on, full of enthusiasm.

'We can get pizza, Chinese, anything you fancy, and lots of booze, we just need to watch where we pick it up, and that old hut where you gave us our BJs ought to be safe.'

I felt my cheeks flare with heat, just for the utterly casual way he'd spoken of what we'd done, as if the almost painful shame of being put on my knees to suck him off was nothing out of the ordinary. He didn't seem to notice, but I made my excuses anyway.

'I'd better catch up with the others. See you later.'

Stacey and Juliette were already at the southern end of the old runway, where broken asphalt gave way to long, damp grass. Mr Straw was nearby, with a clipboard, while each team now had two of the long wooden poles we'd used to build our bridges. I didn't mention what the boys had said for fear of being overheard, while Mr Straw had begun to go over the exercise, tapping his clipboard with a pencil as he explained.

'As you know, this one's called Stretcher Bearers and it's not on the original programme because Mr Parker has decided to customise the regime to your special needs. The task is simple, but it takes initiative and is designed to test your sense of priority. At the far end of the runway, beyond the ditch, you will find the remaining member of your team. You are to treat her as the victim of an accident, apply bandages as necessary and bring him, or her, back here on a stretcher. The fastest team wins, but the victim must remain on the stretcher for the full length of the runway, even if you stop to rest. There is a bonus for applying the bandages correctly.'

Sam Haynes raised his hand.

'Where do we get the bandages?'

'Use your initiative. Now go!'

We ran, my mind already boiling with resentment against

Parker, because it was quite obvious that he'd chosen the exercise specifically in order to show us up. Sure enough, as we reached the slope at the far end of the airstrip we found the four victims on the other side of the ditch, including Wendy. Team C had already reached Daniel, and Chad was peeling his top off under the approving gaze of both Parker and Sergeant Reynolds. I didn't stop, but ran down the slope to get as much momentum as I could before jumping the ditch, which was now about a third full of glutinous red mud. Wendy had a large red X marked on her knee, obviously intended to be her injury. Stacey and Juliette quickly joined us with the poles and I spoke as soon as I could catch my breath.

'He's done this to humiliate us, because we're going to have to take our tops off.'

Juliette shook her head.

'No. He's done this to humiliate us, because he thinks we'll be too precious to take our tops off. Well fuck that!'

She was already struggling out of her top, as was Stacey, for all that she looked furious. I hesitated, wishing I'd put a bra on under my top, as they both had, and sure that two tops would be enough to go between the poles to make our stretcher. Juliette wasn't having it.

'Get it off, Lucy. We need to bandage her knee!'

'I've got no bra on! Use Wendy's instead.'

'I haven't got a bra on either!'

'Just do it, Lucy!'

'But ...'

I didn't finish, my fingers already tugging my top free of my shorts despite the huge lump in my throat and the resentment and shame raging in my head. Juliette was right though, because what Parker wanted more than anything was to show us up as weak, so my top came up and off, leaving my breasts bare to the cool morning air and my face red with shame and rage. I tried to hide my feelings, but I was biting my lip as I made a bandage of my top, painfully aware of my bare boobs and the attention of the men as they realised I wasn't merely in a bra but fully topless.

We were at least too far away from them for me to hear what was said, but I could see them pointing and grinning, fuelling my blushes as I tied the makeshift bandage off. Stacey and Juliette had the stretcher ready, with their own tops stretched taut between the poles, and we quickly rolled Wendy into place. Team C were already on the move, but as they got to the edge of the ditch Chad's foot slipped, tipping Daniel off the stretcher and leaving both of them foundering in the mud. I was laughing as Stacey and Juliette took the weight of the stretcher, delighted to see one of my tormentors get a dose of his own medicine, only for Juliette to bark out a brusque order.

'Get in the ditch, Lucy. Take the end and support it until Stacey's across.'

'But Juliette ...'

'Do it!'

I'd been making ready to jump, but at her command I found myself scrambling down to the ditch and plunging in, up to my knees in cold, slimy muck.

'Stop making stupid faces and take the fucking stretcher!'

'It's cold!'

'Don't be such a little princess.'

I'd taken the stretcher anyway, allowing them to leap across without getting muddy and slowing themselves down. It took all my strength to support Wendy across, but I managed it and began to scramble out as they lifted her to start up the

161

slope. As I paused to catch my breath I glanced at our rivals. Team B were level with us and Team C were just getting across. Team D still hadn't got their victim onto the stretcher and seemed to be arguing about something, expect for Billy, who was surreptitiously eyeing my chest, always the pervert despite having had me up my bottom just the day before.

He noticed my attention and gave an embarrassed grin, which I ignored as I pulled one leg free of the mud, bracing myself to climb out, only for my foot to slip back, so suddenly I had no chance at all of catching myself. I went over backward, my legs in the air as I hit the surface, bum first, my squeal of shock abruptly cut off as my head went under the surface. For one terrifying moment I couldn't see or breathe, or get any purchase on anything at all, before my hands found the bottom and I pushed myself up, to rise dripping and filthy from the mud, my hair sodden and foul, my body plastered with muck, slippery red goo dripping from my shorts.

It was a long moment before I even dared open my eyes, but when I did I realised I hadn't gone right under, not quite. The mud and water had gone in my face and over my tummy, but it hadn't completely covered my chest, which left my boobs sticking out like a pair of small pink blancmanges. Somebody laughed, and when I thought of how I must look I could hardly blame them, but that did nothing to reduce my appalling embarrassment. I had to get away, and fast, splashing across to haul myself free on my hands and knees, with cold, sticky goo squashing up into my fanny and between the cheeks of my bottom as I climbed out onto the grass.

Most of the people who could see me were now laughing, including Parker, driving my humiliation to new heights as I threw myself up the slope and after the now distant figures of Stacey and Juliette. I was on the edge of tears, filthy, half naked and freezing, mud squashing in my cunt, my boobs bouncing wildly as I ran, and calling Parker every filthy name I could think of. When I caught up with Stacey and Juliette I passed them without even slowing down, although by then I was only a couple of hundred yards from the end. Mr Straw was there, trying to pretend he wasn't staring at my bouncing pink boobs and failing badly, but I ignored him, crossing the line and turning for the showers, only to find myself forced to make a full show of my body to the compliments of Teams B and C as I ran past.

I'd sprinted the whole way and was forced to slow down, so I put my hands over my chest in a vain effort to preserve a last tiny shred of modesty, only to realise it made me look even more comic than when I was running with them bare. Even the supposed victims sat up on their stretchers to have a good stare, and while Alastair at least had the decency to congratulate me on having the guts to complete the exercise, he was enjoying the view as much as the rest of them. As I reached the first of the buildings I turned, to see that we'd managed to come in second, quite possibly because I'd provided a distraction, which gave me at least a little bit of satisfaction as I limped on towards the shower block.

My entire body ached, the mud in my hair was starting to dry and I'd got some up my cunt, while my feet were squelching in my filthy shoes with every step. I got straight into the shower, without bothering to undress, turned the water on full and hot, then slumped down onto the tiles. As I began to strip I was seriously considering going to see Parker as soon as I was dressed and giving him a piece of my mind that would make the dressing down he'd given us in the morning seem feeble. Unfortunately I knew what he'd say, that if I was worried about going topless I should have worn a bra, that I could have refused in any case and simply forfeited any points for the exercise, and that I'd managed to fall in the mud entirely of my own accord. I'd then be left with a choice of swallowing my pride or going to court, which meant dragging the whole affair out in public, while it was all too easy to imagine the judge taking his side.

There was another problem too, entirely of my own making, and very private. With my clothes off I was left sat nude in the bottom of the shower, with no choice but to spread my thighs and slip a finger in up my cunt to make sure I was clean. As I did it I was trying hard to keep my thoughts away from sex, but it wasn't easy. Compared with my usual fantasies of being spanked, made to suck men's cocks or simply fucked, what had happened was trivial. It wasn't even as if I'd really had no choice in the matter, but that was beside the point. I'd been made to go topless in public, in front of fourteen men, and for all that I despised Parker it was impossible to ignore that one of my favourite fantasies had become reality.

I wanted to masturbate, but I was determined not to do it, even though he would never know what he'd done to me. There was irony in the situation too, because he'd set out to humiliate me, and he'd succeeded, but my reaction was the exact opposite to the one he'd have been hoping to provoke. Despite that, I felt that giving in to my feelings would be giving in to him, and as I continued my shower I was determined not to allow my fingers to sneak back between my thighs where they were so badly needed. I knew the girls would be along reasonably soon too, and did not want to be caught masturbating over what should have been a purely negative experience.

When I was finally clean I put my wet shorts back on,

wrapped one of the miserable little towels around my chest and scampered back to our hut. I was just in time, with the others already coming towards us across the grass, and I was still trying to get properly dry when Wendy came in.

'Are you alright?'

'Just about, thanks. So we came second?'

She'd been about to open her arms to offer me a hug, but I knew that once in her arms I'd either dissolve in tears or want sex, possibly both, so I stood up to fetch some fresh clothes as she replied to my question.

'Yes, but it was pretty close, except for Team D, who didn't even finish.'

'Why was that? I saw they were arguing about something.'

'You saw that Paul had a Motorhead top on? Apparently he got it at some particular concert. Graham tried to make him use it for the stretcher and he refused to take it off.'

'Why was he wearing it in the first place, if it was so special?'

'Oh you know Paul, and apparently he doesn't own any sports kit.'

'That I can believe. Did we get our bonus?'

'Yes, and Team B didn't, because their bandage fell off, so we're level top for today's exercise, but they're top overall.'

'That's something. So much for Parker's precious Team C.'

'He's got them in his office now, which is blatant favouritism.'

'Yes, I suppose it is. He doesn't call Team D in, not for losing anyway. Speaking of which, the reason Parker came round looking for drink is that Paul and his friends got caught trying to smuggle in some of their own, or rather they tried to have it delivered. They want to know if we'd like to have a party.'

She seemed a little doubtful.

'I suppose we could, if we can find somewhere safe, and not all of Team D.'

'No, just Paul and Billy, I expect, but perhaps we could invite some of the other men?'

'Maybe, or John?'

'John would be good, and there's another guy I met on our first night down in Devon. I don't actually know his name, but he's OK.'

Juliette and Stacey came in and we explained the situation to them. They both responded with cautious enthusiasm, concerned for me, but otherwise in a good mood, which helped to pick me up. When we went down to Mess for lunch everybody else was already there, and as I walked in most of them began to cheer and clap, not mocking me, but with genuine enthusiasm, and as I saw the sour expression on Parker's face I realised that for all my embarrassment, I was the one who'd won.

* * *

The afternoon schedule involved a series of indoor exercises and a run on the assault course, which Parker manipulated to allow Team C to regain their lead. We did reasonably well in the circumstances, and I'd added to my personal score. Mr Straw had been keeping tally and approached the four of us as we watched Team D on the assault course, speaking to Juliette.

'Right, A, I still need the individual scores from this morning's exercise. You scored thirty-six in all, so how do you want to apportion them?'

Juliette obviously hadn't thought about it and took a moment to consider before replying.

'Evenly, I suppose. Nine each.'

Both Stacey and Wendy nodded, but I didn't think it was fair.

'After what happened to me? I think we should get points according to the effort we each put in.'

Both Stacey and Juliette rounded on me, evidently unimpressed, but Wendy spoke up.

'That's fair. After all, I didn't really do anything at all. Lucy can have three of my points.'

Mr Straw looked to Juliette, who hesitated once more, then shrugged.

'Fine, if that's your choice, Wendy? In that case, twelve to Lucy, nine to me and Stacey, six to Wendy.'

'Girl O twelve, A and G nine, E six. Remember to use your designated letters.'

He said it with a little grin, whereas I knew Parker would have given us a little lecture, then left. A splash and a curse signalled that Billy had fallen off the rope swing, as usual, and we went back to watching the assault course. I'd got used to it, and was only a little wet and muddy, but started for the showers anyway, not bothering to wait for Parker's debriefing. He ignored me, although I was sure the incident would find its way onto my report, along with what was already an extensive list of misdemeanours and failures, but I'd decided that my only defence lay in persuading Mr Scott that I'd been deliberately picked on. Not only was it true, but the more petty criticisms Parker put on my report, the easier it would be for me to demonstrate that he was being unreasonable.

Mr Straw was ahead of me, carrying the bits and pieces of equipment we'd used during our exercises, and as I reached the level of the big Assembly hangar I saw him disappear into the Stores. He emerged a moment later and made for the office, leaving the Stores door wide open. I knew he'd be putting down the day's scores on the main record sheets, which was sure to take at least a few minutes, certainly long enough for me to pinch a puff stick and a couple of hanks of rope, maybe even some spare towels. Everybody else was still at the far end of the assault course, well out of the way, and I was running immediately.

Time seemed to slow down as I dashed for the hut, but it was the work of an instant to snatch up what I wanted. Only when I had everything did I realise that our personal possessions were there too, each little pile carefully labelled with our letter. It seemed too risky to take our mobiles, let alone our bags, but I decided to risk one debit card, which they were hardly likely to notice. Now well pleased with myself, I fled, keeping to the shelter of the shower block before making a final sprint for our hut. I was grinning triumphantly as I hid the card, the three lengths of hemp and the long puff stick in my bed, and having trouble keeping a straight face as I headed back for the showers.

Mr Straw saw me, just as he came away from locking up the Stores, but he plainly didn't suspect a thing. The others joined me in the showers, but I didn't admit to my little theft, nor over dinner. Only when all four of us were seated on our beds with the hut door securely locked did I exhibit my ill-gotten gains.

'Look what I've got, one of my debit cards, an extra towel each, one cane and three long pieces of rope, which means that somebody is in big trouble.'

I was looking right at Juliette, for all that it took an effort to meet her gaze, but she simply laughed.

'Why me? I think you ought to be the one in trouble, you

little thief! And why didn't you get our cards too?'

I wasn't having the tables turned on me so easily.

'Uh, uh, for a start I owe you a spanking and a caning, and I won today, which gives me the right to have you tied up while you're punished.'

'It does not! You only won because Wendy gave you three points, and it's hardly fair to punish her for that, let alone me!'

I was still determined, but I was struggling not to sound sulky as I replied.

'Not just this morning, this afternoon too. Come on, stop trying to wriggle out of it, Juliette. At the very least I owe you a spanking and twelve of the cane!'

'But you didn't get the most points this afternoon, Wendy did, and I was equal.'

'I'm still ahead for the day, and I still owe you a spanking and the cane. Come on, Juliette, play fair, or I'll ... I'll invite some of the boys to watch.'

'You will not! I admit you owe me a punishment, but not in front of any men!'

'Why not? You made me suck Paul and William off, and they both saw I'd been spanked. I'd like to do you in front of them.'

Stacey had been listening without comment, but finally decided to speak up.

'That's not really fair, Lucy. You like cock.'

'It was one of the most humiliating experiences of my entire life!'

'You like humiliation too.'

I made to answer, but I knew it was true, and that I was beginning to sound like a spoilt brat. Juliette carried on.

'OK then, you can spank and cane me, but no men, and

169

the right to revenge, immediately afterwards, if that's alright with you, Stacey?'

I wasn't having it.

'It's not alright with me! You take your punishment, Juliette Fisher, and then you get down on your knees and you lick ... you lick my ...'

I came to a faltering stop. She was looking at me, her expression cool and haughty, as if what I was saying was no more than insolence. Wendy tried to come to my rescue.

'I'd like to play, but I don't want anybody to feel upset. Why don't we draw straws?'

Stacey nodded.

'That's fair.'

'No it isn't! I still owe Juliette ...'

She cut me off.

'I'm up for that, and if Princess Lucinda won't play, then she can sit and sulk while she watches.'

'I am not sulking!'

She ignored me and went to the door and outside, quickly returning with four pieces of grass in her clenched first. I noticed she was very careful to keep her grip as she locked the door again, and decided I knew what she was up to.

'OK, I'll play, but Juliette has to choose last as she's holding the straws.'

'Don't you trust me, Lucy?'

'No, I do not. I've known you too long.'

'Charming, I'm sure. Fine, I'll go last. You can even go first.'

She held out her fist, with the ends of the four pieces of grass sticking up. I was sure she'd be trying to trick me, but it was hard to judge whether she'd have put the short one nearest to me in the hope that I'd make the simplest choice, or furthest away in order to try and catch me out. Two were in the middle and I pulled one out at random, to find myself holding what could only be the shortest of the four. Sure enough, she was grinning as she opened her hand to display the remaining pieces of grass, all twice as long.

'Lucy loses!'

I put my hands up, starting to panic as Stacey and Wendy stood up.

'No, stop, hang on, I did win, and ... look, let's stick to the rules?'

Stacey shook her head.

'You lost, Lucy, fair and square.'

'Yes, but we agreed ...'

They were standing around my bed and I began to move backward, my panic growing as I struggled to find some reason they'd accept for letting me off.

'Look, this isn't fair at all! We agreed on the rules, and ...'

Juliette shook her head.

'Never mind the rules. Let's get her, girls!'

'No! That's not fair! I won! It's my turn ...'

My words broke to a squeak as they grabbed me, pushing me back on the bed and quickly spreading me out, one limb to each corner. Stacey was holding one of my legs but had also got hold of one of the hanks of rope and I realised they were going to tie me up.

'Hey, no! Stop, you can't do this, it's not fair! Stacey!'

'Shut up. Juliette, hold her arms.'

'Let's strip her naked.'

'Fair enough. Wendy, get her jeans and panties off or we won't be able to spread her out properly when she's bare.'

They set on me, Juliette and Stacey holding me down while Wendy tried to get me out of my clothes. I did my best to fight, wriggling in their grip and telling them over and over again that it wasn't fair and that if anybody was going to be punished it should be Juliette. It did no good, partly because there were three of them, two much stronger, but also because I lacked the will to succeed, or even struggle with any real determination. I lost anyway, my jeans unfastened and stripped off, my shoes and socks tugged away, my panties pulled down and off, my top and bra wrenched up and over my head to leave me spread out stark naked on the bed. Juliette seemed to have taken charge and gave the next order.

'Turn her over, girls, and put a pillow under her tummy, then we'll tie her up.'

I began to wriggle again, but they quickly got me in position face down and bottom up with a pillow under my hips to make sure I was showing everything from behind. Stacey had my hands, but there was no real fight left in me and I didn't even bother to close my legs as they lashed my wrists to the bedstead. My ankles followed and I was completely helpless, barely even able to kick in my bonds, with my bottom well lifted and a little open and my pussy on full show. Juliette stood back, triumphant, my discarded panties dangling from one finger.

'What were we saying this morning about noisy spankings?

I had to protest.

'Who said anything about spanking me!?'

She just laughed.

'Of course we're going to spank you, silly, but we don't want nasty Mr Parker to hear you getting it, do we? That's why your panties are going in your mouth, again. Open wide.'

'No, Juliette, please …'

'Pinch the little brat's nose for me, Stacey.'

I knew it was hopeless, but that didn't stop me squirming in my bonds and trying to turn my head away as they grappled with me, and the moment Stacey managed to get a grip on my head and pinch my nose between her fingers my mouth came wide. Juliette crammed my panties in, leaving just a scrap of material hanging out before she tied them off with more of the rope, then stood back once more.

'What a sight! Well Princess Lucinda, how do you feel now?'

I gave her what I hoped was an angry glare, but she merely laughed and extended a hand to stroke my bare bottom, at which Wendy spoke up.

'She is right about the noise though. What if Parker hears the smacks?'

'He didn't hear anything before, and besides, what's wrong with giving a brat a well-deserved spanking? Maybe we should invite him in to watch?'

I shook my head, urgently, for all that I knew she was only joking. Again she laughed, still stroking my bottom as she went on.

'Not Parker, no. He doesn't deserve the treat, but I can't help remembering how she said she'd like to do me in front of Paul and Billy.'

Again I shook my head, if less forcefully, and she continued.

'I'm sure they'd love to watch, a pair of perverts like them, and they already know you get it, so it's not as if you've anything to hide.'

Stacey finally broke in.

'Stop tormenting her, Juliette. We can't go and get them anyway, not without letting the other two find out something's going on, and it's hardly fair to let them watch too.'

'Oh, I don't know. I'd happily spank her in front of the

whole camp, if I thought we could get away with it, and it would be panties down. Wouldn't that be nice, Lucy, a bare-bottom spanking in front of all the boys?'

For the third time I shook my head in denial, but I didn't mean it, already imagining my shame as she held me firmly in place across her knee to peel down my knickers in front of everybody. Only the thought of Parker seeing made me rebel, but Juliette's hand had moved between my legs to stroke my cunt. I tried to fight the sensation, but couldn't, and was soon sticking my bottom up for more, at which she applied a gentle smack to my cheeks.

'Slut. You'd love that, wouldn't you? Oh, I know you'd put up a fight, and I'm sure you'd protest like anything, but it would all be fake, wouldn't it, Lucy? Oh, yes it would. What do you think, Stacey? Would she enjoy a nice public spanking?'

She was still stroking my sex, one long finger making little, slow circles on my clitoris, and I'd begun to whimper into my panties and push my bottom higher still, no longer even attempting to hold back my emotions. Stacey knew me well enough to recognise the signs, and I'd explained my fantasies to her often enough, so she knew how to respond to Juliette's question.

'I'm sure she would, but that's not really the point, is it? Of all the people I've ever met there's not one who needs regular spanking as badly as Lucy does. I think we should do it anyway, whether she likes it or not, and why stop at getting her bottom bare? I say we should march her out into the middle of the airfield, invite everybody to come and watch, then strip her nude. We could make her parade herself like that, before taking turns to spank her, and maybe even letting some of the boys have a go?'

As she spoke she began to spank me herself, applying firm, regular swats to my bare bottom as Juliette masturbated me. It wasn't hard, and barely made a sound, but it was enough for me to know that I was being spanked, especially alongside the pictures she was putting into my head. I could see it so easily, with all the men gathered around, laughing and joking amongst themselves as I was frogmarched out onto the field, stripped, and made to do exercises in the nude, including star jumps to make my boobs bounce and wobble, to the men's delight, and touching my toes to show off my anus and the rear view of my cunt, which would get every single one of them stiff. Juliette was now rubbing hard and I was beginning to wriggle my bottom against her hand as she went on.

'In fact, it would only be fair if we let them all spank you. Not Parker, of course. We'd have him and Chad tied up, head to toe with their cocks out so they could suck each other off, just to be kind, but well out of the way.'

Wendy had been watching in silent awe, but chimed in at last.

'Yes. In one of the mud pits on the assault course. I bet they'd still suck. We'd make Lucy do it as well, to any of the men who'd got turned on by watching her being spanked.'

Juliette laughed.

'Good idea! After all, it's not their fault she's got such a wriggly little bottom, is it, or that she's had to be spanked? It's only fair they get a bit of fun out of her.'

I was sure I was going to come as I pictured the scene, me kneeling nude, my red bottom sticking out behind, tears of humiliation rolling down my face as the men lined up to have their cocks sucked. My thighs started to go tight and I gave my bottom an encouraging wriggle, only for Juliette to stop.

'Oh no you don't, my girl, not yet! First, I intend to give you the cane, six-of-the-best, Lucy darling, plumb across those sweet little cheeks. After that, I think I'll roll you over so I can sit on your face. Then you can come, while you lick my bottom.'

I tried to call her a bitch, but could only manage a muffled sob, which just made her laugh. Stacey was still spanking me, and I was hoping she'd decide to assert herself as my girlfriend and frig me off in defiance of Juliette's cruel suggestion for my fate. She chose to assert herself, but not in the way I'd imagined.

'If anybody's going to sit on her face it's me, at least first, but I agree that she ought to be caned. That's not so noisy, is it?'

'No, not like spanking, and you get much more out of your victim for each stroke.'

They'd both been sat on the edges of my bed as they molested me, but now stood up, leaving me squirming in pained apprehension for what was coming. Wendy took Juliette's place, cuddling up to me and stroking my hair and back, but even that only went so far to soothe my feelings as I twisted my head around to see what the others were doing. Stacey had picked up the puff stick and was about to pull the piece of green-dyed cotton wool off the end, only for Juliette to stop her.

'No, no, leave that on. Think how comic she'll look!'

Stacey grinned and glanced at her hand, which showed a mark of deep forest green on the palm. I was trying to make eyes at her and mumbling through my mouthful of panty material, hoping to at least be allowed to negotiate my punishment, but she ignored me completely, laying the thin hard stick across the cheeks of my bottom. It was impossible not to feel resentful, when I'd been right on the edge of orgasm, but I tried to be good and pushed up my hips once more, making my bottom as inviting a target as I could in the hope of getting my caning over and done with. I was beginning to feel the need to go to the loo as well, which didn't help. Stacey gave me a couple of gentle taps, just to take aim, only to lift the cane from my bottom as she spoke.

'On second thoughts, let's each give her two strokes. Wendy.'

Wendy took the cane and once again I lifted my bottom, only for Juliette to speak up.

'Not like that. The tip of the cane will curl round her hip and might cut her.'

'Oh. Sorry.'

'Look, put the puff there, just where her cheek meets her hips. Not too high, either, or you might hit the base of her spine. Too low's not so bad, but it hurts like crazy on the thighs and you'll suffer if she ever gets to do you in turn. Lay the cane across where her bumhole shows, with the puff just touching here. That's it.'

I'd held my position as they spoke, growing increasingly frustrated, while the expression of uncertainty on Wendy's face was anything but reassuring. Juliette saw that I was looking.

'Put your face in the sheets, Lucy. Look, Wendy, I'll show you a trick. She hates this. Press the cane across her bum, like that, then lift it, but don't give her the stroke immediately. Make her wait, then do it when she's not expecting it. Yes, look, look at the way she clenches her cheeks, thinking she's going to get it!'

All three of them laughed, and Juliette carried on.

'Another thing she really hates is when you pretend you're

177

going to give her the stroke but miss on purpose. I used to love doing that to her.'

I thought Wendy would do it and I was determined not to give them the pleasure of seeing me react, but I had put my face in the sheets. When Wendy finally brought the cane down it was full across my bottom and so sudden it caught me completely by surprise. It was also hard, making my body buck and jerk in my bonds and laying a line of fire across my cheeks, while I was left shaking my head and gasping through my panties as she spoke to me.

'Was that OK, Lucy?'

Juliette drew a patient sigh but Stacey spoke up.

'It was fine, darling. Remember, you're punishing her. You don't need to ask if it was OK. Come on, give her another one, a bit harder this time.'

I gave an angry little wriggle, but Wendy took no notice, laying the cane across my bottom once more, lifting it, and swishing it through the air just above my cheeks. Despite my efforts at resistance my body had gone tight in anticipation of the cut, squeezing my already full bladder, and they laughed once more for my reaction and my muffled curses. I put my face back in the sheets, trying to be well behaved in the faint hope that it would make things easier for me. Again the cane pressed to my bottom, again it was lifted and again Wendy missed on purpose, only to bring it down an instant later, full on target, to leave me bucking and writhing in my pain as all three dissolved into laughter. Juliette then spoke.

'Great fun, isn't it? I love caning girls, and Lucy best of all, because she's so pathetic about it. Oh, and you should see your bum, Lucy. It's pink and green. My turn.'

A sob escaped my throat, of fear but also of less simple emotion at the thought of being caned by Juliette once again.

She plainly didn't care, enjoying my naked body and my help-less reaction as she began to tap the cane across my cheeks, only to suddenly lift it and bring it back down, far harder than Wendy had done. As the cane bit into my cheeks my entire body jerked hard, and if I hadn't had my panties tied off in my mouth I'd have screamed the hut down. I'd nearly wet myself too, and was fighting to control my bladder even as I writhed my hips in a futile effort to dull the stinging pain, while I was left shaking badly and gulping on my wet panties. I'd never heard Juliet's voice sound so cruel as she spoke again.

'Now that is how to cane a naughty girl. Stay still, Lucy.'

I struggled to obey, but I was clutching the sheets and sobbing as she lined up another stroke, with my cheeks and anus squeezing in pained anticipation. Juliette gave a soft chuckle.

'Look at the way her bumhole winks! Come on, Lucy, don't be such a baby. There's no need to snivel like that over a little caning. Stop it, or I'll really give you something to cry about.'

Her voice was full of cruel delight, bringing all the memo-ries of how she'd made me her plaything flooding back, and of just how cruel she could be. With that I lost control, kicking my feet and jerking my wrists in my bonds, fighting to make myself understood as I begged for release through my mouthful of soggy panty cotton. Stacey realised and spoke, asking Juliet to hold off, but it was too late, as the cane lashed down across my bottom. Again I jerked violently at the impact, not once but several times, completely out of control, and it was only at the touch of Stacey's hand on my cheek that I managed to stop jerking stupidly against the ropes holding me to the bed.

'Juliette, you're a vicious bitch. Are you alright, darling?'

I gave a weak nod, eager to reassure her, even as Juliette answered.

'It's what she likes. That's the thing with Lucy. You have to push her right to her boundaries to really get her off. You'll learn.'

Stacey didn't reply, but I could just imagine the look she'd have given Juliette. She'd taken the cane though, laying it across my cheeks for what was to be my fifth stroke. I tried to relax, only to find the pressure in my bladder rising suddenly, so that I was forced to tighten my pussy just as the cane hit. Stacey's stroke wasn't nearly as hard as Juliette's but it still hurt and I was still left shaking badly, although with only one to go, and from my lover, I managed to put my bottom on offer properly, with my hips thrust well up and my thighs cocked open a little.

'Good girl. You see, Juliette, she responds better if you don't hit her too hard.'

With that she brought the cane down, in a sharp, fast arc that ended not across the flesh of my bottom but right in the soft groove between my cheeks and my thighs, and across the lips of my cunt. Every muscle in my body seemed to lock, a scream broke from my throat into my wadded panties and at the same instant my bladder gave way, spraying piddle from my cunt, all over the bed and all over Wendy. She screamed in turn, in shock and disgust, but I barely heard and I couldn't have stopped myself anyway, because I was bucking wildly up and down on the bed, completely out of control, all four limbs jerking in my bonds and spurt after spurt of piddle squirting from my cunt. I'd still have been screaming too, but all I could manage was a choking noise that echoed the soft, wet bubbling of my pee as it came out, in little, hard gushes, to wet the bed and to wet the floor.

They watched, in horror and delight, with Wendy batting at her sodden clothes, but only when my urine had died to a weak trickle and my pained reaction had given way to muffled sobs for the way I'd disgraced myself did anybody speak. Juliette's voice was as cool as ever as she addressed Stacey.

'Well, yes, I see what you mean about how she responds. I never managed to make her do that.'

Stacey's voice was hard as she answered.

'Shut up, Juliette. You're not helping. Are you OK, Lucy?'

I managed a nod, although it was a lie, but Stacey began to undo the knot holding my panties into my mouth, only for Juliette to reach out and stop her.

'Not yet, Stacey. Trust me.'

I knew what she was going to do, but I couldn't resist and went limp, uncomplaining as she pulled up her sleeve and slipped a hand between my thighs.

'Give her a cuddle, you two, and make it sexy.'

Stacey hesitated only a second, then she'd come to sit down by my head, taking me in her arms. Her hands went under my chest and she caught up my breasts, stroking and squeezing gently as she began to kiss my face and neck. Wendy was busy taking off her soiled clothes, and continued to strip, peeling off her bra and panties to go nude but for socks and shoes. She came close, opposite Stacey, to stroke my hair and back, with her little, high breasts pushed to my face.

With Juliette's skilled fingers working on my cunt and the others cuddling me the awful shame of wetting myself quickly began to fade, leaving an overwhelming sense of arousal and complete helplessness. I was surrendered to them, the three girls who'd taken me and stripped me nude, tied me to my bed, spanked my bottom and taken turns to cane me until at last, in my pain and vulnerability, I'd let my piss go in full view and all over my bed. Now they were stroking me, touching me, exactly how they wished, two to soothe me and one to cajole my soaking cunt up towards orgasm.

Juliette took a moment to tickle my anus, then began to touch my beaten flesh, running her fingers along the six raw welts that decorated my bottom. Her thumb was in my cunt and I could already feel my muscles starting to squeeze on it as Stacey took hold of my head to bury my face between her full breasts. That was too much, a gesture so loving, so motherly, and from the girl who'd hurt me the most and made me give way to the most appalling, disgraceful act. I came, in a long, powerful orgasm that made everything they'd done to me worthwhile a thousand times over.

Chapter Eight

As I stood on parade in the cool spring morning I was praying that whatever exercise Parker had for us it did not involve the display of my bottom, at least not in front of anybody but the other girls. My flesh showed six clear welts, most of them set quite low, so that even in my relatively modest swimming costume it would have been blatantly obvious that I'd been beaten. The marks showed around the sides of my panties too, and even a skirt or running shorts would have been risky, especially with the likes of Paul and Billy around, so I'd opted for tracksuit bottoms despite what promised to be a hot day.

I'd expected Parker to be in a bad mood, but as he stepped towards us he looked cheerful, which was almost as worrying as the state of my bottom. For one awful moment I wondered if he might have discovered what was missing from the Stores, or some other evidence of our delinquency, but to my relief he launched straight into his usual morning pep talk.

'Good morning, although I suspect that for the less able among you it's not going to be very good at all. Today is the day we separate the men from the boys, the soldiers from the sissies ...'

Paul's voice broke from the ranks.

'What about Chad?'

Parker stopped, his smug expression changing to a blend of anger and puzzlement before he replied.

'What? What are you talking about?'

Paul carried on, his voice mild and courteous.

'Well, you said you were going to separate the soldiers from the sissies, but it seems to me that the two terms are not mutually exclusive. After all, Chad is a soldier, at least in the sense in which you appear to be applying the term, but he's also a sissy.'

Parker had been going slowly darker as he listened to Paul's explanation, while Chad had turned round.

'Are you calling me a sissy?'

'Yes, in that you enjoy taking a passive role – or a submissive role, if you prefer the term – within the context of a male-on-male homosexual relationship. Don't get me wrong, I'm a firm believer in every adult being allowed to express their sexuality in their own way, and if sucking cock on your knees is what gets you off, then that's not a problem. However, if today's exercise is going to involve sorting out which of us enjoys giving fellatio, then I think there are certain issues ...'

Parker finally found his voice.

'What the hell are you talking about, you fat moron!?'

'Dividing the soldiers from the sissies. Or am I mistaken in supposing that Chad visits your hut on most nights to give you long, lingering blow jobs while he masturbates?'

Daniel and Sam Haynes were holding Chad back as he tried to get at Paul, his face purple with rage, but it was obvious Paul knew what he was talking about and Parker was struggling to find a way out that didn't involve immediate violence.

'Stand to attention, Man C! Man M, see me in my office after the exercise.'

Paul gave a casual shrug.

'Fine, as long as you don't expect me to suck you off.'

Chad had obeyed the instruction and now stood at attention, his face still coloured up. Parker gave Paul what was obviously supposed to be a dangerous look, but as he carried on his voice was a great deal milder than before.

'We'll ignore that outburst, for now, and perhaps after this exercise some of you will be a bit less full of themselves? Right, where was I ...'

'You wanted to know which of us were sissies.'

It was Wendy who'd spoken, to my astonishment. Most of us laughed, but Parker had got himself under control and contented himself with a quick glare in her direction before he went on.

'Today's exercise. Today's exercise is designed to test your personal resources – your stamina, your intelligence, your ability to think for yourselves, and much more. You will be taken, individually, to carefully chosen locations, your drop points, all within twenty miles of the camp. Your first task is to reassemble as a team. Your second task is to get back here. You ought to be able to do that before sunset. If you can't, tough. You will have no equipment whatsoever, no compass, no map, nothing, except for water, a single ration pack and an emergency blanket. The first team back gets forty-eight points, the second thirty-six, then twenty-four and twelve. Any team that comes back incomplete gets nothing. Anybody who comes in alone gets a twelve-point penalty for themselves and their team. Any questions?'

It seemed straightforward, although I had a nasty suspicion that I'd be taken somewhere awkward, or at the very least that Parker would have chosen the drop points to help his favourites and hinder those of us he disliked. Once he'd answered a few questions and we'd been dismissed, the four of us came together outside, with the other teams nearby. Stacey had the same concern as me.

'He's sure to drop us as far apart as he possibly can, so let's meet at Venncott.'

Juliette agreed.

'Yes, at the pub, for lunch. Lucy can use her card. You've got it, haven't you?'

'Yes, safely hidden, and that's fine, if I can get there.'

Stacey objected.

'That'll cost us time, and we're not going to be able to get back fast enough anyway.'

'Yes we are. I'm going to hitchhike.'

Wendy looked doubtful.

'Do you think that's safe?'

'Yes. If you only stick your thumb out for women, old couples, or whatever. It's just common sense. Anyway ...'

She carried on, but Paul was beckoning me over to where Team D had gathered, with Billy next to him and the other two a little apart. I couldn't help but remark on his earlier behaviour.

'That was very funny, Paul, and I'm glad you did it, although what I told Billy about Parker and Chad was supposed to be in confidence.'

'Yeah, well, sorry about that, but we went and had a look for ourselves too. Boy, does that Chad like to suck!'

'But why say that to Parker, and in front of everybody! He already hates you.'

'I see it this way. If he's going to give me a bad report, and he obviously wants to, he can't very well do it without

mentioning what happened, because it was in front of everybody else, including Dan and Alastair. So he either has to
give me a good report, and say I tried my best despite being
a fat bastard, or he has to admit he likes getting his dick
sucked by twinks.'

'Twinks?'

'You know, young, good-looking gay men, like Chad. I
don't think Parker's cool with being gay, somehow, let alone
having it get around the circuit.'

'He's bi. He made a move on me, but yes, I was thinking
the same thing, more or less. The more extreme his report,
the easier it will be to explain away as sheer nastiness, and
of course we can stick up for each other.'

'Cheers. Scotty's never going to believe you're anything
other than the perfect prissy PA. I used to think so too, until
the other day. Anyway, how about a similar deal for today's
exercise? We can help you get back with minimum hassle.'

Billy chipped in.

'Yeah, in return for a spit roast.'

I felt my cheeks flare scarlet and Paul gave Billy a clip
around the ear before going on.

'Ignore him, he's a retard, but yeah, we were thinking of
that sort of deal.'

'I ... I'm sure that's very sweet of you, but we might be
miles apart.'

'Uh, uh, all three of us are being dropped on the far side
of Dartmoor, not close together admittedly, but ...'

'How do you know that?'

'Because we hacked into Parker's system last night, while
he was getting his BJ. He's worked it all out so it'll be really
tough, but we have GPS, and a car.'

'A car? How did you manage that?'

'We hired it last night. They may have our cards, but all the details are in my head, and for an online transaction that's all you need.'

'Oh, right. I actually have a card, carefully concealed.'

Billy gave a low sigh.

'I bet it's down your panties.'

I went pink again and he gave a dirty little snigger. Paul glanced down as if to inspect my pussy.

'Is it? I was wondering why you were in tracksuit bottoms.'

'Yes it is, if you must know. Anyway, what do you suggest?'

I was blushing hotter than ever for the thought of why I was really wearing tracksuit bottoms, although they did help to conceal the card I'd pushed down the front of my panties in case of just the sort of exercise that Parker had come up. It also occurred to me that if I let my knickers down for them they'd realise I'd been caned, although they already knew I got spanked, so with them it would be merely humiliating rather than a disaster. Paul carried on with his explanation.

'You're being dropped at a car park near the Willsworthy firing range, almost exactly on the far side of Dartmoor. There's a military road, and I think Parker's hoping you'll take it, but it only goes a little way past the range, then peters out, so you'll have to go right across the moor. You'd be better off going around to the north, but that's something like twenty-five miles. Our car's going to be ready for collection next to the war memorial at Mary Tavy, which is due south of your drop point along a straight road. You can't go wrong, and it's a silver Golf, safely anonymous. Be there for your lift, and if it's OK with you, maybe you'd like to entertain us on the way back?'

Billy's head was bobbing up and down, while his face was split into a huge grin. I drew a heavy sigh, just for form's sake, although the shame of what they were proposing was more than I could resist, especially when both of them had already had me.

'OK, you little perverts, I'll see you there. You can drop me at Venncott, OK? By the way, where are my friends being dropped off?'

Billy's grin grew sly.

'What's it worth to know?'

'Come on, boys, play fair! Anyway, you ... you know you can do as you like with me.'

Paul gave a happy sigh.

'That's what I like to hear. You are the best, Lucy. Wendy's being dropped off near Sidmouth, on the coast. Stacey's high up on the Exe and Juliette's furthest away of all, in the Blackdown Hills. Parker's really got it in for you lot.'

'I know. Thanks for your help.'

I wanted to kiss him, but it would have looked suspicious and I contented myself with a happy smile. They slapped their palms together in triumph as they walked back towards their teammates, adding to my already soaring sense of humiliation. To all intents and purposes they'd pushed me into sex in return for a lift, always one of my favourite fantasies and now to be realised for the second time in a few days. Stacey was coming towards me.

'What was that all about?'

'Just some friendly advice. They hacked into Parker's computer ...'

I gave them their drop points, just in time before Mr Straw came over to give us our supplies and check that we weren't carrying anything we shouldn't be. Both Parker and Sergeant Reynolds were patting down the men they were checking, but for once we were allowed to keep our dignity, body searches obviously being a step too far. Mr Straw then glanced at his clipboard.

'Girl A and Girl E, you're with me. G, you're with Sergeant Reynolds. O, you're with Mr Parker. Let's go, girls.'

I wasn't at all happy about being in Parker's minibus, but I did have Paul and Billy with me, as well as Chad and Sam. We barely spoke as Parker drove south and then west, to drop Chad off in a heavily wooded valley which I had to admit was a long way from the camp. Sam came next, on a tiny lane somewhere on the south moors, after which we drove for miles with Parker never saying a word until he drew the minibus to a halt in a lay-by high on the shoulder of a barren hill.

'Out you get, M, and you've got five miles less than the last two, so no whining.'

Paul took a look around, at the open, grey-brown moor stretching away to the north as far as the eye could see in a jumble of huge, bare hills broken only by tumbled rocks and patches of vivid green bog.

'You bastard.'

Parker merely pulled the minibus door shut and we moved on in silence once more. Billy was dropped at a tiny village in the lee of another huge, bleak hill and I found myself alone with Parker and feeling far from comfortable. We'd gone about a mile before he spoke.

'Look, I know we got off on the wrong foot, but you're a pretty girl and I was a bit drunk, OK?'

I had a nasty suspicion I knew where the conversation was going and I felt my stomach tighten. My answer was cold.

'Nothing needs to be said, thank you.'

He gave a click of annoyance.

'Oh come on! You and me, huh? You're the best-looking

chick in the camp, and well, I can tell you need a man, not some boy.'

I would have liked to reply with a crack about him and Chad, but I was feeling scared and didn't want to antagonise him.

'I'm sorry, but I'm not interested.'

'Hey, come on! Look at me. What do you see? I'm all man, Lucy, and I want you.'

I ignored him, staring out of the window at the passing fields, with not another person in sight or another vehicle on our road. He carried on, his voice harsh.

'Yeah, so it's true, I let Chad suck my dick. And do you know why Chad likes to suck my dick? It's because he knows a real man when he sees one, and I know you do too, Lucy, deep down. I'm what's called an alpha male, Lucy, the boss, the kingpin. I'm the one who gets sucked, and you'd love to do that, wouldn't you, if you can just get over that silly girlish pride of yours. Now come on, what do you say?'

'Please drop me off here.'

'Oh no you don't. We both know you want it, and you're going to get it, right up your pretty cunt, after you've sucked me hard. In ten minutes you'll be begging for more.'

'Oh no I won't. Anyway, I'm … I'm a lesbian. Stacey Atkinson's my girlfriend.'

'Yeah, yeah, yeah, I've heard it all before. You like other girls, so what? I like other men, when they're good looking and know their place. A butch girl like Stacey, I can see you'd get off on her, but what about me, huh?'

I didn't answer, at once furious and scared, both by what he was saying and by his driving, which had become increasingly reckless as his temper rose. When we reached a main

191

road and he was forced to slow down behind a lorry I tried to reason with him.

'Please, Mr Parker, try and understand. I'm not attracted to you, and that's that.'

He didn't answer immediately, but gave me a single angry glance before taking advantage of a straight piece of road to hurl the minibus past the lorry. I hid my face in my hands, sure we were going to crash, and he laughed.

'How was that? Doesn't that make your cunt cream, you stuck-up little bitch?'

We reached another village, and as we passed the war memorial I saw a silver car parked a little way down a side lane. Parker had gone quiet, and I was hoping he'd given up as we climbed a long hill back up onto the moors. From the ridge I could see for miles in every direction save the west, where yet bigger hills formed a ragged horizon. Some way to the side was a line of pale squares arranged on top of a bank, presumably targets for a firing range, and I realised we'd reached our destination. I was already undoing my seatbelt as Parker pulled off the road. He spoke with a sigh.

'There's no need to be scared, you stupid tart. I'm no rapist. What is it with you girls? You're so fucking precious! I mean, it's not like you don't enjoy a dick up the cunt, is it?'

I was already climbing down from the minibus and decided I could afford to answer him back.

'It's not me, you arrogant pig. It's you, your attitude. No woman would want to have sex with you, ever.'

'Plenty have, doll, plenty have. OK, if you're going to be a bitch, let's put it another way. It's fifteen miles back to the camp from here, and that's in a straight line, right across the highest part of Dartmoor. You can walk it, in maybe seven or eight hours, or you can pull out those pretty little tits and go down on my cock for a few minutes. Do we have a deal?'

'No we do not! Just fuck off, you disgust me!'

'Hey come on, it's only a blow job! Everyone has to suck cock sometime, Lucy.'

'Speak for yourself.'

I slammed the minibus door and made a hasty retreat to the edge of the car park, just in case he lost it completely. To my immense relief we weren't alone, with a family sitting in a parked car nearby and an elderly couple approaching us along the military road with an enormous dog following behind. I was fairly sure they'd heard what Parker had said, and found myself blushing, but I was still glad they were there, and all the more so when he drove away without giving me any more trouble.

For a long moment I stood as I was, shaking badly and wishing there was somebody to give me a hug, before I could bring myself to look at my surroundings. Paul had described the place well, with the military road leading into the moor and in just the right direction, while the main road ran north to south. Without his advice, and help, I'd have been in for a long, hard slog, nothing I couldn't cope with, but nothing I was particularly keen to do either. The car was a far better option, not only because it would be fast and comfortable, but because we'd have outwitted the horrible Parker.

I did wonder if Paul and Billy would allow me to at least postpone the dirty payment I had to make for my trip, because I wasn't really in the mood, but as I walked back across the hill my feelings gradually settled down. Parker's behaviour had been appalling, and he was unspeakably arrogant about his looks, which made me wonder how he'd feel knowing I gave what he so badly wanted to the very sort of person he despised the most. Not that I was going to tell him, but I'd know, and that would go some way towards lifting my spirits.

By the time I reached the village I was determined to go through with it, and hoping Paul and Billy would give me the little push I needed to give in. I wanted to be held as well, by somebody who actually liked me instead of seeing me as nothing more than a pretty object to rub his cock in, then spunk on, which more or less summed up Parker's attitude. Stacey would have been ideal, but Paul wasn't a bad substitute, especially as he was so much bigger than me, and even Billy was better than nothing. They also worshipped me, in a perverted sort of way, while Parker expected worship he didn't deserve.

Unfortunately nobody else was at the car and I was left standing in the road feeling sorry for myself until the appearance of a distant, globular figure who had to be Billy. I gave him a hug and a kiss the moment he reached me, to his surprise, and if his hands went straight to my bottom then being groped seemed a small price to pay for my comfort. He had a good feel of my bum before detaching himself and fetching the keys from the coach station opposite, allowing us to drive back and collect Paul, who'd only moved as far as an ice-cream van parked up to cater for the tourists. A double cone with two flakes left me with a slight sugar rush and able to open the bidding.

'Well then, boys, what's it to be?'

Paul shrugged.

'I suggest we find somewhere comfortable. After all, we've got all day, all night if we want it.'

'How do you mean?'

'Parker's obviously hoping we'll get stuck out on the moor after dark. Why else give us emergency blankets? Wouldn't it be a laugh to be having fun in some nice hotel while he thinks we're freezing our knackers off on the moor?'

I didn't bother to point out that I didn't have any knackers, but shook my head.

'I promised to meet the girls at the Venncott Arms. Stacey's determined to do as well as she can, and so am I, really, just to show that bastard Parker up. He made a pass at me.'

'Are you alright?'

Paul's arm came around my shoulder, which was like being embraced by a bear, and suddenly there were tears flooding down my face. Billy stayed as he was, looking concerned but also embarrassed, but I couldn't stop myself, pouring out my feelings into Paul's chest as he stroked my hair. He spoke only when I finally pulled away.

'I'll kill the bastard, I really will. He's such an arsehole. He didn't touch you or anything, did he?'

'No, nothing like that. Sorry, I'm in a bit of a state.'

'That's OK, let it all out, and if you'd rather not …'

I shook my head, even as I was wiping the tears from my eyes.

'No. I want to play, but be nice, yes?'

Paul nodded. Billy merely looked puzzled and I kissed the tip of his nose before turning back towards the car. The car park was crowded and a lot of people were looking at us, setting me blushing until we were safely out of view. We hadn't reached a decision about where to go, but Paul turned east, in the general direction of the camp. I wanted a lay-by, or anywhere private enough to let me go down on them, one by one while the other kept watch, but Paul had other ideas, pulling off at a fairly grand-looking country hotel at the bottom of a pretty valley.

'I would spend the night, but I really can't …'

'We can. I'm sick of those bloody huts. I want a decent

bed, and a hot bath, and a pint of fucking beer! Don't worry, I'll drive you to Venncott and drop you off after lunch.'

He parked and I climbed out of the car, wondering if the place would even let us in. Fortunately they seemed used to walkers and accepted my card without complaint, allowing us to book a double room in the names of Mr and Mrs Smith, something I'd always wanted to do. They didn't even seem concerned by the presence of Billy, perhaps assuming he was only with us for the afternoon, and we were soon upstairs, where I immediately turned on the bath, an old-fashioned castiron thing so big it looked as if I'd be able to float without touching the sides.

Neither of them objected to me going first, but watched in delight from the bedroom as I stripped, having deliberately left the door open. By the time I was out of my panties Billy had got his cock in his hand, stroking a stiff little erection as he let his eyes feast on my body.

'Can we come in with you?'

'Don't be silly. The bath would overflow.'

'No, I mean to watch. I've always wanted to watch a girl have a bath. I mean, for real. I've seen plenty of pornos.'

'I bet you have. Come on then.'

I'd already climbed into the bath, immersing myself slowly in the hot water, which was pure bliss after so many hastily snatched showers in water that was never more than warm. There was good soap too, in place of the little hard bars we'd been using, and complimentary bottles of body lotion, shampoo, conditioner and more. I used it all, luxuriating in the water and deliberately showing off as I soaped my legs and feet, my breasts and belly. All the while both Paul and Billy watched in near silent fascination, speaking only to compliment my body or ask me to show off a little more.

Paul soon had his cock out too, and I reached over to take him in my hand, squeezing his lovely thick shaft and giving him a little tug to help him towards erection.

Billy looked as if he was ready to come, just for the sight of me naked in the bath, so I took my breasts in my hands, soaping them and teasing my already stiff nipples as I locked eyes with him. He made an odd little grunting noise and began to wank harder still, only to suddenly stop, panting as he spoke.

'No, I mustn't ... not yet. I haven't even seen your bum yet ...'

I laughed and rolled over in the water, to stick my bottom up above the thick layer of soap suds that covered the surface. Billy gave a weak groan and began to stroke his cock again, but only gently. I wondered if I could make him lose control and reached for the soap once more, to rub it over my cheeks and in between, deliberately showing off my anus and pussy lips. He swallowed and the motion of his hand on his cock had grown faster once more, so I locked eyes with him again and slid a finger in up my soapy bumhole.

'Oh fuck, you dirty bitch ... go on, do it, Lucy, right in.'

His wanking had grown furious again as I obliged, pushing my finger deep in up my bottom, in full view of both of them. Paul was now hard, his huge cock rearing up from his open trousers with his balls bulging out beneath, making me want to take him in my mouth and suck, or maybe let him inside me, even up my bottom. The thought made me shiver and set my bumhole tight on my intruding finger, so I began to talk, teasing myself as much as them.

'Do you know Billy had me up my bottom, Paul? He caught me unawares in the woods and he buggered me. I said not to tell, but I bet he did, and I bet you'd like to do it too.'

It was his turn to swallow, both of them now wanking hard at their cocks, and I realised that if I didn't let them have me soon they'd waste their spunk watching me in the bath. I pulled my legs up, lifting my bottom higher out of the water with my legs set apart to show it all off behind as I went on, now breathless.

'Go on. Get in. Fuck me, Paul. Fuck my cunt, or fuck my bottom if you want to.'

He didn't need telling, already tearing at his clothes, but Billy looked a bit forlorn, immediately making me feel guilty.

'You too, Billy. Put it in my mouth and you can spit roast me, just the way you wanted to.'

I opened my mouth for him as he came forward, to take his cock in and suck, even as Paul scrambled into the bath behind me. The water sloshed over the edge, but I no longer cared, keeping my bottom high as he pushed his erection in up my ready cunt. They shared a high five as they began to use me, rocking my body backward and forward on their cocks with the water splashing against my tits and belly. Paul began to slap my bottom as he fucked me, then abruptly spread my cheeks, showing off my soapy, open bumhole.

'OK, up the bum it is, if that's what you want?'

All I could manage was an urgent nod on my mouthful of cock, because Billy had taken a grip in my hair and was fucking my mouth. I wanted to beg Paul to take it slowly too, scared by the thought of taking a cock as big as his up my bum for all my excitement, but it was too late. His knob was already pressed to my anus, slippery with soap, then in, stretching me wide to give me what I'd asked for. The soap stung like anything, but there was nothing I could do but take it, gulping on Billy's cock with my eyes watering. At least it kept me slippery as Paul crammed himself inch by inch up my rectum, until at last I felt his balls squash against my empty cunt.

'That's good. I'm right up her bum … right up.'

He broke off with a sigh, gave my bottom another hard slap and took hold of my hips to pull me close, now jammed in as deep as he'd go. I felt completely bloated, as if the head of his cock was about to come out of my mouth and leave me spit roasted in earnest, but they were using me hard and there was nothing I could do but stay in my rude kneeling position with my bottom spread to Paul's cock and Billy's deep in my mouth. Both were getting urgent, and it had begun to hurt when Billy suddenly grunted, whipped his cock free and gave me the full contents of his balls in my open mouth and over my face, to leave me gagging on spunk even as Paul called me a filthy bitch and stopped pumping himself into my rectum.

Billy stuffed his cock back into my mouth and both were holding me as they milked themselves into my body, letting go of my hips and my hair only when they were fully done. I'd put a hand back to my cunt on the instant, snatching at myself and babbling at Paul the moment Billy's cock had once more slipped free of my mouth.

'Don't you dare take it out, you bastard! Keep it in me, Paul, right in up my dirty bottom … right up … Bugger me, Paul, and spank me while you bugger me. That's it, harder … harder … hurt me, spank me like the dirty little brat I am …'

My voice broke to a cry as my bumhole went tight on his cock and I was there, riding my orgasm in breathless ecstasy as he buggered me, with his friend's spunk still dribbling down my face and my fingers snatching at my empty cunt to bring me to peak after peak until I could take no more and collapsed down into the water.

Chapter Nine

Parker was having trouble keeping his temper and I was having trouble keeping back my giggles. When we four girls arrived back at the camp the previous afternoon at what we judged to be a sensible hour, he'd been suspicious but unable to prove anything. We'd raced up through the woods and across the airfield to ensure that we were suitably sweaty and dishevelled, but it hadn't really been enough to give the impression of twenty miles or more across country. I'd been subjected to particular scrutiny, but on Paul's advice I'd got my shoes and socks muddy with Dartmoor peat, and on Billy's added an artistic rip to my top to hint at the curve of one breast. He didn't seem to notice that I'd washed my hair.

We'd been the first back, and he'd had no choice but to award us our full measure of points. Team B had followed just over an hour later, all four of them completely exhausted, and Parker's suspicions had grown stronger still. We'd already gone in to dinner when Daniel arrived, to say he'd been waiting for the rest of Team C for over two hours. Three more people had limped in after dark, but of Chad, Paul and Billy there was no sign at all. We'd gone to bed, and had discovered at breakfast that shortly after midnight Chad

had made a plaintive call from Dawlish lifeboat station, over ten miles off course, asking to be rescued. It had taken Parker well over an hour to fetch him. After breakfast we were put on parade. He spent a long time looking us over before he spoke.

'I said yesterday that we'd be doing an exercise to separate the men from the boys, and do you know what that really means? Men finish, or they go down fighting. Boys quit, and boy do we have a bunch of quitters here. Yes, Team A, I'm referring to you. I don't know how you did it, and I don't want to know, but you cheated. In the circumstances, I have no choice but to adjust yesterday's scores. You're disqualified and receive a forty-eight point team penalty, twelve points each.'

Juliette didn't bother to raise her hand.

'What do you mean? We got back first, didn't we?'

'Yes, Girl A, you got back first, an hour ahead of Team B. They could barely stand. You looked as if you'd been for an afternoon stroll, and Girl O looked like she'd visited a fucking salon along the way!'

His voice had risen close to a shout as he spoke, but that didn't bother Juliette.

'That's completely unreasonable. We won, according to the rules you gave us.'

'No, you did not. You cheated. You may have got back first but you did not play according to the spirit of the game. You quit, all four of you, cadging lifts or something. You're quitters, all four of you! What are you!?'

He was shouting, his face just inches from hers, and for a moment I thought he was going to get a knee in the balls, but Juliette stayed cool.

'We're the best team here, and kindly don't spit in my face, you revolting little man.'

Parker went crimson, and I saw that both Sergeant Reynolds and Mr Straw had stepped forward as if they were expecting to hold him back, but he managed to get control of himself and stepped away. After a moment fiddling with the pages on his clipboard he started again.

'As I was saying, Team A is disqualified. Team B, you stuck to it and you pulled through, so you're the winners with forty-eight. Team C also stuck to it, and in fact Daniel … Man K was the first back to the vicinity of the camp. Had it not been for Man C sustaining an unfortunate injury …'

Juliette interrupted.

'He was in Dawlish! He went in completely the wrong direction, and you said that anybody who came in alone would get a penalty!'

Parker ignored her.

'… they would have come in second, quite possibly first. Team C, thirty-six points. That's what I mean by trying, Girl A, not giving up, not taking the easy way out.'

'He rang you from the lifeboat station!'

Parker had already turned his back on her as he continued.

'At least we can all agree that Team D score zero.'

Juliette didn't and was starting to protest when Paul himself walked in, holding a bag of chips, closely followed by Billy, who was eating a burger. Both looked fresh, their clothes clean, their chins free of stubble. Parker looked them up and down, then drew a heavy sigh.

'And where have you two been?'

Paul made an airy gesture.

'Oh, here and there. As the exercise was obviously fixed to make sure we and the girls lost, we decided it would be nice to stay at a hotel. Dinner was excellent, although on reflection I might have gone for the duck rather than the steak …'

'Shut up! What were you doing at a hotel? How did you pay?'

'I have my ways. Chip?'

'No I do not want a chip! Right, now you're all back, let's get on with it, shall we? I had planned to give you an easy day, but after what's happened I've decided to make you see once and for all that there's a very real difference between real goddamn men and fat, useless slobs, and that when the chips are down it's the men who come up trumps.'

Paul raised a finger and swallowed the chips he'd been eating in order to speak.

'You shouldn't mix your metaphors.'

'What!?'

'You were mixing your metaphors. The expression ...'

'Shut up, you imbecile! By God I'll wipe the smile off your fat face if it's the last thing I do. Drop and give me twenty!'

'Twenty what?'

'Press-ups, you moron!'

'No thanks. I never exercise after eating. It's bad for the digestion. Speaking of which, what are we up to today? Billy and I were thinking it might be fun to have a cocksucking competition, as that way Chad might have a chance ...'

Parker hurled himself at Paul, but Sergeant Reynolds had been watching and separated the two in an instant, before taking Parker outside. Paul nodded and took another chip before going on.

'He's good, that guy Reynolds, army training, I suppose. So what are we doing today?'

Mr Straw stepped forward to pick up Parker's clipboard, throwing a glance towards the door before he began to examine it.

'Um ... we were going to be doing a series of mental exercises, but that's been replaced with a track and field programme, gym too: hurdles, archery, weightlifting, boxing ...'

* * *

We lost, unsurprisingly, although we didn't do as badly as we might have done. Parker only reappeared in the middle afternoon, and was his usual obnoxious self, as if nothing had happened. He didn't bother to hide his satisfaction as we came in third or last time and time again and simply pretended not to notice when Stacey won at archery, or when Paul managed first place in the weightlifting due to his sheer bulk. Otherwise everything went to form and he finished the day with a nasty little speech about knowing our physical limitations. I was so used to his manner I was barely listening, until he reached his conclusions.

'... and some of you don't seem to appreciate this. Some of you seem to think that physical ability doesn't make any difference, but I'm here to show you that it does. Yes, Man M, I'm looking at you, and you, Girl O, and you, Girl A. You have just the sort of arrogant, stupid attitude I despise, with no respect whatsoever for your obvious superiors, but by God you're going to learn it, if it's the last thing I do!'

His voice had risen as he spoke, close to a shout, and I found myself caught off guard and unsure what to say. I glanced at Juliette, but she seemed indifferent. Paul merely yawned, and Parker's face had begun to go dark again as he went on.

'For the rest of the course you're all on KP, which means kitchen patrol for the ignorant among you. That means you work in the kitchens and in the Mess, under the direct supervision of Sergeant Reynolds. It means you do the food preparation, or at least those parts of it you can be trusted with. It means you serve at meals, and includes addressing your superiors as sir and maintaining a generally respectful attitude. It means you clean up afterwards, including taking out the slops – your job, I feel, Man M – and washing up, Girl A perhaps, and scrubbing the floor, which I would say suits you very well, Girl O, down on all fours where you belong!'

I found myself blushing hot for his words, not so much because they echoed my fantasies, but for the implications. Perhaps he was just trying to put me down, but perhaps he knew more than he was letting on. Perhaps he'd even peeped in on our hut while I was being spanked, or watched while I was made to take Paul and Billy in my mouth. Worse still, if he did know, and had the slightest inkling of what being made to behave like a servant would do to me, he was sure to try and take advantage. Not that I'd give in, not to him, because for all my submissive needs I'd never go down to anybody unless I wanted to. There would be no obedience to him, not from me.

He finished by telling us to fall out and then marching from Assembly. I began to follow, determined to make it very clear that I had no intention of accepting my punishment, only to be brought up short by Juliette.

'You're not going to bother to argue with him, are you Lucy?'

'Well, yes. I have to …'

'No you don't. Just ignore him. What's he going to do?'

Paul was close by and had overheard.

'Exactly. Our reports are already going to be as bad as he can possibly make them, so there's no point in arguing. I say we go down to the pub.'

I hesitated, tempted by the idea but not sure Parker would recognise it as a gesture of contempt or a show of cowardice.

'At least I have to speak to him first.'

Paul shrugged.

'If you're going to speak to anybody, speak to Sergeant Reynolds. All you'll get from Parker is more bollocks-speak, and you saw how he lost it with me.'

Juliette agreed.

'That's the way to do it. Undermine Parker's authority.'

I'd been thinking exactly the same thing.

'That's true, and besides, we'd have to report to Reynolds for this kitchen patrol thing anyway. I'll just tell him we're not doing it, and why. He seems to have some common sense.'

'Do you want us to come with you?'

Paul shook his head.

'No, it's better if Lucy goes alone. Why give Parker the satisfaction of a big reaction? Make it casual. I wouldn't bother at all, myself.'

Juliette considered for a moment, then nodded.

'That's good. Are you OK with it, Lucy?'

I wasn't, but I nodded in turn. Stacey, Wendy and Billy had been listening to our conversation and added their good wishes as I made for the door. I hate confrontation, but it was plainly necessary and as I walked down towards Mess I was rehearsing what I was going to say. Unfortunately he wasn't there, but I knew that if I waited I'd soon start to lose my edge and so continued towards the hut where he lived.

It was one of three set back a little among the trees and well away from the main barracks area. There was a small porch and veranda at the front, with a window to either side of the door. Both were lit with a dull yellow glow. I could hear music too, very faint, but when I knocked there was no response. Determined, I pushed the door open, to find myself in a small, spartan sitting room with just a single comfortable armchair. In the chair was Sergeant Reynolds, stretched out at full length, his head tilted back and his eyes closed. He had earphones on, and was still dressed as he had been that afternoon, except that his fly was open and his underpants had been pushed down to expose an impressive erection, which he was nursing with a pair of girl's panties – my panties.

My initial gasp of shock failed to penetrate his reverie, but even as I began a hasty retreat through the door a thought had occurred to me. I stopped, wondering if I dared do what my dirty mind had come up with, all the while with my eyes fixed in fascination on his huge, dark erection and the scrap of pale-pink cotton wrapped around it as he masturbated. It seemed insane, or at least insanely inappropriate, but on the other hand it seemed certain to succeed. I had to do it, and before I could lose my nerve I spoke up loud and clear.

'Would you like a hand with that?'

His body jerked as if somebody had plugged him into the mains and I found myself stifling a giggle even as I backed away a little in case he didn't take kindly to the interruption. Yet there could have been no mistaking what I'd said, nor the tone of my voice, and he pulled himself together remarkably fast, his tone more cautious than embarrassed as he answered me.

'You're serious?'

There was really only one response, as I didn't want to go into the issue of why he'd stolen my panties, or what he was doing with them. I knew the answer to both questions, and while his behaviour was hardly respectful there was no mistaking his desire. He'd dropped the panties when I spoke to him, and tucked his cock away, but he was still stiff, too stiff to hide the bulge of his erection. I got down on my knees, retrieved the panties and pulled out his cock, to wrap them around his shaft once more. He looked surprised, but there was no more resistance than you'd expect from any man with a girl wanking at his erect cock.

Despite my wicked plan I felt small and dirty, on my knees to a panty thief, masturbating him with my own stolen knickers. That was good in its way, especially as he was so strong and fit, but I felt I needed a little affirmation for my behaviour, or at least to make sure he knew how privileged he was. I also wanted to enjoy the experience and give myself something to fantasise over once I was done.

'Do you like this?'

The answer was obvious and he merely nodded.

'It's nice, is it, feeling my panties on your cock?'

Again he nodded, but I wanted more.

'Do you just like girls' panties, or is it because they're mine? Come on, tell me!'

I sounded breathless even to myself, and he must have realised I was deliberately turning myself on, but it still took him a moment to answer.

'Because they're yours ... you're so sexy.'

It couldn't be more than half true, but it wasn't the time to argue, while the implications of what he'd said had brought my sense of shame up like a rocket. The little pink panties wrapped around his cock hadn't come out of my knicker drawer, or even been discarded when I'd undressed. They'd been pulled off during a spanking and crammed in my mouth to shut me up until I'd been finished with. I had to know if he'd seen.

'Did you ... were you watching? Did you see what ... what happened to me? Tell me, I don't mind.'

Again he hesitated, before giving a sudden, urgent nod.

'I heard you. I heard noises from your hut and I went there. I meant to tell you to be quiet, but I heard odd noises, smacks and cries. I looked in, around the curtain, and ... and I saw you playing dirty games.'

I gave a low moan, imagining how I must have looked to him, a complete stranger, panties down across Stacey's lap while I got my bare bottom smacked, and with two other girls thoroughly enjoying the view. He'd have seen every detail of my cunt and anus, watching my pathetic struggling as I got my bottom slapped up to a hot, pink flush, and maybe far worse.

'Did ... did you see me with the boys?'

He nodded and something inside me seemed to snap. I'd meant to toss him off in my panties, nothing more, and use what had happened as a bargaining chip, but the thought of him watching me being not only spanked but then made to suck off Paul and Billy was too much. Not that I had long, his cock was now a straining tower of flesh in my hand, the dark, veiny shaft rock hard beneath the soft panty cotton, the helmet glossy with pressure. I leant forward, to plant a single gentle kiss on the very tip of his erection, before I took him in my mouth, as deep as I could manage, sucking eagerly as I continued to tug on his shaft. His hand closed in my hair as he spoke.

'Oh you sweet little bitch! You love this shit, don't you? You really love it? Come on, darling, let's do it properly. Let's have those cute little titties out. Let's have that sweet little backside showing behind.'

'You bastard.'

I'd pulled back from his cock, and even as I spoke I was lifting my top to show off my breasts for him. My shorts followed and I was bare behind, my naked bottom thrust out as I showed off my body for his amusement and my own soaring sense of shame. Now virtually naked, I went back to sucking, taking his cock deep once more and using my panties to stroke his balls and shaft. He gave a low moan, then began to talk again.

'That's my little one. That's my cocksucking little panty babe. Yeah, I bet that feels better than your friends' little cocks, doesn't it, doesn't it just? That's right, Lucy baby ... that's right ... suck my cock.'

I was doing my best, and still trying to hold off from the final disgrace of slipping a hand between my thighs to masturbate while I sucked him. What he was saying was outrageous, openly getting off on me when he'd stolen my panties and I'd caught him masturbating in them, but it was wonderfully demeaning. It really brought home what I was doing as well, sucking off a panty thief with my naked tits jiggling to the motion and my bottom bare behind, a bottom he'd seen spanked by a girl and in front of other girls. He'd seen me suck too, seen me being made to suck, on my knees with my smacked bottom stuck out behind. Really I was no better than he was, and with that realisation I gave in.

My hand went back and I was rubbing at my cunt as I wanked him into my mouth. He saw and called me a bitch again, and what he'd said before, a cocksucking little panty babe, as if the little scrap of pink material wrapped around his cock was as exciting and as important as my living body. At that I started to come, picturing how he saw me, no doubt how many men saw me, and other women, as a set of pretty curves decorated with sexy clothes, all designed to get their cocks stiff and to make them want to fuck us.

It was desperately humiliating, and not something I could

normally have coped with at all, but in the circumstances just right. I'd put myself in the situation, for my own ends, which made me feel I deserved everything I got, and more. Just as I'd used my body to get what I wanted, so had he, making me into his panty babe. As my body went tight I was picturing myself as exactly that, a cute little fuck dolly dressed up in pretty pink panties, ready to be used at his convenience. It didn't matter that he'd peeked in while my girlfriend spanked me, or watched in secret as I was made to suck two other men to orgasm. He had the right to enjoy my body, naked or clothed, and if he'd stolen my panties to get off in, then that was just tough. On that thought I hit my peak, just as he too came, filling my mouth with spunk, all of which I just gulped down, too high to stop myself as I deliberately filled my belly while still rubbing at my aching pussy.

The degrading fantasy I'd built up in my head as I masturbated collapsed as my orgasm died, but he had me firmly by the hair and even as my guilt washed in I was still swallowing spunk like a good little tart ought to, which left me shame-faced and gasping as he finally allowed me to pull back. Nor was I the only one, his face now split by an embarrassed, uncertain grin.

'Sorry about that. I got a bit carried away there.'

I wasn't really in a position to reply until I'd swallowed once more and wiped my lips with the panties I was still holding, and he spoke again.

'That was good though, yeah? And I'm sorry I stole your panties, only you really got me going.'

I threw them at him.

'Keep them, enjoy yourself.'

He caught them, his grin now unabashed as he went on.

'You are a bad girl, you know that?'

I began to adjust my clothes as I replied.

'I suppose I am, for the right person … when the time is right, but if you fancied me, why didn't you just ask?'

'It's against the rules. We're not supposed to get it on with the clients.'

I'd stood to pull my shorts up, but quickly sat down again, on one of the hard chairs arranged in perfect symmetry around a table. After what we'd done I was sure I could talk to him openly, while he was hardly in a position to try and push me around, or likely to want to. If anything, what he'd said suggested he might be more on my side.

'That doesn't seem to stop Parker.'

'Yeah, well, he's the boss. It's always one rule for them and one for us, isn't it? So it's that guy Chad this time, is it?'

'This time?'

'Yeah, he always gets it on with somebody, maybe a girl, maybe a boy, but he likes fit blonds and he likes ones who're into body image.'

'With Chad it looked more like body worship. Stacey and I watched him getting his cock sucked and you should have seen Chad's face.'

'I can imagine. Yeah, body worship, that's his bag. I'm surprised he didn't go for you.'

'He did. He tried it on at The Plough, where Stacey Atkinson and I stayed the night before we arrived. He was too brash for me, so I turned him down.'

'So that's why he's got it in for you.'

'Yes. In fact, that's what I came to talk to you about. He's put me, and Juliette Fisher, and Paul Yates, on something called kitchen patrol, which you're supposed to supervise. We're not going to do it, any of us.'

To my surprise he laughed.

'He tried to put you on KP? He loves to do that, usually with the fat boys.'

'Well he's picked the wrong people this time. It's just not going to happen.'

He gave a thoughtful nod before replying.

'I've got to do my job, but if you won't do KP, then I guess you won't do KP and the worst he can do is throw you out. Anyway, he was well out of order today, when he went for that guy Paul.'

'So you'll stick up for us?'

'Like I say, I've got to do my job, and believe me, I need my job ...'

'You didn't seem worried when you frogmarched Parker out of Assembly earlier.'

'No? Can you imagine what would have happened if Parker had hit that guy?'

'Well, yes ... my company would have sued, naturally, and ... OK, I see what you mean, you've have ended up without a job anyway and not much chance of getting another one.'

'Dead right, and that's not the first time it's happened. You see, Parker reckons anyone who's not A1 fit ought to be ashamed of themselves, and he doesn't get it when they don't see it the same way. So yeah, that's why I pulled him back, and he knows the score, but I need to stay on side, so I'll tell him you've refused to do KP and let's take it from there.'

'OK.'

I kissed him and left, full of mixed emotions, for my own dirty behaviour and his. I was also pleased with myself for defying Parker but worried about the consequences. As I walked back I was telling myself that my report couldn't possibly be any worse than it was going to be anyway.

Logically, I knew that the entire KP episode would be one more piece of evidence to lay before Mr Scott to show that I'd been unfairly treated, but that didn't get rid of the unpleasant, slightly sickly sensation I always suffer from when I've been deliberately disobedient. Fortunately I had support, with Paul and the girls waiting for me outside our hut, all eager to know what had happened.

'Well, I've solved the mystery of the panty thief for a start.'

'Who was it?'

'Not Sergeant Reynolds!?'

I waited until we were inside before I replied, enjoying their attention.

'The very same. He was ... using them when I came in!'

Stacey seemed puzzled.

'He was wearing your knickers?'

'No, he was using them to help himself come.'

Wendy was horrified.

'What, to ... to do his business in? The dirty bastard!'

Paul took a more practical view.

'Perfect! He'll do anything you say rather than let that get out.'

I held up my hands, smiling.

'That won't be necessary. I explained the situation and he understands our position. He's a bit worried about his job, as Parker seems to call the shots, but he agreed that we can't be forced to do kitchen patrol.'

'I bet he did! Come on, Lucy, you could have the guy running about for you like a puppy!'

'That's blackmail, Paul.'

'Sounds good to me.'

'Besides, it would only be his word against mine, and believe me, he's on our side.'

Juliette had been watching with her mouth twisted up into a wicked little smirk, and finally spoke up.

'I'm sure he is, Lucy. You are such a little slut!'

'What are you talking about!? I didn't ...'

'Why have you gone bright pink then? I know you, Lucy.'

I shrugged, suddenly unable to speak for embarrassment as Paul burst out laughing, while Wendy and even Stacey were looking shocked.

'Lucy, you didn't!'

Juliette answered her.

'Oh yes, she did. Just look at her blush, always a dead giveaway with our little Lucy. So how far did you have to go, slut?'

I forced myself to answer, for all that I could no longer raise my eyes to meet hers.

'I ... I just gave him a helping hand, that's all.'

'With your panties?'

I managed a feeble nod and she too began to laugh, holding onto Paul for support. Stacey finally came to my aid.

'Give her a break, you two.'

Paul made to apologise, although his body was still shuddering with suppressed laughter, but Juliette wasn't finished.

'Isn't she lovely? She catches a guy wanking off in her panties and what does she do, smack his face, kick him in the balls? Oh no, not Lucy, she offers him a hand job!'

She sat down on her bed, shaking with laughter as Stacey answered her.

'Come on, Juliette. You're not being very fair.'

Juliette took no notice.

'Oh, but I am. What a little trollop! Mark you, she always was. Even when I first knew her she never seemed to have

216

any knickers on, and you knew she was just waiting to have her skirt pulled up ...'

'Juliette.'

Stacey's voice had a sharp tone I was more than familiar with, and I held back from the admission I'd been about to make. What Juliette was saying was turning me on, and she knew it, but she'd completely failed to catch the warning note from Stacey. I hung my head and began to snivel, which provoked fresh laughter from Juliette, just as I'd hoped. Stacey's sympathy came immediately.

'Don't cry, Lucy.'

Again Juliette laughed, crueller than ever.

'Oh come on, Stacey, you know what she's like! She's always blubbering when she's getting her bottom smacked and she loves every minute of it. That's what she's after, a good spanking for her filthy behaviour, so why don't you give her one, or I will.'

'I'll give you one in a minute, Juliette.'

'Don't be silly. Come on, let's spank her.'

She'd got up, and was coming towards me, clearly intent on carrying out her threat whether Stacey joined in or not. I squeaked and backed away, so that her full attention was on me as she passed Stacey.

'Juliette, no!'

It was an order, given in Stacey's best barrack-room voice, but Juliette took no notice as she reached out to take me by the wrist. I was pulled up, but Juliette had her back to Stacey, a big mistake. One hard jerk and her shorts were down, showing off her panties to the room. A push and she was sprawled over my bed, bottom up, her gasp of outrage breaking to a grunt as she went down, but she'd managed to twist around before Stacey could get on top of her. I scrambled out of the way and Wendy shrieked, Juliette cursing as she tried to push Stacey back, but I could have told her it was no good. In just seconds she'd been put in an arm lock and twisted back over, face down on the bed as Stacey straddled her back, her panty-clad bottom pushed out to the room, to me and Wendy, and to Paul, who was watching in rapt fascination. Juliette continued to struggle, her full cheeks wriggling in the bright-red panties that clung to every contour of her bottom, until she realised she was only making an exhibition of herself. Only then did she speak.

'No, Stacey, not me.'

I knew exactly what she meant, and even then it seemed horribly inappropriate, but not to Stacey.

'Why not? You spank Lucy, so why shouldn't you get it yourself?'

'No ... Stacey, please! It doesn't work that way!'

'You were going to take it from her.'

'Not like this. No, Stacey, please ... and anyway, she likes to be spanked, I ...'

'Like to do the spanking, I know, but like my old man used to say, if you want to dish it out, you have to know how to take it. And besides, Lucy owes you one, doesn't she? So, Juliette, either she spanks you or I do. Take your choice.'

Juliette's face was set in consternation, and instead of answering she gave a sudden, hard jerk, but Stacey kept her grip and carried on.

'Come on, Juliette, what's it to be, me or Lucy?'

'Bitch! OK, OK, you can spank me, but not in front of Paul.'

'Fair enough, as you don't like boys. Paul, would you be kind enough to step outside for a moment while I spank this brat?'

218

Paul nodded and withdrew without protest, which I was sure meant he would be watching through the window. Juliette must have guessed too, but seemed to think she'd salvaged enough pride by having him leave the room, speaking again the moment the door had closed.

'OK, get on with it, if you really have to, you vicious bitch!'

Stacey laughed.

'That's a very silly way to speak to a woman who's about to spank your bottom, Juliette, as you of all people should know, but isn't there a little ritual we ought to go through first?'

Juliette knew exactly what Stacey meant, and gave an angry little squirm in response, but said nothing. Stacey wasn't satisfied.

'Yes, there is, isn't there, Juliette? There's a little ritual that involves pulling the victim's knickers down to humiliate her. Lucy insists on it, and I believe you're the one who introduced her to it, aren't you?'

Juliette didn't answer, at which Stacey planted a single hard smack across the bulging panty seat. My heart jumped at the sight, not just to see a smack landed on a girl's bottom, but to see a smack landed on Juliette Fisher's bottom, and as it landed she'd given a little squeak of pain followed by a sob, just the way I might have done. There was a huge lump in my throat and I'd started to shake, but I couldn't look away as Stacey took hold of the waistband of Juliette's knickers.

'OK, if you're going to be obstinate, I'll just have to spank you that little bit harder. Right, panties down then, Juliette, nice and slow, and all the way, all the way down to your knees, so the girls can see everything.'

She'd spoken slowly, and as she'd done so she'd peeled Juliette's knickers down, exposing the full, naked globe of her bottom, with her cheeks spread to show off first the neat little star of her anus, which I'd been made to poke my tongue up many a time, then the plump swell of her pussy lips. I'd licked that too, even more often, but for all the occasions I'd buried my head between her thighs or had my face sat on, I couldn't ever remember seeing her wetter. Wendy gave a nervous giggle as she saw, but Stacey laughed openly.

'Oh my, oh my! You are soaking, Juliette, absolutely soaking! Could it possibly be that big, bad Juliette gets off on having her botty smacked?'

Juliette finally reacted.

'Shut up, you bitch! I can't help it, any more than you could.'

As she finished she began to sob, her whole body shaking in reaction to her shame, just the way I would have done, no better, no more dignified. Stacey put her hands to Juliette's cheeks and gave them a little wobble, stretching her anus wide, which immediately made the little hole contract, winking just the way mine does when I'm in a similar position. I finally found my voice.

'That's right, be rude with her, Stacey, and spank her hard!'

'I intend to.'

With that Juliette's spanking began, one hard slap and then another, with Stacey using a hand for each cheek, to make the flesh bounce and spread. I watched in fascination, my eyes riveted to her bouncing cheeks, the lewd winking motion of her anus and the way the flesh of her cunt pulled to the smacks to make her wet hole squeeze, squashing out white juice. Wendy was no less enthralled, staring open-mouthed and no doubt as horrified and excited by the sheer intimacy of the display as me, as well no doubt as imagining herself in the same shameful position. Juliette knew what a spectacle she was making of herself too, from all the girls she'd dealt with in the same way, principally me, and she took it sobbing and gasping between little heartfelt cries for the harder smacks. Only Stacey seemed cool, applying a hard, matter-of-fact spanking to Juliette's dancing bottom and not speaking again until both cheeks were an even, rosy red.

'There we are, girls, one well-deserved spanking, but I don't think we're quite finished yet, do you, Juliette? No, we're not. Twelve strokes, wasn't it, if you'd like to fetch the cane, please, Lucy?'

Juliette shook her head, but she didn't try to escape. She was still sobbing hard though, and if it hadn't been for the blatant evidence of her arousal I couldn't have done it. Even then it seemed wrong as I went to extract the cane from its hiding place, yet I was determined to go through with it. As I came back she lifted her head, her eyes wide and moist with tears, pleading with me, but she made no effort to get Stacey off her back and said nothing.

Her bottom was pushed out, a perfect target, with her reddened cheeks well spread and slightly lifted. I tapped the cane across them, taking aim just as she had so often across my own bare rear cheeks, determined for all that it felt so wrong, lifting the cane and bringing it down with a firm thwack across her bottom. Her answering scream immediately broke to a heavy sobbing, and at the same instant a glorious sense of release swept through me, as if a spell had broken. I'd done it, applied a cane to Juliette Fisher's bottom, something I'd been sure I'd never dare to do, and I'd enjoyed doing it.

I gave her another stroke, easier this time, to lay a second welt across her beautiful bottom, her bare bottom, with her panties pulled well down and her cheeks red from spanking.

After that it was easy, and an absolute delight, every stroke, every squeal and sob, every wriggle of her bottom a thrill. I had Juliette Fisher, the girl who'd made me her plaything, the one I could never disobey, on her knees with her panties pulled down as I caned her.

By the time I'd given her the first four I was laughing, while she was crying bitterly into the coverlet of my bed, but the juice from her cunt was now running freely and I was not going to stop. After the sixth stroke I pulled off her panties and forced them into her mouth, gagging her in the same humiliating way she liked to use to shut me up during my own punishments. With the eighth I treated myself to a leisurely feel of her bottom, enjoying the heat of her flesh and the way she squirmed as my fingers traced the welts I'd left with my cane. When I'd given her the tenth I pushed two fingers in up her cunt and began to spank her as I fucked her hole, now laughing in delight for what would have been unthinkable before.

I gave her the eleventh across the back of her thighs, deliberately hurting her to pay her back for all the cruel things she'd done to me, but the choking, agonised gasp she let out in response was too much for me. She'd spat her panties out as the cane hit, and she really began to bawl, crying her eyes out as the sobs wracked her body, and even Stacey looked worried. I gave the last stroke anyway, harder still, and as the thin cane smacked down across her flesh it broke, clattering away across the floor as she screamed in pain.

Stacey was already half standing, and looking very uncomfortable, but I knew what Juliette needed and had opened my arms for her as she twisted around on the bed. She came to me, the tears streaming down her face as she cuddled into my chest. I was stroking her hair as I jerked my top up to let her get at my breasts, and whispering into her ear to soothe her as she took one nipple into her mouth and began to suckle. She was clinging to me like a drowning kitten as she fed, and that might have been enough for her, but not for me. After a moment I pushed my shorts down and wriggled them free of my legs, before sitting back on the bed and urging her gently down.

'Come on, Juliette, you know what you have to do.'

She obeyed, filling me with a sense of triumph as I spread my thighs to accommodate her, on her knees on the floor, her naked, well-whipped bottom thrust out behind as she buried her face in my cunt and began to lick. Both Stacey and Wendy were still watching, as fascinated as ever, but now with their arms around each other's waists as they sat side by side on the bed. I gave them an encouraging smile as I tightened my grip in Juliette's hair to make her lick harder. She responded by pulling up her top and bra to bare her heavy breasts, completing her exposure. I knew just how she felt, nude back and front as she licked, and I knew what I'd have been doing if I was in the same position.

'You can play with yourself, Juliette, we don't mind.'

Her answer was a muffled sob, but she'd put a hand back between her thighs to get at her cunt, with the other stroking her breasts and pinching at her nipples. The rhythm of her licking broke a little as she began to concentrate on her own pleasure, but I didn't mind, because I still wasn't finished with her.

'Do you remember what you did to me in the car, Juliette? And that time in the loos after hockey. That was my first time, Juliette. I was still a virgin and you made me ... you made me lick your bottom. Well, now you're going to lick mine.'

I let go of her hair and bounced over on the bed, presenting her with my naked rear view. She looked up, her face still wet with tears and her mouth smeared with my juice, pleading with her eyes to be let off, just as she had before I'd given her the cane. I shook my head.

'Uh, uh, oh no you don't. You lick, Juliette, and while you're licking, you bring yourself off. Now come on, get your tongue up my bottom hole, now!'

She swallowed, but she couldn't resist, any more than I'd been able to when she made me perform the same shameful act. I moved back a little to make it easier for her and suddenly she leant forward, to bury her face between my open bottom cheeks. My mouth came wide in ecstasy as I felt her tongue touch my anus, to lick at the sensitive little hole, then push deep, probing me as she began to masturbate once more. I closed my eyes in bliss, revelling in the sensation of having my bottom licked, yet what really mattered was that it was Juliette who was doing the licking.

I'd begun to break the spell, just as she was breaking to me, rubbing eagerly at her cunt while she kissed and licked at my bumhole. She was going to come too, already panting out her excitement and squirming against her hand in rising ecstasy. I let it happen, looking back between my legs to watch as she clutched and smacked at her naked breasts, every last ounce of her precious dignity lost as she hit her orgasm with her tongue stuck as far up my bottom as it would go.

She seemed to take forever, shudder after shudder running through her body, to leave her flesh slick with sweat and marked red from her nails, but even as she came down she didn't stop licking. I made myself comfortable, my bottom pushed well up and my face in the covers to let her get at my pussy and my anus at the same time. She took the hint, using her tongue to make long, slow strokes the full length of my slit, but growing quickly faster. That was enough. My mouth came wider still, my muscles began to tighten and in just seconds I was there, a perfect orgasm with the girl who'd made me her slave using her tongue on me from behind. With that I knew the spell she'd had me under was completely broken, Juliette Fisher reduced from cruel goddess to well-beaten, bum-licking little slut, just as she'd done to me.

My climax was so strong I nearly collapsed, but just as I'd begun to come down there was a heavy thud from outside and I realised somebody else actually had, presumably Paul. That meant he must have watched the entire filthy escapade, and all my shame came flooding back, to leave me giggling and blushing as I rolled over to take Juliette into my arms once again. She responded with a kiss.

Chapter Ten

'So, certain people refuse to do their KP?'

Parker's question was obviously supposed to be rhetorical, but he was looking right at Paul and he got an answer.

'That's right, and the same goes for any other punishments you might have in mind.'

Parker gave him a dirty look but didn't reply immediately, instead walking up the line and back again. Ever since I'd caned Juliette I'd been feeling strong and confident, so much so that I was hoping Parker would decide to pick on me, but it seemed to be Paul who'd really got under his skin. I was fairly sure I'd get my chance though, as Parker was obviously trying to work out how to get the better of us. He was also angry, and it showed in his voice as he went on.

'If there's one thing I hate it's people who won't face up to their responsibilities. Yes, that means you, M, A and O. I'm in charge here, and I made a decision. You've been accepted onto my programme, and so you should abide by my decisions. Come on, tell me, Man M, why won't you face up to the consequences of what you've done?'

Paul shrugged.

'Er ... well, we didn't do anything, did we? Except for

piss you off, that is, which is more or less inevitable with a noxious little egomaniac like yourself.'

Parker stuck his face close to Paul's.

'What did you call me?'

'A noxious little egomaniac, not to mention a fascist bastard, a misogynist pig, and a prize buffoon. Shall I go on?'

Paul had been ticking off the points on his fingers as he spoke, and for a moment I thought Parker was going to lose his self-control again. I saw that Sergeant Reynolds had moved a step closer, but Parker pulled back and carried on.

'You are bang out of order, Man M, but I am going to give you, and your girlfriends, one last chance to get back in my good books, just because that's the kind of guy I am.'

He seemed to me suspiciously forgiving, especially in view of what Paul had just said, and Juliette and I shared a doubtful glance before he went on.

'You think you're as good as the guys in Team C, and Team B too? Well, this is your chance to prove it. You're going to pair up, each of you with one of the boys from the decent teams. You can even choose your partner, and you can't say fairer than that. You can also choose what you do, any physical challenge you care to name, only your opponent gets to choose one as well. Each challenge is worth twelve points, so it's nice and simple. That goes for all of you except M, A and O. With you three I want to give you a chance to show that you can face up to your responsibilities. You win both challenges, or even win one so it's a draw, then we call it quits. You fuck up, you do your KP like good little boys and girls. Is that a deal?'

He'd decided it wasn't such a good idea to talk to Paul and was right in front of me and Juliette, staring at us with his face set in a nasty grin. It was obvious he was trying to show us up, and I was sure Paul would tell him to go to hell, or just laugh at him, but I didn't feel I could back out. I also felt I had a fair chance.

'Yes, that seems fair.'

His grin grew nastier still as he turned to Juliette.

'Well? You're the mouthy one, how about it?'

'I'll give it a try.'

'And how about Man M then?'

Paul shrugged.

'Yeah, if the girls are going for it, why not?'

Parker turned his smirking face to me for a moment before stepping back and picking up his clipboard.

'That's settled then. Next, we choose partners. Girl A?'

Juliette leant forward to glance down the line of men.

'I'll have Sam Haynes.'

It was a sensible choice. I could easily see Sam letting her have a win so that she could get off the KP, which made me wonder why Parker had let her choose first. He marked his clipboard then carried on.

'Man D?'

Graham chose and Parker moved on.

'Girl E?'

Wendy went for Alastair, another one I'd have liked to pair up with, and I realised what Parker had done. Paul and I would have to choose last, and with only three people in Team C one of us would have to pair up with an instructor. The other would almost certainly be with Chad. Parker's grin had taken on a manic touch by the time he got to Paul.

'Man M?'

Paul smiled back.

'Looks like Chad for me then.'

Parker gave a satisfied nod and turned to me.

'Which leaves our own little Girl O, all on her lonesome. What a pity. Never mind, darling, I'll play with you.'

He was standing right in front of me, his legs braced apart, but I resisted the temptation to kick him in the balls, for all that I didn't like his attitude at all. I couldn't help but think of what had happened before, and yet even when he'd had me alone in his van he'd held back from assault. He'd also be out to humiliate me, but I knew I could cope with that, while I'd begun to form an idea of how to beat him. I met his gaze.

'So, what would you like to do then? How about something nice and macho like truck pulling ... no, I know, tossing the caber. You should be good at tossing.'

Paul laughed, and one or two others, while I found myself blushing for my own rude words, but Parker ignored me, shaking his head.

'No, that would be too easy. I want to show you that a real difference exists between you and me, other than the obvious. We'll try out on the mat, gymnastics, three standard routines with Mr Straw as judge. That's a pretty girlie sport, don't you think? Now how about you? Come on, anything you like.'

'OK. Follow my leader.'

He looked puzzled.

'What, the kids' game?'

'Yes, unless you don't think you can cope?'

'Sure I can cope. In fact, let's go.'

I'd expected him to insist on doing the gymnastics first, or at least to let the other pairs get going. He was obviously too fired up to care, jogging on the spot and then following as I made for the door. My plan was only half worked out, and I'd been hoping to complete it while we did his half of the challenge, but I was at least sure of my first move. I crossed the airfield, moving at an easy lope, into the woods and down to where the stack of rock I'd climbed before stood among the pines.

The rope ladder was still in place, but I ignored it, running around to the back and starting up as I had before, climbing free until I could pull myself onto the top. Parker had waited at the bottom and for one moment I thought he wasn't even going to try, before he took a tentative handhold and began his ascent. I watched, half hoping he'd fall, but also with a touch of guilt in case he managed to injure himself, or worse. Yet he obviously wasn't going to back out, and despite falling back once and grazing himself on the rough surface he finally joined me at the top.

It had been a tough climb, and a dangerous one, so much so that I thought his attitude might have softened, but he merely gave me a triumphant glare as I started down the rope ladder. My first trick had failed, but I wasn't finished and started down the slope at breakneck speed, running along fallen logs and hurdling obstacles in the hope that he'd take a fall. Instead he kept up, easily, his mocking voice following me through my every attempt to shake him off. I'd meant to splash across the river at the valley bottom, but it seemed pointless and I used the bridge instead, across to the Venncott Arms, through the bar and into the Ladies. Parker hesitated only a moment, then followed, laughing.

'That's a typical girl's trick, that is, but it ain't going to work, not on me.'

I'd been hoping it would, but another thought had occurred to me. The windows were set high in the walls, small squares surely too small for him to squeeze through, while I could at least make the attempt and, if I failed, move on to something

231

else. I hauled myself up, wincing as the catch jabbed into my flesh. My shoulders barely fitted, and I had to hold myself in an agonising position to squeeze my boobs through before tipping forward, face down and several feet above the tarmac of the car park. Quite a few people were looking at me too, as my hips stuck for a moment, and I was forced to wriggle like an eel to get the meat of my bottom under the frame, but when you've been spanked in front of an audience a few inquisitive stares don't bother you.

Unfortunately they didn't seem to bother Parker either. He was sneering confidently as his head appeared, and he'd quickly pulled himself up, to jam his shoulders into the gap. Just as I'd hoped, he didn't fit, but he wasn't giving up, grimacing as he struggled to force himself through, and to my disappointment I realised that with enough effort he was going to make it. I needed new tactics, but even as I was wondering what I could possibly do that he couldn't I noticed the white car with the blue and yellow squares on the side just coming out of the village. It was more than I could resist.

Parker was still struggling to get his shoulders through the window as I ran up the shallow grassy bank to flag the car down. To my rising delight I saw that one of the occupants was a woman, with sergeant's stripes on her sleeve and a no-nonsense expression on her face. As the car drew to a stop I spoke to her, making the best of my expensively educated accent and putting in all the indignity I could muster.

'Excuse me, officer, but that man followed me into the Ladies.'

They didn't think to ask why he'd then decided to climb out again through the window, or for one of them to stay with me to check my story. Both made straight for Parker, while I decided that it would be better if I wasn't around to answer any questions they might have. As the female officer began to remonstrate with Parker and the male attempted to pull him through the window I was running again, back across the river and up the hill, just as fast as I could go.

I didn't stop until I'd reached the safety of the trees, only then looking back, to find Parker being assisted into the back seat of the police car. He was protesting vigorously and pointing towards me, but the police didn't seem particularly interested, so I gave him a cheery little wave and moved on. I was still on my natural high for giving Juliette the cane and breaking the spell she'd had me under for so long, and after seeing Parker taken away by the police it got better still. I was singing as I climbed up through the woods. I knew the police might very well want a word with me, but even that didn't seem to matter.

Everybody else was still busy with their exercises, with Paul and Chad sweating it out over weights in the gym and none of the other girls around at all. I wanted to celebrate, and I didn't want to be in the camp in case the police turned up, so I quickly showered and changed, by which time Paul had beaten Chad and was able to call me a cab. The only place I knew aside from the Venncott Arms was The Plough, so I asked Paul to tell the girls where I'd gone before I gave the cabbie his instructions.

By the time I arrived I'd come down a little, and I felt a bit silly all on my own, but the first person I saw was the man Stacey and I had nicknamed Redbeard the Pirate. He was mending a wall which some careless or drunken motorist had hit on the way out of the car park, and he looked even bigger and stronger than I remembered him, with the muscles of his arms and torso working under his shirt as he lifted stones into place. The last time I'd seen him I'd sucked his cock, without even knowing his name, so I was blushing a little as I approached, but he recognised me immediately.

'If it isn't my little damsel in distress. I hoped I might see you about.'

'I've been at a sort of training camp, over towards the moors. Um ... I don't even know your name.'

'Reuben Miller, and yours?'

'Lucy Salisbury.'

We shook hands, which seemed a bit silly when I could remember the taste and feel of his erection in my mouth, but he seemed content to make small talk, so I settled down to watch him work. I love watching men do physical labour, especially if it involves both effort and skill, and it was a pleasure to see the way he managed to fit the stones back together until the wall was complete once more, with only the new mortar to reveal that it had ever been damaged. By then it was lunchtime, with delicious smells drifting from the hotel kitchens, so I offered to treat him.

'... on me, just to say thank you for the other day.'

'Oh, you said thank you, and very nicely.'

It was the first hint this time of anything sexual between us, although I'd been hoping he'd make a move on me since shortly after my arrival. I found myself smiling and blushing in response, and after that nothing really needed to be said. We ate together, talking casually of this and that over filled baguettes and local beer, which he drank as if it was water. By the end I was a little tipsy, as well as horny, but it didn't seem to have affected him at all. He knew I was his if he wanted me though, and didn't hold back, kissing me as we reached his van. For a moment I thought he was going to make me suck him off again, this time in broad daylight, but instead he opened the door and helped me up into the passenger seat with a firm pat to my bottom.

He lived at the far end of the village, in a small square house surrounded by building equipment, the ground grey with cement dust and the air rich with scents that brought me images of rough, uncompromising men. Indoors was an equally masculine environment, making me feel small and vulnerable, yet also intensely sexual, although I was already pretty well helpless in the face of his sheer bulk and power. I had his cock out the moment we were through the door, and into my mouth, sucking earnestly as I struggled to get his belt undone. He seemed a little taken aback at just how eager I was, but settled against the wall, stroking my hair as his cock began to stiffen in his mouth.

I was enjoying my suck, but the heavy belt that held his trousers up was giving me ideas. Soft and thick, it looked just the thing for use on a bad girl's bare bottom, and I could see no reason why that bottom shouldn't be mine. Once he was stiff I pulled back, rose and took him firmly by his erection, to lead him into the nearest room. He was plainly ready to fuck me, pulling me into a kiss as he fumbled my top up to get my breasts bare, but I wanted more and pushed back a little as he tried to get my jeans down.

'Would you … would you like to beat me with your belt?'

'Beat you?'

'Yes, across my bottom. You can do it quite hard.'

'Well, I'm not sure …'

'Please? Or at least put me across your knee and spank me like I've been a naughty little girl.'

'You are that, for certain.'

'Go on, then, spank me like the little brat I am, then make me kneel for a few hard ones with your belt.'

'You city girls, I don't know.'

He sounded doubtful, but that hadn't stopped him sitting down on the nearest chair and tipping me over his knee, with his erection pressed firmly to my side, perfect conditions for a spanking. It was just what I needed, because for all the extra confidence making Juliette go down to me had provided I still wanted to be on the receiving end, especially with a man like Reuben. I gave him an encouraging wriggle and his huge hand settled across my bottom, squeezing gently. He began to touch me up, enjoying my flesh with a casual intimacy, then to smack, not hard, but for him a pat was enough to make me gasp. I stuck my bottom up, eager to show I was willing, and got a harder swat for my reward, before he'd suddenly taken a firm grip around my waist and pulled my jeans down with a single hard jerk.

My button was already undone, and everything came down, panties and all. He gave a grunt of satisfaction for the sudden exposure of my bare bottom, then began to spank in earnest. Being stripped so rudely had sent a shock right through my body, but it was nothing to the one I got when his hand came down across my defenceless rear cheeks. I was used to Stacey, who spanked hard but always with the aim of turning me on, while I'd trained her very carefully, and my Magnus, who was a skilled and dedicated spanker. Reuben was nothing like them. He just spanked me, as if he was giving me a real punishment, held tight across his knee while he walloped my bottom with smack after smack from his enormous hand. I could barely breathe, let alone speak, and he'd given me a good two dozen before he realised that my frantic squirming and piglike squeals might mean he was doing it too hard.

By the time he stopped I no longer had the strength to

get up, but could only lie limp and shaking across his lap, panting for breath and shaking my head in shocked reaction. Yet as the pain faded to warmth the lecture I'd been about to give him on how to spank a girl properly died on my lips. He'd given me what I truly needed, a good, hard, old-fashioned spanking, delivered without thought for how I was supposed to cope with it, and it felt great. I'd asked him to treat me like a brat, and he had, leaving me with my head swimming and desperate to please. He'd also seen my cane marks.

'Someone been at you already then?'

He sounded curious, and a little doubtful, but I was confident he'd be turned on by what had happened.

'My friends caned me. I lost a bet.'

He gave a low whistle as I got up, now shaking badly. I turned to show off my bottom, allowing him to inspect the six red welts the girls had given me as I continued.

'They tied me down and beat me with a stick, three girls.'

'Why you little trollop!'

The spanking had been too sudden to start my tears, but they began to come as I went to the sofa, to kneel down with my bare bottom pushed out for his attention. He was right, I was a little trollop, and ashamed of myself for all that I couldn't help it, with the tears rolling down my cheeks as I asked for the belt.

'Beat me, Reuben. Never mind my tears, just beat me.'

He looked concerned, but only for a moment, rising as he saw how acquiescent I was, to pull the thick leather belt from his waist. I watched, genuinely frightened but eager too, my body shivering in fear and apprehension but my bottom pushed well up and my knees apart to make an open show of my cunt and anus. His cock was still hard too, rock hard, sticking up from his fly, as much a threat as the belt he'd now doubled up in his hand.

He didn't need to ask if I was ready. My pose said everything, for all that I was sobbing hard and shivering with fright. He came close, took a moment to tug my top a little higher to make sure both my breasts were on full show, then measured the belt up across my bottom. I hung my head, clutching the sofa as I waited, my already well-smacked bottom lifted for the belt, the air cool on my wet, blatantly exposed sex and between my cheeks, making my anus tickle.

I heard the swish of the belt even before it hit, and my mouth came wide in a scream of pure fear that broke to pain as the thick leather strap cracked down across my bottom cheeks. The pain was too much to cope with, sending me into a frantic jiggling dance, which left him hesitant but trying not to smile for what must have been a ridiculous sight. Only when I'd got back into position with my bottom thrust well out did he measure up for a second shot, with my cheeks squeezing in anticipation, my bumhole winking and the contractions of my cunt pushing out juice to trickle down my thighs.

Again the belt cracked down across my bottom, and again I screamed and jumped, but I was soon back in my lewd, vulnerable position for the third. It came in harder still, leaving the muscles of my legs and belly jerking so badly I couldn't hold myself up. He did it instead, his patience exhausted as he grabbed me by my hips and jammed the full length of his cock deep in up my ready cunt. If he spanked hard he wasn't much gentler when he fucked me, ramming himself in and out with furious speed, his hands locked hard in the flesh of my hips.

There was nothing I could do, jerking like a ragdoll on his

erection with my tits bouncing and my hair flying in every direction, while his belly was smacking hard on my aching bottom with every thrust. I couldn't even speak, only gasp and grunt as I was used, a helpless fuck toy in his massive hands. He didn't even try to pleasure me, but he succeeded, for all that he was treating my body as no more than a pretty receptacle for his cock, and his spunk. I'd been pushed close to orgasm by the time he came, and if I'd been able to get my hand back to masturbate it would have only taken a touch to bring me off. Instead he came first, with a single loud grunt as he filled me with so much spunk it erupted from the mouth of my cunt with the next push, to spatter my thighs and bottom cheeks as I screamed in reaction.

I thought he'd crush me, his massive balls pressed to my pussy as he finished his orgasm deep inside my body, and when he finally let go I slumped down on the sofa, my bottom still stuck high but my limbs like jelly. It took a moment before I could get myself back under control, and then my hand had gone back and I was rubbing at myself, my bottom spread wide to him, both cheeks red with the welts from his belt, my open cunt dribbling his spunk down onto my fingers as I masturbated in front of him. He watched, fascinated, twice calling me a dirty bitch, and then he began to use the belt on me again, cracking it down across my cheeks to a hard, even rhythm that could have only one result. Even if I hadn't been rubbing myself I'd have come, beaten to orgasm by the man who'd used me so well, and with my fingers busy in my slit it was better still, and ruder, showing off without a trace of modesty or dignity as I brought myself to a long, shuddering orgasm.

* * *

It was nearly six by the time we got back to Camp Aspiration, after a long afternoon of cuddling and slightly less vigorous sex, mostly with me on top to spare my poor bruised bottom cheeks. Reuben had insisted on taking me back, and as we drove I'd told him what had happened between Parker and me since the incident in The Plough. He listened quietly, with no more than an occasional low, protective growl, but had to laugh when I told him about the incident with the police that morning.

My answering smile was more than a little nervous, as we were approaching the camp and I was dreading the prospect of finding that the police had been looking for me, or that Parker was back and after my blood. Reuben stayed with me, and as I climbed from the van close to where Stacey was talking to Sam Haynes I was quick to ask for information, although both of them were grinning. Stacey was quick to reassure me.

'No, no police and no Parker. Paul tells me you got him arrested for going into a ladies' loo?'

'More or less, yes. Do you remember Reuben, from The Plough?'

She looked a bit surprised and shot me a knowing look, but greeted him in a perfectly friendly manner. I let myself relax a little as I asked my next question.

'What happened with everyone else? What about this KP business?'

'That's all fine. Paul beat Chad weightlifting, but lost in a straight sprint, so that's a draw. Juliette and Sam struck a deal.'

Paul himself was approaching, along with Billy, both grinning from ear to ear.

'We have booze, or we will have as soon as it's delivered.

Who's up for a party?'

He didn't seem in the least bit concerned for who'd over-heard, and I couldn't help but glance around for Mr Straw and Sergeant Reynolds. Paul saw and laughed.

'Don't worry about it, Lucy. We've got 'em fixed. Graham opted for orienteering at night and Mr Straw's gone with him, and well, you know how likely Panty-Pincher Reynolds is to drop us in it. Anyway, it looks like Parker's going to be spending the night in the cells, thanks to you!'

I smiled and nodded, not entirely happy with the situation but content to go along with everybody else. Reuben didn't seem to be in any hurry to leave, but wanted me to show him around the old airfield, which had still been in operation when he was a child. I obliged, only to get humped for the fourth time that day, down on my knees among the pines on the far side of the runway.

It was starting to get dark as we walked back, now hand in hand, and there was still no sign of Parker. Everybody was in Mess, where they'd thrown together a rough and ready dinner and set out several bottles of wine and cases of beer. Even Chad seemed to be getting into the spirit of the thing, with a can in his hand as he talked with Daniel, while Wendy had obviously been as busy as me, sat on John Runyon's knee as he fed her crisps. Reuben turned out to know him from school and the four of us were soon chat-ting happily, with my blushes rising for being with two men who'd both had me and were sure to find out about each other before too long. Neither said anything, and it was left to Paul to give me away, coming over, beer in hand, to joke about the way Wendy and I had ridden John's quad bike, blissfully unaware that Reuben was anything other than a man who'd given me a lift.

'Both at the same time, you've got to hand it to the man!'

I'd gone red on the instant, as had Wendy, and Reuben gave me a distinctly peculiar look, but then laughed as he addressed John.

'Trust you, you randy bastard. You always were the one to get in first!'

John gave me an interested look.

'You too then?'

Paul thrust out the can he was holding, clinking it against Reuben's.

'Join the club!'

I'd been scarlet before, but now I was crimson, while Wendy had dissolved into giggles for my embarrassment. Her bottom was sticking out over the edge of John's leg, a target I couldn't resist. I gave her a solid smack.

'You can laugh, Wendy! You let John have us both together.'

Reuben gave a thoughtful nod.

'Now that I'd like to have seen.'

He took a swallow of beer and the five of us were silent for a moment before Paul spoke up.

'Hut Twenty-six anybody?'

Reuben and John had no idea what he meant, but I did, and so did Wendy. Stacey and Juliette were both busy, surrounded by a group of hopeful men, although in Juliette's case at least I knew they were wasting their time. With what was on offer, I couldn't resist, and took both Reuben's hand and Paul's, to make it very clear that I was keeping my options open. Neither objected, allowing me to lead them outside, with Wendy and John following. My heart was in my mouth as we walked up between the huts, to that same one where I'd been put on my knees to suck Paul and Billy.

I wanted the same treatment, more or less, but with two girls and three men I had little choice but to take charge. Wendy certainly wasn't going to, full of nervous excitement but clinging close to John as we closed the hut door behind us. Inside, it was almost completely dark, with only the lights from other distant huts casting a wan yellow glow. Somehow that made it easier as I sank down into a squat to pull Paul's and then Reuben's cocks free of their trousers.

Neither seemed worried by the presence of the other, a very different reaction to what I'd have expected from most of the men I knew, and an encouraging one. I popped Paul in my mouth, taking him as deep as I could while I stroked Reuben's shaft, then changed places. It was my fifth time with Reuben in the space of a few hours, and not surprisingly he was slow to react, still only half hard by the time Paul was sporting a full erection.

Wendy still seemed shy, but that hadn't stopped John, who'd pulled up her top and bra and taken out his cock to make her stroke him while he explored her breasts. I was keen for her to join in properly, if only to spare myself the embarrassment of being such an obvious slut, and went over to kiss her, then to take one hard nipple into my mouth. She couldn't help but respond, and the boys were all for it, crowding close as I suckled her. When she lay back a little into John's arms I went lower, reaching up under her skirt to pull down her panties, allowing me to roll her legs up and bury my face in her sex. She gave a single weak moan, still unsure of herself, but as John straddled her head to lower his balls into her mouth her knees came wide, leaving her panties stretched taut between them as I continued to lick.

Paul was fumbling with my jeans and Reuben already had my top up, pawing my breasts and rubbing his half-stiff cock on my side. My jeans came open, and down. Paul pushed close and he began to rub his erection on the seat of my panties before suddenly tugging them down to use my naked bum slit instead. I stuck my hips out, eager for more despite my aching flesh, but if he noticed that I'd been beaten he said nothing, merely rutting in my slit for a while before slipping a hand under my belly to lift me high enough to allow him to slide his cock into my cunt.

I turned my attention to Reuben as Paul began to fuck me, taking him in my mouth once more. He was getting stiff again, and had soon begun to push his cock so deep I was struggling not to gag. I'd given Wendy a good lick and she'd lost her reserve, now lapping eagerly at John's cock and balls as he rubbed himself in her face. Her legs were still wide open and I slid two fingers into her, although I was starting to have trouble concentrating with Paul now pumping into me from behind and Reuben getting increasingly excited as he used my mouth. They were both getting rough with me, and it was all I could do to stay in position, while every smack of Paul's belly on my bottom gave me a sharp reminder of my belting.

Not that I minded, not when I was being manhandled by two really big men, and it didn't look like either of them was going to stop in a hurry. When Paul did finally pull back it was simply to strip off my lower clothes, then lie down on the floor and pull me on top of him, twisted round so that I was riding him cowgirl style, with his hands on my bouncing breasts as we fucked. That left Reuben free, his cock now fully hard and Wendy's cunt spread ready in front of him as she continued to work on John with her mouth. He didn't even ask, but simply took her by her panties and slid himself in up her hole, provoking a low moan, half resignation, half pleasure.

I was bouncing on Paul's cock as I watched my friend being fucked and made to suck at the same time, enjoying the show but wishing I was the one with two men to use me. A moment later and I was, as John dismounted, saw the position I was in and fed his erect cock straight into my mouth. At that Reuben jerked Wendy's panties free from her legs and mounted her properly, with her thighs cocked wide to accommodate his massive hips as he thrust into her. I already wanted to come, and moved forward a little, to grind my cunt against Paul's flesh as he fucked me and I sucked John's cock.

My pleasure had already begun to rise towards orgasm when I heard the click of the door, then Billy's voice, full of longing as he begged to be allowed to join in. Reuben was about to tell him to leave, but I beckoned him in, my head too full of dirty thoughts to resist, while I knew that my open bottom cheeks would give him the perfect target for his spiky little cock. Sure enough, he got it out immediately, already stiff, and I realised he must have been watching us through the windows. I wiggled my bottom for him, making Paul laugh and drawing a grunt of mingled amusement and disgust from John.

A sharp pang of shame hit me for the tone of his voice, but that only made me want to be buggered all the more, and I pushed my bottom out and spread my knees to make it even more obvious to Billy where he was supposed to put his cock. He didn't need telling, making an odd wet noise in his throat as he squatted down behind me, his belly pressed to my open, bruised bottom. I felt the head of his cock touch my anus, slippery with my own juices, and my ring came open, admitting him in up my bottom.

John called me a filthy pig, provoking another sharp jolt

of ecstasy and shame, but it didn't stop him enjoying his suck, or watching as Billy buggered me with my bottom thrust out against the meat of his belly. Every push of his cock in my anus was pressing me onto Paul's body, while he too was pumping into me and John had begun to masturbate into my mouth, with his hand locked tight in my hair. I was helpless, in the grip of three men, one in each hole and all determined to use my body to spunk in, my flesh shaking to their thrusts, my control totally lost, the rubbing on my clit an exquisite pain from which I had no escape.

My first orgasm hit me from nowhere, tearing through my body in violent spasms, but they barely seemed to notice, pumping into me harder and faster, using me exactly as they pleased. I came again, harder and more painfully than the first time, my body now jerking limp on their cocks, and a third time, leaving me weak and faint. Still they worked their cocks in me, but John was there, groaning in ecstasy, his fist smacking against my lips as he wanked himself off to fill my mouth with spunk. I tried to swallow, failed, and his mess had gone all over the floor and all over Paul, only he was coming too, pumping my cunt full of his spunk with John's still dribbling from my mouth.

Both took their time to finish off in me, and as they loosened their grip I collapsed, rolling off Paul's body to slump on the floor. Billy gave a squeak of surprise as his cock slipped free, but he was back on top of me in an instant, mounting my bottom to jam his erection deep in up the slippery little hole between my cheeks. I was in no state to resist and could only lie there, face down on the floor in a pool of spunk with more of it still oozing from my mouth and cunt as I was buggered. Billy rode my bottom, whooping and yelling in triumph, until he too gave me the full content of his balls, up my bumhole and all over my cheeks, finishing by wiping his cock on my thigh.

I stayed down, barely conscious save for one strange thought floating in my mind, that now I knew what people meant when they said some object was fucked or buggered, meaning it was beyond use. That was how I felt, lying slumped on the floor, naked but for my top and that pulled up over my tits, spunked in and spunked on, bruised and sore, used and abused. I also felt deeply ashamed of myself for being such an utter slut, but I knew I'd soon be bringing myself off to exactly that emotion, while for all my aches and pains and the filthy mess I was in, there was no denying my satisfaction.

They watched Reuben finish with Wendy before helping me to my feet, and having had me they proved to be courtesy itself. Billy was sent to fetch some towels and Paul helped me to clean up before Wendy and I went down to the showers. We were giggling over our naughty behaviour as we entered the block, only to go quiet at the sight of Stacey and Juliette. They were in the shower together, Stacey standing with her face to the wall and her bottom pushed well out, Juliette on her knees with her face buried between my girlfriend's cheeks. Juliette also had a noticeably pink bottom, in addition to the six cane marks I'd given her, and for all my immediate jealousy and shock, that was what stuck out. I gave a loud cough, making both of them jerk around as I spoke.

'Have you been spanked, Juliette?'

She nodded, blushing, and got up. After what I'd done that day I was hardly in a position to criticise Stacey, but she at least had the decency to explain herself.

'Sorry, Lucy, we got a bit carried away.'

'That's OK, so did we, but ...'

Juliette interrupted.

'Actually, I've been meaning to tell you something, Lucy. Stacey's explained how you feel about me, and I probably ought to say I'm sorry. The thing is, having you as my play-thing absolutely saved my sanity, because ... because Angela Barnes used to treat me the same way, regular spankings, six-of-the best, queening, everything, and I needed somebody to take my feelings out on. You were so pretty, and so ...'

'Easy? Vulnerable?'

'I was going to say sweet. Sorry, Lucy. I'm a bitch.'

I nodded, unable to speak, and yet her bottom was not only pink but marked with six cane welts, which I'd inflicted. She'd already been punished. I could also imagine how she would have felt with Angela, when she wanted to dish it out but constantly found herself on the receiving end. It was Stacey who finally spoke.

'Friends?'

This time I managed to find my voice.

'Yes, but don't be sorry, Juliette. All you really did was bring out my natural feelings, and now I've dealt with you it's all OK.'

She didn't reply, but came straight to me, to take me in her arms for a long open-mouthed kiss. Stacey and Wendy watched for a moment, both smiling, before coming forward to join in, all four of our tongues touching together. By the time we broke apart I'd lost my towel and we climbed into the shower together, laughing as Wendy and Stacey compared the state of my bottom with Juliette's. We'd both been well beaten, but I was undoubtedly in a worse state, with the marks of Reuben's belt in addition to my cane welts and an all-over pink flush from the way the boys had used me.

We began to wash each other, with inevitable consequences,

concentrating first on necks and backs and bellies, then on boobies and bums, until I'd gone down to give Stacey a lick with one finger well in up her soapy bottom hole. She came like that, full against my face while the others watched, their arms around each other and Juliette with a hand between Wendy's thighs. Stacey was no sooner finished than Juliette had gone down in turn, to lick Wendy to ecstasy while she knelt with her bottom thrust out and the water cascading down over her reddened, welted cheeks. Her anus was on full show, a tempting target for my tongue, and when Wendy had sat down, splay-legged on the shower floor with a look of dizzy satisfaction on her face, I made my offer.

'Your turn, Juliette. Would you like to sit on my face?'

To my surprise she shook her head.

'No ... well, yes, of course I would, but there's something I'd like you to do, to make me feel better about everything.'

'No, really, those cane marks on your bottom are all the apology I need, and you licked my bum, you bad girl.'

'I know, but I did you lots of times, and like you said, there was that time in the loos. Piss on me, Lucy. It would make me feel better.'

She was still on her knees, in the exact middle of the shower, with water running down her body and dripping from her breasts and hair, and as she finished she hung her head. I went close, not at all sure of myself, to stroke her hair, my pussy just inches from her face. She lifted her head for a moment, to kiss my sex lips, before hanging her head once more, waiting. I glanced at Stacey, who shrugged, and at Wendy, who was wide-eyed with shock and arousal despite having just come. Juliette spoke again.

'Please, Lucy, if you want to. Piss on me, Lucy. Do it all over my head.'

There was real need in her voice, beyond simple lust, while I wanted to go anyway. It still felt an impossibly inappropriate thing to do, for all that had been said, and yet she plainly wanted it, and it was mine to give. I let it come, a trickle at first, mixing with the shower water to run down Juliette's face and hair, then more, and as she realised she gave a single deep sob. At that I let go, my stream splashing over her head, exactly as she had asked.

'There we are, darling, is that what you wanted? Go on, Juliette, play with yourself while I pee all over you, go on.'

She didn't need telling twice, snatching back to get at her pussy, and as she began to touch herself she lifted her head, her eyes tight shut but her mouth wide to catch my stream. I watched in dirty fascination, her upturned face so calm and beautiful, like a girl in some magazine advert, only with pale-yellow urine bubbling around her lips as she deliberately caught my piddle in her mouth. Then she swallowed.

Wendy gasped and Stacey blew her breath out, shocked to see Juliette deliberately drink my piss, but for me the reaction was one of pure, cruel joy. I'd nearly finished, but I made her do it one more time before wriggling to shake off the last few drops down her chest and taking her firmly by the hair to bury her face in my cunt. She was masturbating as she licked me, on the floor at my feet, pissed on and with her belly full of urine, my own Juliette Fisher. It was so dirty, so wrong and yet so perfect I was struggling to take it in even as she lapped at my clitoris and rubbed hard between my legs. I'd pissed on her, over her head and in her mouth, by request, an apology for everything she'd done to me, and one I intended to accept, while hoping she'd do it all again, and more. I screamed as I came, oblivious to who might hear or anything else but my pleasure and what it meant, the final resolution to my submission to Juliette Fisher.

* * *

It took us a while to sort ourselves out and get dressed, but the party was still going on and all of us were badly in need of a drink. Otherwise I was in a dream, thinking happy, satisfied thoughts as the four of us walked hand in hand down to Mess, arriving just in time to hear Parker's shouted voice.

'Where the hell is Lucy fucking Salisbury!?'

It was too late to back out. He'd seen me even as he spoke, and stamped forward, his face set in fury, his voice a roar.

'Right, you demented little bitch! I want a word with you, right now, and then you can get out of my fucking camp, you mad fucking cow, you ...'

He stopped as he found his way blocked by the massive bulk of Reuben Miller.

'Don't you talk to her like that.'

Parker looked up.

'I'll talk to her how I fucking please, and who the hell are you anyway? Get out, now, and that goes for you too. Out, or do I have to throw you out?'

He was looking at John, who'd come over to join Reuben. John spoke, very quietly.

'You can try.'

Parker came forward, to clutch at both men, but they simply caught him up under his arms as if he weighed nothing at all, leaving his feet kicking in the air. He was still yelling at them, demanding that they let go and ordering them to leave, but they took no notice whatsoever. I followed as they marched him towards the open back door, not wanting any real trouble, but by the time I got outside they had him up against the huge metal drum of the kitchen bin. A single great heave and he'd been upended into a week's worth of slops and garbage, leaving just the lower part of his legs on show, kicking wildly as he struggled to get out, and still ranting and raving at Reuben and John, but mainly at me. Somehow I knew it was time to go.

Chapter Eleven

I'd been expecting the summons to Mr Scott's office, but it was very bad luck that it came when I'd been making myself a coffee, forcing me to run the gauntlet of the main floor. Word about what had happened had got out, inevitably, and several dozen pairs of eyes followed my progress. I forced myself to keep my chin up as I crossed the floor, as if nothing had happened, for all that I felt close to tears.

As I got into the lift I was desperately trying to decide on which course of action to take from among those I'd considered, but underneath I knew it was hopeless. I could protest all I liked, and I'd have no difficulty proving that Parker's behaviour had gone beyond the bounds of what was acceptable, but then so had mine, and further by far. The sack seemed inevitable.

Nevertheless, I rapped smartly on the familiar door and entered in response to his invitation, to find not only Mr Scott but the Chair herself, Mrs Grierson, and two other directors. Hope flared for a second, with the thought that it hardly took such a senior group to give a mere PA the sack, only to collapse at the realisation that their presence probably meant there were going to be even more serious consequences than I'd anticipated. Mr Scott looked up at me.

'Ah, Miss Salisbury. Do sit down.'

'I prefer to stand, thank you, sir.'

He looked surprised but didn't comment, instead shuffling the papers on his desk, among which I could see my Camp Aspiration report. It had been written in red ink. He picked it out, glancing over the first page before speaking.

'You seem to have had quite a time. Let's see ... "no team spirit whatsoever", "a disruptive influence from the start", "cheating at every opportunity", "utter contempt for rules and regulations", "refusal to accept orders or fit into the hierarchy". It goes on for quite a while, as you can see, but I'm sure you get the gist of it?'

'Yes, sir. Sorry, sir. The thing is, sir, that ...'

He raised a hand and I went quiet as he continued.

'I don't need to hear your excuses. I've already had all that from Paul Yates, who managed to get an even worse report than you did, which is quite an achievement. Alastair Renton and Daniel Chambers also confirm what happened, at least in outline. Did you really persuade a farmer to give you a lift on his quad bike when you were supposed to be running?'

'The rules didn't say anything about not taking lifts, sir. I thought I was using my initiative.'

Mr Scott gave what might have been a chuckle or possibly a sceptical grunt, and would have continued had Mrs Grierson not posed a question.

'I understand that you also smuggled drink into the camp?'

There was no point in denying it.

'Yes. We didn't see why we shouldn't. We felt that Mr Parker's rules were unnecessarily harsh and, well, I like a glass of wine in the evening.'

'So you deliberately went against a policy to which you'd agreed in writing?'

'I felt it was unreasonable, but I didn't want to make an issue of … of my disobedience.'

From the way she was looking at me I expected her to ask if I knew what happened to disobedient girls and go on to say that they got spanked, but she merely nodded and made a note on the pad in front of her. Mr Scott took over once more.

'Setting aside the details, it seems to me that when faced with a difficult decision you prefer to follow your own way rather than obey the rules. Is that a fair comment?'

'Yes, sir.'

I could hardly have denied it, in the circumstances, and could feel a sense of impending doom as he continued.

'I see. The thing is, Miss Salisbury … Lucinda, that Mr Parker is well known for his confrontational style, and while he's hardly popular among his contemporaries in the management training game, we've found him extremely useful. You see, he claims to separate the men from the boys, but what he actually does is separate the sheep from the goats. You, Lucinda, have shown yourself to be a goat, if you'll excuse the analogy. In view of this, we'd like to offer you the number two position at our Paris office.'

9 780007 533343